YELLOW HAMMER
An Asian Thriller

by
Valerie Goldsilk

This novel is entirely a work of fiction. The names, characters and incidents portrayed in it are the work of the author's imagination. Any resemblance to actual persons, living or dead, events or localities is entirely coincidental.

First published by Thaumasios Publishing Ltd. in 2020

Copyright © Valerie Goldsilk 2020

No part of this book may be reproduced or transmitted in any form without permission in writing by the publisher.

Other books by the same author

Negative Buoyancy
The Oldest Sins
Sins of Our Sisters
Sins of Our Elders
The Reliable Man
Reliable in Jakarta
Reliable in Hong Kong
Classified As Crime
Dragon Breath
Perfect Killer
Fatal Action
Random Outcome
Reliable in Danang
White Bishop

About the Author

Valerie Goldsilk is English and has lived in Hong Kong for over thirty years. She is now retired but used to run her own business, travelling frequently around Asia working with factories. Her better half is a former Hong Kong police inspector.

To Kevin - a much bigger role for you in this one.

To Roger Plant – Copy Editor.

To Jonathan Hall – Alpha Reader.

To Richard Vines – you always said I needed a proper editor.

To Tom Morris – I always enjoy recounting the story about your landlady.

To Tim - everybody knows E Squadron does not really exist.

To Dougie - I thought you might find your cameo amusing.

To the real landlady and landlord of The George in Girton.

To the real Harris Hall - thank you for many mellow, sun-drenched afternoons lounging on the edge of the cricket field.

"Now you listen to me, I'm an advertising man, not a red herring. I've got a job, a secretary, a mother, two ex-wives and several bartenders that depend upon me, and I don't intend to disappoint them all by getting myself 'slightly killed'."

Cary Grant in North by Northwest

Try and leave this world a little better than you found it, and when your turn comes to die, you can die happy in feeling that at any rate, you have not wasted your time but have done your best.

Lord Robert Baden-Powell

You will, I am sure, agree with me that... if page 534 only finds us in the second chapter, the length of the first one must have been really intolerable.

Sir Arthur Conan Doyle

1

There are three ways to kill a man: silently, painfully and publicly.

Colonel Wendy Shen of the People's Liberation Army's Strategic Support Force, Department 3 was an expert in all the ways and her reputation preceded her. She was also skilled in the art of luring men into love, but she was nearly forty now so she preferred training younger girls for this kind of mission.

"You must not wear clothes that are too sexy," she was telling the two girls in the classroom. "Men will think you are a slut. They do not want to fall in love with a slut. You must always look decent. He must believe at all times that he is seducing you."

Both of the girls came from Jiangsu province and had the tall slim, pretty features of Shanghainese fashion models. They both had porcelain skin, large double-lidded eyes and a small mouth. They had long, lustrous black hair that fell to their shoulders and they wore dark blue military overalls and serious expressions on their young, unblemished faces.

"All men are pigs," Colonel Wendy Shen continued. "Whatever they say, whatever they do, however politely they behave, all they are thinking about is what it must be like to have sex with you. What it will feel like to penetrate you. How it will look as they stand over you, watching you suck their penis."

The girls nodded intently.

Wendy asked, "Are you both still virgins?"

"Yes, miss."

"Good. Don't give up that prize too easily." Wendy clicked on the remote and the face of a Chinese man in his fifties appeared on the large screen at the front of the classroom. "When you complete your training, one of you will be chosen to become the mistress of this man. His name is Guo Shu Ping. According to Forbes Magazine, an American publication that likes to list the wealthy, he is the 87th richest man in China. But he spends most of his time in London, in England."

"Will we travel to London, Colonel?" the girl they called Jing Jing asked. She was slightly taller than the other one, whose nickname was Lei Lei, but otherwise they could have been sisters.

"If you are chosen, you will go to London," Wendy said.

"But my English is terrible."

"English is not what Mr. Guo will find entrancing about you."

The two girls giggled.

"Will we be allowed to go shopping in Harrods?" Lei Lei asked.

"If Mr. Guo takes you shopping there, then yes."

"And we can visit Buckingham Palace?" Jing Jing said

"I don't think Mr. Guo gets invited for tea by the Queen. You will probably drive past it because Mr. Guo has a big house in Belgravia."

There was a knock at the door and a young man in uniform informed Wendy that General Zhao wanted to see her. When she entered his office, he was sitting behind a large desk with a view of the drill square at the front of the building.

"How are the new girls coming along?" General Zhao asked. He had recently been promoted, as had Wendy, and his epaulettes were heavily starched and bright.

"They are pretty and stupid," she said.

"You were once pretty and stupid," the General said.

"I was never pretty."

"Foreigners always liked your face very much."

Wendy smiled politely.

Zhao said, "Guo Shu Ping is not very discerning when it comes to girls. If a girl is tall, pretty, giggles a lot and has a vagina he will fall in love with her."

"Men can be so smart in business and so stupid with romance," Wendy said.

Zhao shrugged. "Keep me informed how the training goes. The reason I asked to see you is that we have located the man you say was responsible for your last two missions nearly going wrong."

"You have found Scrimple again?" Wendy sat up with sudden animation.

"We have several sightings of him. Identity is confirmed. What do you want to do about him?"

"Kill him. I want to kill him. If I have your permission?"

General Zhao gave her a smile and nodded slowly. "Perhaps."

2

Theo Scrimple, formerly of the Royal Hong Kong Police but now employed by the Security Service, MI5, as the manager of one of their safe houses, was sitting in his garden and reading a Jack Higgins thriller. It was an old paperback he'd found lying on the bookshelf in the living room. The story started with a Catholic priest who had a Tommy gun in his Gladstone bag. Then there was an Irishman who had an Enfield in a shoulder holster and a pretty girl in a Mercedes.

The village was called St. Mary Bourne and the house he ran was an old thatched cottage with four bedrooms. Five minutes' walk up the road was a pub called the George Inn which was funny because his mate Kenworthy had a pub in Cambridge called the George. Scrimple spent an hour every evening in the pub and when he felt like a change he sometimes took his VW Polo to any of the next villages, all of which had pubs with varying degrees of charm.

It was a mild spring afternoon and he'd just finished a cup of tea. The sky was mainly blue with a few clouds, there were some birds chirping on the trees at the end of the long garden and he was wondering when his guests might arrive.

His mobile rang. A man called Winchcombe, who was his usual contact at the head shed, said, "They've just left here so it will be a while yet."

"Who are they this time?" Scrimple asked.

"Some North Korean bloke that did a runner while he was on a trade mission in Manchester."

"Who's his Handler?"

"It's Tchaikovsky. You've not met him before. He's a good lad. Unless he's interrogating you."

"He's the one they call the Nutcracker Suite?"

"I think it's supposed to be the Sweet Nutcracker," Winchcombe said.

"What's his real name?" Scrimple asked.

"Fred something or other."

"And who's security?"

"That'll be a bloke they call Pacino."

"And what's his background?"

"He's one of the Hereford lot. They call him Pacino because he's got a big scar across his face. Like the film Scarface."

"That's fine. I don't suppose they will want dinner then?"

"Probably not," Winchcombe said and provided some more operational details before they ended the call.

The front door bell rang five minutes later. Scrimple went to answer it. He checked the security monitor, saw it was Esmeralda and buzzed her in.

"Hey there," he said. The woman smiled at him. She was about five foot tall, brown as Belgian chocolate and twice as sweet. He wrapped his arms around her and gave her a wet, slobbery kiss. Esmeralda had come to the United

Kingdom from the Philippines to work as a nurse in the NHS. Her husband had run off with another woman so she left her teenage children with her mother and got on a plane. That had been five years ago. She went back home once a year for Christmas. She was not quite forty but looked ten years younger. Scrimple had met her in a pub in Andover and after a while she'd moved in with him and took care of all the domestic chores around the safe house.

"How many guests today?" she asked.

"Three men. No dinner needed."

"I got some nice steaks from Asda," she said.

"They can have them tomorrow," Scrimple said following her into the kitchen where she dumped the shopping bags. "The main guest is from North Korea so he's probably only ever had dog meat to eat. A real bit of beef might freak him out."

"Really?" Esmeralda said and stared at him in confusion.

"Just joking."

"I never had a real steak until I came to live in England," she said.

"Chicken Adobo. That's what you probably lived off in your province."

"We ate a lot of Jollibee burgers."

Scrimple laughed and went back outside. He checked the time and wondered if he might pop over to the pub for a pint.

He'd been running the safe house now for nearly a year. Kat Pedder had arranged for him to be hired as part of a bigger deal that was made between her boss and Bill Jedburgh. He didn't know all the details but Jedburgh had disappeared and nobody seemed to know where he was.

Perhaps Kat and her boss had an idea and Scrimple was sure that Julian McAlistair would know how to get hold of the man. His estate, Ryden Hall, had been put on the market.

Scrimple's son Torres had given up his studies at Cambridge. They had talked it through with his mother, Eva and it was just too dangerous to remain in the UK given what he had witnessed and that the killer was still at large. Torres found a Master's course he liked at Fordham, which was a Jesuit university in New York and he was enjoying his new lifestyle in the Big Apple. Scrimple was planning to visit him during the summer.

"I'm just going for a pint," he said to the girl, ran through the security checks and went out through the side door. He'd gained some weight since living in England. He wasn't as fat as he used to be but his habit of a pint or two every evening didn't help. He tried to go for a run several times a week but when it rained it was difficult to get motivated. He'd also shaved off his beard. Esmeralda didn't like it.

When he got to the George Inn the usual faces were at the bar. "It's that bloke from Hong Kong," said Charlie who was a retired bond trader with a big house up on the hill. When he wasn't playing golf he was in the pub. Sitting next to him was Roland who owned 500 acres of farmland and always liked to talk about how his land was better quality than that of his neighbour the Earl of Carnarvon.

"Can I get you lads a top up?" Scrimple asked, sliding up on his usual stool.

They both said yes and the landlord, a taciturn fellow called Frank nodded and did the honours.

The official story was that Scrimple was retired from the Hong Kong Police Force. He was on a decent pension and had bought the house with some money inherited from a great-aunt. The occasional guests that came every few weeks to stay at Scrimple's house were rarely seen. They were not supposed to go out and usually arrived and left under cover of darkness.

"So how do you fancy Man City's chances this season?" said Roland.

Scrimple took a measured sip from his pint of bitter. "They'll win the cup of course."

Charlie guffawed. He was more into the Rugby but always took great pleasure in talking down Scrimple's team.

"I'll put it on your tab," Frank the landlord said.

"What do you think the Chinese are up to with this Belt and Braces program they're rolling out in Africa?" asked Charlie.

Scrimple shrugged. "I think you'll find it's called the Belt and Road Initiative and it's just an infrastructure project. It's the new Silk Road of connectivity or something like that."

"It's just a way for China to rip off the Africans and get them locked into expensive loans, isn't it?" Charlie said.

"I've no idea," Scrimple said.

"What's your opinion of the Chinese then? Are they out to take over the world?" Roland said leaning over.

"They want to compete with the Americans. They want to get back to where they were a few hundred years ago,"

Scrimple said. "We gave them a bloody nose during the Opium Wars and they can't forget that."

"So why did we have to give Hong Kong back to them in 1997?" Roland asked.

"It was the easy thing to do. Britain didn't want colonies any more. Wasn't politically correct."

"Just like that, we gave it back to them? How come they didn't throw you out of the police in 1997?"

Scrimple smiled. He'd explained some of this before to the same audience but it was a topic they regularly revisited. "China committed to no change for fifty years. So we all stayed in our jobs."

"Why didn't you stay out there?" asked Roland.

"I did for a little while and then I thought it might be fun to be back in old Blighty."

"You must be barmy. I wouldn't live in England if I didn't have my family responsibility for the farm," said Roland. Scrimple nodded absently. Roland was always whingeing about the poor quality of life in England but he had a big villa near Puerto Banus in Spain and spent three months a year down there.

Scrimple's mobile buzzed in his pocket and he checked it. He walked to the other end of the pub before he hit the green button.

"I'm coming into London for a meeting with my UK publisher," said Julian McAlistair. "Got a few days to kill. Are you busy? Fancy meeting up somewhere for dinner and a few bottles of vino?"

"Depends on when. I'm running a sort of bed and breakfast so I can't get away too often."

McAlistair lived in Thailand. He had married the heiress of a Thai family fortune, resigned from the Royal Hong Kong Police and now led a life of leisure.

"How about Friday evening? Come over to London and I'll get you a room at my club."

"Have you heard from our mutual friend?" Scrimple asked.

"The dangerous one? I have as a matter of fact. That's what I want to talk to you about."

Scrimple felt a cold poke of fear in his ribs. "What about?"

"I'll tell you when I see you."

"I need to check with the girlfriend if she can hold the fort but Friday should be fine."

3

Guo Shu Ping was fond of telling people that there were three ways to be successful in business: Be first, be smarter or cheat. He had seen it in a film. If you were all three, he would snigger, then you had the best chance of consistently beating your competition.

Last week he'd bought the Beaverbrook Golf Club and was enjoying all the attention this was bringing him in the financial press. Not that he played golf. He thought it was a stupid sport for boring people but he understood that there was money and kudos to be earned from being involved with the sport. He didn't drink French wine. He preferred single malt Whiskies. But he still owned three vineyards in Burgundy. They were not a great investment but it was fun to helicopter in occasionally and be fawned over by the French staff.

Mr. Guo had made his fortune in pharmaceuticals. Mostly generics such as acetaminophen, aciclovir, ramipril, atorvastatin, allopurinol and warfarin, as well as all the supporting ingredients that were part of the manufacturing process. China made 85% of all generic drugs and Mr. Guo was one of the first and one of the smartest in the industry. It was rumoured that he was not averse to cheating at times but nobody had ever managed to prove that he was skimping on the active ingredients in his generics. His customers, such as the British National Health Service, simply did not have the resources to check all shipments and there was always an explanation if a batch was not quite showing the right readings during quality testing.

In London he owned a house just off Eaton Square Gardens which - as he enjoyed telling his friends in Shanghai - was round the back of the Queen's cottage.

This morning Mr. Guo was having breakfast in his elegant dining room, attended by his Slovakian butler, Bohumir. Mr. Guo was wearing a white Ralph Lauren Polo shirt under a tweed jacket, which was his usual attire. He wasn't big on sartorial expression but would dress up when he attended public functions and he had some excellent suits from Savile Row. He was a small, corpulent man with a round, chubby face that was perfectly smooth so it was hard to tell how old he was.

Bohumir had come to London in his youth, spoke excellent, idiomatic English and had graduated from the International Butler Academy based in Simpelveld in the Netherlands with the highest marks. He was also a competent practitioner of Krav Maga, the vicious martial art that originated in the Jewish quarter of Bratislava in the 1930s. This Mr. Guo all knew from when he had first interviewed and hired his employee.

"What time is the meeting with Lionel Woodcote?" Mr. Guo asked in his thickly-accented but fluent English, looking over the top of the Financial Times he was reading.

"At eleven, sir, in the Caledonian Club." Bohumir had been to elocution classes so he sounded like Jeeves although if one listened carefully there was still a slight Slavic tinge to his vowels.

Mr. Guo nodded. "I don't like this omelette today. Tomorrow ask Chef to make me Wonton dumplings again."

"Very well, sir. And which car would you like to use?"

"The Bentley Mulsanne. The weather is looking nice."

"I'll have Peter get it ready."

"Afternoon I want to go and see my son. He is playing football."

Bohumir smiled formally. "He's a very good football player."

"I am happy he plays football. But why doesn't he study harder? The school only give him B, B and B. I pay big money and he should have A, A and A."

Mr. Guo's son was twelve and attended a boarding school in Berkshire called Harris Hall. It was a traditional preparatory school for boys and fed into all of the famous old public schools such as Eton, Winchester and Sherborne. One of Mr. Guo's English business partners had recommended the school and over twenty percent of the students were Asian. Harris Hall was about an hour west of London so if they had a quick lunch they should get there in time for the matches.

"This Woodcote, I don't like him, Bohumir," Mr. Guo said, folding away his pink newspaper and pushing his plate away. He picked up his cup of Chinese tea and slurped the hot liquid.

"Anything you want me to do?" the butler asked.

"Keep eye on him. He asked me for money last time and this time I think he will ask for more money."

"He's a procurement official. It is what they do."

"The English always think their shit smells no stinky. They say we are corrupting in Asia but they are just as bad." Mr. Guo fixed his man with a sharp look. "He asked for one hundred thousand pounds last time. The stupid man doesn't even have a secret bank account. He wants cash."

"Maybe he hides it in a steel box in the garden."

"I told him that is not the price. The man before him never asked for more than fifty thousand."

"And what did he say, sir?"

"He laughed at me like I'm a stupid foreigner who does not know the price for anything."

"Are you sure you don't want me to send someone to have a talk with him?"

"No, no. It is not time for that sort of talk yet. I will decide after our meeting. If he can sign a bigger purchase order I can be happy."

4

It was nearly ten by the time the guests had arrived from London and all Scrimple had done was shown them to their rooms. The North Korean man was short, skinny and appeared permanently frightened. The Minder was tall, scar-faced and scary while the Interrogator was bland, charming and well-spoken.

Scrimple had made sure all the alarms were on, the house was locked down and then sent a secure message to Winchcombe confirming status. MI5 used an encryption App called Ganymede which had recently been introduced and it could be used for both calls and short messages with images. Apparently it used a 4096-bit RSA encryption algorithm but as far as Scrimple could tell it worked mostly like Signal.

When Scrimple came to bed, Esmeralda was already tucked under the duvet. She had been looking at the screen on her phone. "My cousin has been having problems at her work," she said.

"This is the cousin who came to the UK last month to work as a maid? Or the cousin in Hong Kong? Or the cousin in Dubai?"

Esmerelda frowned. "The one in England. Her employer is not giving her enough food to eat and she hasn't been paid yet."

"Who is her employer?" Scrimple asked as he slipped under the duvet. The house was old and creaked at night. In the winter it could be bitterly cold when the heating wasn't on or the boiler broke.

"She never said but I think it is an Indian couple." She shook her head in frustration and put the phone aside. "I told her to study nursing like me but she was always wild and got pregnant by her boyfriend when she was eighteen. Now all she can do is work as a maid."

"Is she pretty?"

"She used to be but she was getting fat."

"If she's pretty she can always get a nice man." He tweaked her bum. "Someone like me."

"Don't be naughty," his girlfriend said. They had made love the night before knowing that the house would be full for a week or two. They didn't make love when they had guests because Esmeralda was vociferous at the moment of orgasm and the walls were thin. In the early days of her moving in, there had been some embarrassing mornings in the breakfast room. Scrimple wasn't sure if he loved her yet but on a scale of 1 to 10 she was moving along steadily towards the top quartile.

"Do you think they will all want eggs and bacon tomorrow?" she said.

Scrimple already had his eyes closed. "Just offer them the usual. I think the Rice Krispies have nearly run out."

The next morning they came down for breakfast at eight.

"Mr. Park here would like something with rice," said Tchaikovsky. The North Korean smiled and bowed at Esmeralda. It appeared he had decent English skills.

Pacino, dressed in a tracksuit with a shoulder holster that held a Sig Sauer semi-automatic pistol, sat down at the long oak breakfast table.

"It's not bad here, sir. I heard good things about this place from some of the other lads."

"No need to call me, sir. Everyone calls me Scrimple."

"Right. They tell me you was in the Hong Kong Police?"

"I was for many years and then left to go into business." Scrimple passed Pacino and the others the little laminated breakfast menus. "Are you serving or former SAS?"

"I'm full-time with E Squadron now. My boss is Major Tom Rieves."

"It's not a secondment then?" Scrimple asked.

"They like me so much, they won't let me go." Pacino laughed and poured himself a cup of tea from the pot on the sideboard.

"Done any good stuff?" Scrimple asked.

The soldier smiled. "Can't talk about it. But the work we do in E Squadron has its hairy moments."

Tchaikovsky came and sat next to them. He just had a piece of toast with marmalade. He was dressed like an old fashioned school master in a tweed jacket with leather patches, an olive pair of cord trousers and brown polished brogues.

"Just want to confirm, Scrimple, usual drill. Pacino will work with you on all the security and I'll just get on with Mr. Park."

Scrimple nodded. "The study is all set up for you. You've got two big leather armchairs. If that's how you like to sit. Or you could sit behind the desk and he sits in the chairs. Coffee, tea and biscuits will be laid out in the living room so you can take a break any time you want."

"I'll need to plug into your broadband connection because we may want to bring a translator in on some of the conversations. There will be technical stuff and Mr. Park's English isn't up to it."

"Password is in the folder on the desk. Is he a high-level guy?"

Tchaikovsky shrugged. "He says he is. Biochemist, Professor. It will be my job to find out if he's telling fibs and is just the janitor."

"It's strange that he was allowed to travel to the UK. I thought nobody is ever allowed out of North Korea," Scrimple said.

"There was a big delegation and they had lots of minders. Happens quite regularly apparently. Not very common that one manages to slip away. I'll be delving into that one a bit." Tchaikovsky gave a cold smile. He was a strange one, Scrimple decided but then most of the interrogators they'd had stay as guests were a bit odd. It wasn't a specialisation you signed up for in MI5. It was something one drifted into by accident.

Esmeralda came out of the kitchen with two plates of bacon and eggs followed by Mr. Park who had been discussing his culinary desires with her.

Pacino looked pleased. "That's the best part of this job," he said. "The grub."

"Esmeralda prides herself on her cooking. She's also a fully qualified nurse."

"I won't be cutting off any limbs or extracting fingernails on this job," Tchaikovsky said, buttering himself another piece of toast. "So we shouldn't need any medical assistance."

Pacino rolled his eyes at Scrimple who gave him a smile of complicity.

"What weapons do you have in the house?" Pacino asked Scrimple a bit later when Tchaikovsky and the Korean had left the room.

"Gun safe in the cubbyhole under the stairs. I'll give you the combination later. We've got two Glock 17s with 100 rounds of ammo and two L119A2 Close Quarter Battle assault rifles with enough ammo to turn a car into a sieve."

"Are you qualified on both of these pieces of kit?" Pacino said.

"I've had training but frankly it's not my thing."

Pacino nodded and asked: "In the Hong Kong police, did you ever have to shoot a man?"

"Hong Kong was, still is, a really safe city. Not much need to pull your gun on duty." Scrimple knew it was an evasive answer. He felt Pacino deserved a bit more and maybe it would help to give him more confidence in Scrimple and the running of the safe house. "I did have to fire my gun a few times," he added.

"Did you shoot to kill?"

Scrimple shrugged. "Yes. I had no other choice."

"How did it feel afterwards?" Pacino asked, giving him a hard stare. "Did you get nightmares?"

"How did it feel?"

"To kill a man?"

"It felt good. He was a man who deserved to be killed."

"Do you dream of him sometimes?" Pacino said.

"Rarely," Scrimple replied.

"I had to kill the man who did this to me," Pacino said touching the long, vicious scar on his cheek. "Little black turd. It was in Libya in 2012." He stood up and brought his empty plate into the kitchen.

5

Mr. Guo sat in the back of his Bentley Mulsanne and listened to music over a set of Bose headphones. He had a weakness for ABBA and The Beatles. Bohumir, dressed in his customary black suit and white shirt, was in the front next to the driver.

The meeting with the government procurement official had gone well. He was a greedy, stupid man and Mr. Guo thought he would be found out soon and replaced by someone hopefully less greedy and more intelligent. In China, bribery was a way of life. Everybody was seeking rents, a little cream on top of every transaction however small it might be. If you wanted to get your child into kindergarten you bribed the principal. If you wanted your child to sit in the front row of the classroom you bribed the teacher. If you wanted a good table at the restaurant you bribed the head waiter. Nothing much had changed since the days of the old Emperors. Mr. Guo had learnt since he was a young boy how to offer a bribe discretely. How to ask for one cautiously. One must not be heavy handed and one must always be respectful to the other party in the transaction.

But foreigners were always so crass. They were so direct. They were ... simply foreigners, crude and ill-mannered and with a sense of their own importance that was entirely misplaced given the current geo-political situation. China was the second most powerful country in the world. It dominated trade and controlled supply chains. Most countries - and especially one like Britain - had no production capability left, no expertise in making anything anymore and were entirely at the mercy of China.

Mr. Guo enjoyed the quality of life in London. His home city was intensely polluted and the traffic was always appalling. London had a nice sense of tradition and as a rich Asian you were treated like a king in most places. The inhabitants of London knew which side their bread was buttered on. They welcomed the money that rich Asians, Arabs and Russians brought to their city. The jobs it created and even the taxes it helped to pay.

He checked his gold, diamond encrusted Rolex Day-Date and noted that they should be on time. His son's football match started at 2.30 p.m. Harris Hall was a small boarding school with only 120 boys. It had been founded in the 1830s and had traditionally been a feeder school for Winchester. These days it still sent a few clever boys to Winchester every year.

The Bentley swept down off the M4 and fifteen minutes later it turned in through a discrete set of gates onto a half mile drive that led through a pleasant wood where the boys were allowed to roam free at weekends. The driver took the car past the main school buildings and up to the sports fields where he parked not far from the cricket pavilion. A line of other cars, mostly BMWs and Range

Rovers, was already arranged neatly on the side of the road.

"What is the other school they are playing," Mr. Guo, tossing his headphones aside, asked Bohumir.

"I believe the school is called Ludgrove."

"Yes, this should be a good match."

Bohumir had opened the door for his boss and handed him a set of Wellington boots which Mr. Guo slipped into. He was then helped into his Barbour jacket to complete the outfit.

The two men walked across the sports field. There were four pitches being used by boys playing matches but the central pitch was where the first team played. Harry Guo had been coached in the sport since he was five years old when he had expressed an interest and shown an aptitude. Mr. Guo had arranged for professional soccer coaches to be flown in from Senegal, Cameroon and France who began drilling the young Chinese lad so that by the time he started school in England his ball skills were astonishingly advanced compared to the local English lads.

The Headmaster, also dressed in Wellington boots and a wax jacket with a black Labrador in pursuit, hurried over to pay his respects to Mr. Guo. Only last term the Chinese businessman had donated a substantial sum of money for the new drama centre which would be built next to the putting green.

There were about ten other parents watching, mostly mothers, because it was a Wednesday so the fathers would be at work in their banks and international law firms.

"So nice to see you, Mr. Guo," said the Headmaster.

"My son score any goal yet?"

"They have only just kicked off."

"Ludgrove is a much bigger school. They have more boys to choose from," commented Mr. Guo.

"That is true. But we have the Harris Hall spirit and we feed them better food than Ludgrove."

"Ha-ha," said Mr. Guo. His son had told him how appalling the school food was and he required regular supplies of pot noodles to be able to survive the week.

"How is your business?" the Headmaster asked.

Mr. Guo smiled and nodded. "If British people keep sick then my business keep good. Everybody need our medicine. And we have very good medicine that your NHS is buying."

"I'm sure it is, Mr. Guo," the Headmaster said, then excused himself to welcome another parent who had just arrived.

Harry Guo was a tall boy for his age. He was a midfielder and at that moment had just taken possession of the ball and was moving rapidly up the right side of the pitch. Mr. Guo glowed with pride until a tiny Ludgrovian defender slid adeptly and cut Harry's legs out from under him, releasing the ball to the other side.

"*Ni hao*," a young woman's voice said next him. "Is that your son?" she said in Mandarin.

Mr. Guo glanced at her and a smile crept over his features. She looked very young to be a mother. And so very pretty. And tall. He turned to the young Chinese woman and confirmed that it was his son who had been doing so well until he was cut down.

"I am the nanny of Jiang Peng. He just started here this term," she said.

"My name is Guo."

"Nice to meet you Mr. Guo," the girl said. "My name is Jing Jing. There are many Chinese parents at this school."

"It is a famous school," Mr. Guo said, trying to keep one eye on his son while making a detailed appraisal of the nanny. "Have you come to Britain long?"

"Oh, no. I've only just arrived a few weeks ago. I am very fortunate to have been offered this job."

"Are you homesick yet?" Mr. Guo asked.

"Not yet. It is still so exciting being here. We learnt about England at school and then to be working here is wonderful."

"What business does your employer do?"

"I don't know, Mr. Guo. I think he is doing investments. I studied as a nurse so don't know anything about these things."

"And where do you live?"

"They have a house in Windsor. Jiang Peng is allowed to come home every weekend. But only I live there. His parents are in Shanghai and only come once or twice a month."

Mr. Guo beamed at her, then quickly checked and found that his son was once again in possession of the ball.

"He is a very skilful player, your son," Jing Jing said. "Were you a good football player when you were young?"

"No, my sport was Badminton."

"I love Badminton. I played for my university," she said.

Mr. Guo gave her a long appraising look. "You must come to visit us in London when the boys have Half Term.

Perhaps we can play Badminton at my club and then have a nice dinner."

Jing Jing blushed and said she wasn't sure if that would be possible because her employers were very strict.

"Nonsense. I am sure the boys would enjoy meeting up and having some real Chinese food together." Mr. Guo smiled and noticed that her breasts thrust firmly against the thin fabric of the fashionable coat she was wearing.

6

Scrimple wasn't a great fan of taking the train. He could take a train from Andover or Newbury directly into Paddington but the few times he'd tried it he found the trains late, dirty and overcrowded. So when he had to visit London, which was rare these days, he drove his little VW Polo. If he didn't hit the rush hour it took less than two hours and the German motor was comfortable enough on the M4 motorway.

His employer paid for the car, leasing it under a shell company so it was new, clean and economical. For Scrimple, who hadn't driven much in all the years he lived in Asia, it was always fun to take the car out when he had some time off from managing the house.

Winchcombe, his boss for all intents and purposes and his only contact at MI5, had given approval for Scrimple to have Friday evening off. Esmeralda was there to do the cooking and the housekeeping and Pacino was in the house to provide security, while Tchaikovsky and Mr. Park sat in the study and had their long, taped conversations.

Scrimple had asked one of the other interrogators once if they uploaded the recordings to the cloud every evening and he had simply laughed.

"Most of these defectors are just a bunch of self-important losers. They talk endless shit and half the time there is no value to whatever intelligence they claim to be peddling."

"Really?" Scrimple had been disappointed. He thought he was doing vital work in the defence of the realm by providing a discrete environment for interrogations to take place. And here he was being told that it was mostly horse-manure.

"That's right, mostly just a load of cobblers," the interrogator had said. "So we just put it on the memory sticks and then we wait until it's all done before we have it transcribed and analysed."

There was a Burton Safe built into the wall at the back of the cupboard in Scrimple's bedroom. It was rated for EN-1143 Eurograde 6 and that's where he locked the memory sticks and any other paperwork that the interrogators gave him at the end of the day.

He was looking forward to an evening away. He didn't mind the relaxed lifestyle that he had with Esmeralda in the countryside but sometimes the big city beckoned. He had spent thirty years living in big bustling cities, Hong Kong and Bangkok, where anything could be had at a price and some place was always open to sell you whatever you desired. These days his tastes were mundane, a decent meal and several pints of beer or glasses of wine ticked the boxes and put a smile on his face. That's what he was looking forward to this evening with Julian McAlistair. Some jolly banter and old war stories about when they were young and certainly McAlistair could run up fifty flights of stairs without breaking into a sweat. Scrimple had never been that fit. There had been nine months when he was with the Police Tactical Unit, a Platoon Commander, when he'd lost thirty pounds and felt comfortable to walk on the beach without his shirt on, but later the weight had piled back on because he enjoyed his ale too much. Then he'd been been pretty fit for a year or two while he was working as a scuba instructor but once he knocked that on the head and had come to live in England, the blubbery arms of the soft life grabbed him round the neck and began slowly strangling him. Not that he minded. He wasn't a youngster any more and in a few years' time he'd be sixty.

That was a thought.

There was a bit of a traffic jam around Reading but otherwise the motorway was fluid and he drove in the direction of Shepherd's Bush, parking in the vast carpark underneath the Westfield Shopping Centre. He grabbed his overnight bag and hopped on the tube that took him to Piccadilly Circus from where he made his way to the East India Club, on the corner of St. James's Square.

McAlistair always booked Scrimple into the club when they met up as it meant he could come and go as he pleased. They gave him a decent single room with a shower which had recently been renovated. The club remained reserved for gentlemen. The average age of the members was currently 58. The average age of a bottle of port in the cellar was 38.

Scrimple possessed one suit that currently fitted him, which he had bought at Marks & Spencer. The sleeves were rather long, but he'd made sure it was loose around the waist. It was a size 52. He only wore it for weddings, funerals and dinners in London. Since his mother had passed away he hadn't been to any funerals and none of his friends were foolish enough to attempt matrimony again. Not recently anyway, although he'd heard that Sledge was screwing up his courage to entice an 18 year old Indonesian maid to become wife number seven.

The Hong Kong Police tie was black with diagonal stripes of gold and light purple. When Scrimple had joined it was still the 'Royal' Hong Kong Police Force but the Queen had given up on the former colony in 1997. Scrimple had served a few more years in the Hong Kong Police until it had become painfully obvious that there were no opportunities of advancement for him. For others perhaps - a few of the lads with whom he'd been at Police Training School in Wong Chuk Hang had made it to Assistant Commissioner rank - but not for Scrimple.

But he'd served his time and was entitled to wear the tie and since the only other tie in his wardrobe was a sombre black one, it was the Hong Kong Police tie that he knotted at his neck before going down to the American Bar.

McAlistair was already there, in the far corner, discussing the latest club gin with the manager.

"57 percent alcohol, that must kick like a mule," McAlistair said. The manager smiled pleasantly. He was from Sri Lanka originally but had traveled the world in pursuit of the finest cocktails and being paid to serve them in the most elegant clubs, to the most refined of people.

They were admiring a bottle with a burgundy label that read 'Home on Furlough' Organic London Dry Gin. Apparently it was proving a great success with the members.

"There's the man," McAlistair said, clapping Scrimple on the shoulder, "have a glass of the club Champagne. You look like you need it."

A flute of Champagne appeared as if by magic on the bar counter and Scrimple got stuck into it. McAlistair had always enjoyed the finer things in life and when he married his girlfriend who had taken over running the family business shortly after their wedding, life had taken on a permanent rosy tint for him. He spent his time writing racy little pulp fiction thrillers set in Asia and Stephen Leather, another Thailand-based author, had been mentoring him lately over beers at the British Club, which helped increase his sales. Not that he particularly cared about the money but a man has to have an occupation.

McAlistair was a broad-shouldered, broad-chested man and was wearing a perfectly tailored dark blue suit with a yellow silk tie and a white shirt. On his wrist sat an Audemars Piguet Royal Oak Automatic which Scrimple believed cost as much as the average person in Britain earned in a year.

"How's tricks then?" McAlistair asked and popped a handful of peanuts into his mouth.

"All good. Work is easy and salary comes in every month."

"How's that pretty young lady of yours? Filipina, isn't she?"

"She's gorgeous and her breasts are huge."

"What more could a man want."

"Two Filipinas with huge breasts who are lesbians?" Scrimple ventured and held up his empty Champagne glass so the manager could top it up. Marcel, the Master of Wine who ruled over the club's cellars, stocked them up regularly from the finest vineyards of France and the rest of the grape-growing world.

"So what exactly are you doing at the moment for an agency that cannot be named?" McAlistair asked. In truth, taking Scrimple out for a fancy meal was not solely old comrades meeting to banter about the days of yore. The writer was always keen to learn more about Scrimple's new employer. Scrimple knew that he could be discrete until the third bottle of wine was opened but after that he was usually hard pressed to keep official secrets secret.

He said, "I can't tell you, or I'd have to kill you."

"Right," said McAlistair.

"Running a safe house," Scrimple's resolve to remain professional collapsed rapidly. "Interrogators come with dodgy people and they sit around all day long and talk."

"Remember the day we first met?" McAlistair said. "I bet you learnt more that afternoon about how to interrogate a criminal than in all of your years as a Detective Inspector."

"Yes, what was that guy called again? Ham Gar Chan?"

"How the hell would I know? That was nearly thirty years ago. Chinese male, black hair, black trousers, white shirt. Like all of them."

"Have you been in Hong Kong recently?" Scrimple asked. The bar was beginning to fill up with more middle-aged men in suits. There was also a table of youngsters, men in their twenties, in the corner, who were having a jolly good time. They were similarly dressed in business suits. Scrimple felt like a phoney because he wasn't truly one of them. He had no idea what it felt like to be a lawyer, a banker or an accountant. But then nor did McAlistair and he didn't give a tinker's cuss about anything or anyone. Never had. That's why they'd eventually asked him to leave the police. Too many Triads and rapists had had their fingers broken when they were being interviewed by Detective Inspector Julian.

"Where are we going for dinner?" Scrimple asked.

"We're going to go to Goodman," McAlistair said. "You like steak don't you?"

"Can't get decent steak at my local pub."

"Good, you'll like their 400 gram corn-fed rib-eye."

"Will I?"

"You'd be a fool not to."

7

Earlier that day Mr. Guo had received a phone call that pleased him. The call had been from the girl Jing Jing, the nanny he'd met at his son's boarding school. Jing Jing, sounding somewhat shy on the phone, had explained that it was her day off on Saturday and she was allowed out on Friday evenings. Had Mr. Guo been serious when he invited her out for dinner?

Well, Mr. Guo had been absolutely serious and he arranged to have his driver pick her up outside the house in Windsor where she lived with her employers at 6 p.m. She would be standing by the bus-stop, they had agreed.

Mr. Guo didn't kid himself that it was his good looks or his athletic figure that the girl found attractive. Because, of course, he had neither. He was a man in his forties. But he understood that she was probably lonely and bored in a foreign country and that a mature man of means such as him could be an interesting acquisition for a modern young lady.

It was the oldest compromise in history. It was a truth universally acknowledged, that a single woman in possession of a pretty face, must be in want of a wealthy man.

Mr. Guo grinned in anticipation of an enjoyable evening as he danced around the bathroom getting his hair just right. He thought he would impress her with Western food. Chinese food would be for another date. There was a famous steak restaurant in Mayfair that all his friends had been talking about. Bohumir had already made the reservations.

When he came downstairs, Mr. Guo was dressed in a shiny pale-blue suit with a yellow cravat at his neck. The cravat was by Hermes and the silk material was as soft as a baby's bottom. Not that Mr. Guo had ever touched a baby's bottom. They had always had maids in the house after his son was born.

He went to sit in his study to read some emails on his iPad while drinking an Armagnac. Cognac, he felt these days, was a bit too ordinary. Every one of his friends in Shanghai had always drunk brandy but when one becomes really successful one must stand out from the crowd.

There were some issues with the new golf club he'd bought. The old members were complaining that they had to re-apply for membership. Some of them could not afford the newly increased fees and were not accepting the simple business logic that the club needed to make more money in order to afford a complete refurbishment. People in England could never understand that money did not grow on trees. It had to be earned, it had to be created.

Bohumir came to fetch him when the girl arrived. Mr. Guo wanted to impress her with his house and some of the paintings he had recently acquired, then they would pop over to the restaurant.

She looked prettier than he remembered her. Perhaps when he met her on the school playing fields she had not been wearing make-up. This evening her eyes glittered and her lips were a rich crimson that made Mr. Guo shiver in anticipation of one day being able to kiss them.

"*Ni Hao*, Jing Jing," he greeted her in Mandarin, "welcome to my humble home."

"Thank you for inviting me, Mr. Guo," the girl said. "What a beautiful lobby you have and such a large staircase?" She stood in the middle of the hall as Bohumir took her beige coat under which she was wearing a simple, red dress and red shoes.

"Does your employer not have such a large house?" Guo asked as he invited her into his reception room.

"It is a long flat house. Not small, about ten rooms, but quite ordinary. Not so stylish as yours, Mr. Guo."

"Many modern houses in England are very ugly," he said. "And so poorly built. You have to go for the classical buildings to get good quality. Then spend a lot of money to make them comfortable."

He offered her a drink and she asked for orange juice. Guo waved at Bohumir who disappeared to the kitchen.

"Oh," said Jing Jing, as she stopped by the fire place and stared up at the painting. "Is that a famous painting, by a famous painter?"

"Yes, it is a Picasso," said Guo, pleased that she had noticed. She was obviously an astute and perceptive girl. "It is called Nude Woman in a Blue Armchair. I bought it at Christie's last year. Do you like it?"

"It is … very…," the girl cast about for the word she wanted, "colourful."

"Yes, it certainly is. And very expensive. I paid £18 million for it."

"So much?" Her eyes popped open in amazement.

"These are very good investments. See, I have two more in the dining room. You buy them and can enjoy them for a few years and then can sell them on for double or triple the price."

"That is a good deal," she agreed and went up to the Picasso and studied the colours carefully. Guo thought it was a nice picture and everyone always commented on it. But when he looked at it he didn't see the bright colours, nor its provenance, he saw the £40 million he was hoping to sell it for one of these days. Just last week a man from Christie's had come to examine it and thought they could put it up for £25 million if Mr. Guo were ready to sell. He'd shaken his head and told the man that he would never, ever sell. It was too important a piece of artwork. The man had nodded sagely and asked if he could come by again in six months' time.

Bohumir returned from the kitchen with Jing Jing's chilled orange juice.

"I hope you like to eat steak?" Guo asked her. "I have booked a table at the best steak restaurant in London."

"Oh, I love to eat anything," she said.

Half an hour later they were ensconced in the dark timbered and leathered ambience of Goodman on Maddox Street.

"Can I recommend this 2014 Pinot Noir from the Louise Vineyard in the Chehalem Mountains," said the sommelier. Guo thought that sounded like a fine idea. He hoped that Jing Jing liked wine but wasn't used to regularly drinking alcohol. Pretty girls were so much more fun when they were slightly drunk.

He looked around the restaurant and found every table to be full, as one would expect on a Friday night. There was the subdued hubbub of appreciative conversation. The smell of seared beef from the prairies floated in the air above them.

"Tell me about your business, Mr. Guo," asked Jing Jing.

"Please stop calling me Mr. Guo. We must be friends. We are in England and I have an English name. It is Felix," he said.

She laughed and clapped her hands. The sommelier returned and began uncorking the bottle. Guo started telling her about his company: "We make all sorts of drugs. My biggest customer is the British NHS. Do you know about that? How it works here?"

She shook her head. "I've only been here for a short time. It's still all very strange."

"The NHS is very strange. You see, they have free healthcare in this country. Everyone is allowed to go to see the doctor for free, and they can go to hospital for free and take as much medicine as they want for free."

"I didn't know that," Jing Jing said and appeared puzzled.

"Yes, and because it is free, everybody is very wasteful about everything. They don't care about how many medicines they take, because it is all free. And that," he gave her a wink as he held up his glass of Oregon Pinot Noir, ready for tasting, "is very good for businessmen like me."

Later in the evening, when her cheeks - after three glasses of wine - nearly matched the colour of her dress, Guo told her how he was going to take over a struggling drug company in Porton Down. They were about to make a huge breakthrough in anti-virals but had run out of cash. He was going to buy the company cheap and then would make their new products indispensable. He had formulated a clever plan and was waiting for a man from North Korea to come to England who would be vital in the execution of this plan.

Jing Jing giggled and told him she really had to get back to her employer's house in Windsor before midnight.

8

McAlistair chose an American wine and Scrimple knew it would go down well. He glanced around the steakhouse. Every table was full. There were plenty of American voices, tourists who knew they could expect what they were used to at home here: great big massive portions of USDA certified beef.

A few tables away a Chinese man in a pale-blue suit and a yellow cravat around his neck was entertaining a gorgeous Chinese girl in a red dress. Scrimple stared for longer than was polite. The man looked like your regular mainland businessman; the girl's skin was white as alabaster. She was wasted on the older man although she seemed to be laughing at everything he said, listening intently as he expounded on some subject or other.

Chinese women could be so pretty, Scrimple thought, especially the ones from the North who were frequently tall and elegant. For a moment he was jealous of the plain looking man then he reminded himself that he had nothing to complain about.

He had a good woman.

There had not been many good women in Scrimple's life. There had been lots of cheap women in his life - girls who exchanged a few hours of sweaty fornication for a fistful of dollars - and there had been a few special ones. Sometimes when he felt maudlin and before alcohol cast a rosy shade over his memories he thought of the girl called Mabel and that weird day when he came home from work and found a stranger in his bed.

"Earth to Scrimple?" McAlistair broke into his reverie. "What are you moping about?"

Scrimple shook his head, as if to clear the cobwebs of the past. "Nothing, that Chinese bird there is gorgeous. Wasted on that chubby wanker she's with."

"How do you know he's a wanker?"

"Look at him. He's just going on and on and on boring her with some story about how much money he's got."

McAlistair turned his head a few degrees so he could see the table. "Looks like she's well impressed with him. She can't stop giggling."

"That's just that their style, isn't it? Hong Kong girls used to be the same in the old days. These days they are all feminists and earn more money than their husbands."

"If you say so. I think it's an excellent situation when the woman earns more than the husband. Let women run the world, I say. If all the FTSE 100 CEOs were women you can be sure there would be bigger dividends and less global warming."

Scrimple laughed and reached for his wine glass. "I don't know anything about all of that."

"So tell me about your boss. Is she a woman?"

"Well, you know I can't tell you that, you nosy cunt."

"Why not?" McAlistair goaded him.

"There's this woman Kat Pedder. The one who was following me to try and track down Jedburgh. She's one of these ballsy millennials. With a hard, cocky look in her eye and won't ever take no for an answer. I'd like to bend her over and give her a hard answer." Scrimple stopped himself from giggling at the thought. No, no, that wasn't really how he felt about the woman.

"So is she your boss now?"

"No, she sorted it all out that time. I think it was actually her big boss who swept it all under the carpet. Kat reports to this woman who's been around for ever. I think she's the number two or three by now in the Security Service."

"What's her name?" McAlistair asked.

"Oh, come on, mate. I'm not going to tell you that. Anyway, I think Kat Pedder heads up some new specialised counter-intelligence team that they set up. I've got nothing to do with that. Haven't spoken to her in months." The waiter arrived and they were silent while he placed down their starters: Argentinian prawns with chilli shiso dressing.

"I sort of report to a bloke called Winchcombe and he's the only person I really meet," Scrimple said, digging his fork into the pink seafood. "Apart from the guests that is. That's what we call the people who come and stay in our house."

McAlistair nodded, his mouth full. "Any interesting ones?"

"Not really. There's usually one or two blokes from the SAS that come along for security and they're always a bit of a laugh to chat with." Scrimple glanced over at the pretty Chinese girl and watched as she tried to refuse more wine but in the end allowed her glass to be topped up again. "To be honest, it's all a bit ordinary. Just the way I want it."

"Nothing wrong with ordinary as long it makes you happy."

"It does. I just want everything to be totally boring and ordinary. Have you heard from Jedburgh then lately? You said you had some news."

McAlistair shook his head. "Not really news. Just sends his regards. He's fine and that's it. Not to bother him."

"So where is he?" Scrimple asked.

"He didn't say. Could be anywhere in the world."

"I felt sorry for his girlfriend, Poppy Whatshername. She seemed like a nice woman and then he told her he had to pack up and disappear. She didn't really deserve that."

McAlistair said, "It was for her own protection probably. He was really into her. I know that. He didn't do it because he wanted to move on. It was just the safest thing to do, to walk away. Become a ghost."

"I know what that feels like. Didn't work out that well for me," Scrimple said. He'd taken up a new identity for a while but in the end they had still found him.

"With all due respect, mate, I think Jedburgh's a hell of lot better at all that stuff than you will ever be."

Scrimple shrugged and took a long drink from his wine. The second bottle was already nearly empty. "That's fine by me. I think when you get older you have to accept your limitations."

"Yeah," McAlistair said, with a twinkle in his eye and Scrimple thought he was going to say more. Something along the lines of Scrimple having had to accept his limitations a long time ago.

Fuck them. He wasn't going to obsess about what he could and couldn't do. He was just an ordinary bloke, not some vicious killer like Jedburgh, not some idle kept man like McAlistair. At least he worked for a living. He even had a pension now, although for it to get to any useful size he'd have to be working until he was 77. That was probably going to be pensionable age in the next decade anyway. Fortunately he had some savings tucked away in Asia and he got a regular rent from his mother's house in Yorkshire. And he was managing to save half of his salary these days because rent and food were all covered by the job.

So life, was not bad, Scrimple concluded and stole a glance again at the pretty girl in the red dress. Oh, yes he'd like to give her a good seeing to. The way her face was getting all flushed, the man in the pale-blue suit might be in for a bit of rumpy-pumpy tonight. Lucky, lucky, lucky bastard.

Nothing for it but to drink more. After three pints of bitter Scrimple was useless in the sack anyway and only with the help of the little blue pills that Esmeralda kept in her bedside drawer could he manage to satisfy her conjugal expectations.

"What's the latest with Kenworthy?" McAlistair asked. "He recovered from his gunshot wound okay?"

"I think so. He never mentions it. I haven't spoken to him for a while. He's still running his pub in Cambridge. It's doing okay and he's a bit of a celebrity now for having been involved in that whole mess."

"Should be good for his business," McAlistair suggested. He was looking over Scrimple's shoulder watching something. Scrimple turned in his seat and saw their sizzling steaks coming in their direction as a man called Piers - who hosted a morning television show - and his wife were just being seated. Scrimple recognised the man's face but couldn't recall his surname.

"I should go over to Cambridge and have a weekend with Kenworthy," he mused partially to himself. "He told me he was in a new relationship with some attractive divorcee that he met on Bumble."

"The dating app? Kenworthy remains true to form."

"He said he'd tried them all. When he was using Tinder he'd just get all these horny twenty year olds who just wanted to have a hook-up with an older man for the experience."

McAlistair laughed out so loud that the diners at the next table stared. "You can't believe everything Kenworthy says."

"He reckons he's slept with three thousand women over the years."

"You see, he's just a total bullshitter."

Scrimple shrugged. "Who cares?"

The steaks were in front of them now. They were huge, enough to feed an entire African village for a month.

9

Saturday was a good day to go and visit a company you wanted to acquire. All the workers were at home with their families so only the key managers would be there: The boss and the accountant probably.

Guo sat in the back of his Bentley listening to 'Air Supply' on his headphones as they drove down the M3. Bohumir was in the front seat next to the driver. There was a dreamy smile on Guo's face as he thought about the previous evening that had ended when the girl had to return home. He had enjoyed himself and felt he'd made a good impression on Jing Jing. He hadn't pressed her to come back to his house for a nightcap as he felt there would be world enough and time to pursue their relationship in the following weeks.

The meeting in Porton Down was important and had been arranged for late morning. The journey should take about two hours, mostly down the motorway. They had passed Basingstoke and Andover and were then in deep Wiltshire.

Porton Down had been a top-secret British Government research facility for decades and still housed the Ministry of Defence's Defence Science and Technology Laboratory (DSTL) where they studied Ebola, Anthrax,

West African Lassa virus and much, much more. In fact the man Guo was on his way to see, Professor Malcolm Whyte, had worked at DSTL before he left to set up his own company called Gomeldon Advanced Research & Testing (GART).

GART was located in the Tetricus Science Park, the civilian part of the Porton Down base, along with a number of other similar start-ups and spin-offs. After passing through a series of gates they reached their destination which looked like any other business park in England. It was a modern brick and glass building with parking in front and rear for about eighty cars. A discrete sign announced the name of the enterprise.

The driver slotted the big Anglo-German limousine into the space that was reserved for the Marketing Manager and ran around to open the door for his boss.

The sky was overcast and rain was starting to spit. They were not far from the area called Salisbury Plain where the British Army had trained its men and machines for hundreds of years.

A small man with white, messy hair, wearing a blue blazer and a nervous smile stood in front of the glass entrance doors.

"Hello, you found us alright then?" he asked as Guo waved at him and they shook hands.

"Nice to see you again, Professor Whyte," Guo said. Inside the reception area, by the desk, stood a tall woman who could have been the headmistress of a grammar school. Whyte introduced her as Mrs. Block, the Finance Director. She wore trousers and sensible shoes. Just what one expected from the person who crunched the numbers.

Bohumir was carrying Guo's briefcase, a silver Zero Halliburton, and Professor Whyte led them along a long corridor that ran between a set of level four laboratories on the left and offices on the right until they reached a bland board room that looked out over the rear car park. Mrs. Block suggested she would make the tea or coffee but Guo said he was fine with just a bottle of mineral water. Once they were all settled on opposite sides of the boardroom table, which could seat about twenty people, Whyte thanked Guo again for coming out from London on a weekend.

"It is always good to have these discussions in confidentiality," Guo said, smiling at the two directors. He and Whyte had met twice before in London and fenced a little bit about how GART and Guogene Labs might be able to cooperate. It had become obvious that Guo was interested in investing and Whyte was in desperate need of cold hard cash. So here they were.

"Do you live near here?" Guo asked Mrs. Block and she smiled for the first time and explained that she lived in a small village called St. Mary Bourne which was about half an hour's drive away. As they spoke the sound of a large helicopter could be heard in the distance.

"The Army Air Corps has its main facility at Middle Wallop, very close to here," Professor Whyte said. "They are always buzzing over our heads and we pray the pilots aren't drunk and don't crash."

"Very good," Guo nodded. He glanced over at Bohumir who was dressed in the same black suit he always wore and who sat quietly at the end of the table showing no emotion or interest on his face.

"You know my butler, Bohumir. He's a very good egg. Makes everything smooth for me," Guo introduced his man and both Mrs. Block and Professor Whyte smiled politely. Bohumir nodded sharply and said nothing.

"How is the research going on Gomeldovir?" Guo came straight to the point.

"To be honest, it's, umm, stalled a bit in the last few weeks," said Whyte.

"Yes, you say something like that. What is the problem?"

"As you know Gomeldorvir is a direct-acting antiviral that inhibits RNA-dependent RNA polymerase and has shown inhibitory effects on the coronavirus called SARS and also on MERS."

"Yes, yes," Guo said.

"There are two problems we are facing."

"Yes, yes."

"We don't have any sick people to use it on. We haven't had a coronavirus for several years and because of that," Professor Whyte shrugged and held up his hands in sadness, "nobody will give us any funding to further develop it."

"Explain more," Guo said, although he knew the details, he wanted the man to remind himself why they needed Guogene's help.

"As I said the last time we met. The government does not have any funding budget allocated for this type of research. The big pharma companies are not interested because these are not global diseases. They are geographically isolated, so there is no money to be made. And no private equity investors are interested because unless millions of people are dying there is no point is spending money on research costs that won't be recovered."

"Yes, it is a pity," Guo said and actually managed to look sad rather than jubilant.

Professor Whyte continued: "We think it could be a highly effective broad spectrum anti-viral. We just need more development, more testing and a lot more time."

"In China SARS was a very big problem. Many people died," Guo said, nodding intently. "Maybe something like that will come again."

Mrs. Block joined the conversation: "Nobody seems to think it will in Europe and if it does happen it will be restricted to a limited segment of the population, the old and those with underlying health issues."

"But you have other products in development?" Guo asked, waving his hand to take in the building and all the laboratories.

"Yes, some generics but we had really pinned our hope on Gomeldovir," Whyte said. He was sounding more desperate than the last time they had met and Guo suspected it had something to do with running out of cash more rapidly than they had expected. They had 28 employees and many of them were highly qualified research scientists who were passionate about their areas of expertise. They didn't understand business. They believed a government or rich benefactor should provide all the funding that was ever needed. Then they could create pharmaceuticals that were of importance to the medical community and mankind.

"Mrs. Block, you are the expert with money," Guo said. "How much money do you need every month to cover the salaries, rent and other costs?"

The Finance Director pulled out a piece of paper from a ring binder in front of her and mentioned a number that was just under £200,000.

"Professor Whyte, how much do you think your business is worth?" Guo asked.

The founder and Managing Director of GART looked sheepish. He glanced at his accountant who shrugged. She knew what the balance sheet told her. But that was simply the sum total of all the equipment after depreciation, and not much more.

"I've no idea," replied Whyte. "Maybe £10 million, double that?" He glanced at his accountant again who shook her head. She had an idea of what Mr. Guo might say.

"I think your business is worth very little," the Chinese man said. "You have no profit, no product and a large monthly overhead. So by this time next month you will be bankrupt." He frowned sadly as he said this.

"We have applied for the new government Innovate Pharma fund, you know," Whyte said.

"It will take months before we hear back from them," Mrs. Block reminded him.

"I am very interested in Gomeldovir," said Guo, "and I believe you are a brilliant scientist, Professor Whyte."

The Professor didn't quite blush because he was too stressed out with saving his company, the baby he had created only two years earlier.

"I will buy GART for £2 million," Guo said. "I will have 90% of the shares and you will keep 10% of the shares."

Whyte's face was ashen. To give away all that he had created and be left with only a small sliver. But the alternative was nothing, as Guo knew because he had done his research, there was only enough cash in the bank to survive for two more months. Guo was throwing them a lifeline. And there was no other boat on the high seas. This was the only chance of survival.

"You must have Gomeldovir ready for market within six months. We will do testing in Asia. I will provide all financing if you agree with my proposal."

Professor Whyte stared out of the window at the rear car park. There was one lonely battered Land Rover Defender standing in the rain. It seemed that one of its tyres had a puncture. He glanced at Mrs. Block who nodded. She had one percent of the company and she understood that one percent of a company owned by a Chinese billionaire who might turn it into a success was a lot more than one percent of a bankrupt venture.

Guo snapped his fingers. Bohumir came over with the briefcase, opened it up and handed his boss a four page document in a transparent folder. Guo extracted the pages from the folder and slid them across to Professor Whyte. "This is our Letter of Intent. All of our terms are mentioned in there. I have already signed here. You must sign by Monday if you are interested and then we can start on the due diligence."

The Chinese billionnaire turned his attention to Mrs. Block. "In China we do business very fast. If we can finish due diligence by Wednesday, and agree the text of the

Sales and Purchase Agreement by Thursday, I will be happy to provide a cash advance of £400,000 into the GART bank account on Friday so you can pay salaries next week."

"Very well then," said Professor Whyte after a few moments of silence. Mrs. Block nodded her approval.

10

Scrimple woke up about ten the next morning. He'd missed breakfast but all he needed was a gallon of coffee and something for the hangover.

He staggered out of the club into the sunlight by around eleven and found a Costa Coffee that provided some relief.

That had been another typical McAlistair night of indulgence. After dinner he'd taken them to a discrete strip club called 'The House of the Rising Sun' where skinny Vietnamese girls danced around poles. Scrimple had really wanted to pay attention but it was all a bit late by then and he had probably exceeded the government's recommended limit of 56 units of alcohol per month, in one single night. He had finally got to bed by two or three in the morning.

He'd sent Esmeralda a text when he woke up saying he'd be back after lunch sometime. That was suitably vague. He'd asked her to let the guests know but was sure nobody missed him and that all would be ticking over nicely without him.

He popped into Waterstones and browsed the bookshelves for half an hour. It was a form of exercise that helped to re-synchronise the movement of his arms and legs although he did trip on the stairs on the way up. He found two of McAlistair's books and bought these. He might remember the next time they met to bring them along and get them signed. Perhaps sometime in the future he'd be as famous as Lee Child, and Tom Cruise would play the part of the dashing Hong Kong Police Inspector based on Scrimple.

He laughed at that thought. Obviously still drunk.

By 1 p.m. he was hungry and got a sandwich in a coffee shop at Westfield, then found his car and began gently driving home. Gentle was the operative word for everything today.

Scrimple stopped off for a pee break around Reading and got a copy of the Daily Mail which he read while sipping a Grande Latte. He sent another text message to Esmeralda saying he was on his way. There was no reply so he assumed she was serving or clearing up lunch. He came off the M4 and headed in the direction of Andover. There was a petrol station he always used run by a man called Patel who for some reason had the cheapest BP in the county.

By 4 p.m. Scrimple took the turning by the George & Dragon pub in the direction of St. Mary Bourne. He drove the Polo around the back and activated the remote control which opened the electronic gates that led into the courtyard which was part of the garden and where they parked.

He watched the electronic gates close with a satisfying 'clunk'. They were not regular gates although they appeared quite ordinary. Scrimple got his overnight bag from the back of the car and walked gently towards the kitchen door. It was slightly ajar as it usually was when Esmeralda had been cooking.

"I'm back," he said. He didn't yell because he didn't want to disturb the interrogator and his North Korean customer in their work. The table was laid for a meal and the new Rice Krispies box was still on the side table next to the toaster.

"Hello, I'm home," Scrimple said and walked through into the corridor. He couldn't hear any voices coming from the study but that was normal because it had been professionally sound-proofed. Winchcombe had even mentioned something about a Faraday cage but Scrimple wasn't sure exactly how that worked.

He wondered where Pacino was. As the man in charge of security he should have been sitting somewhere with an eye on the doors or the road. A little twitch of insecurity shot across his mind, wondering if perhaps there was something going on between Esmeralda and the soldier. Perhaps they were in the bedroom, having a quick fumble, not expecting Scrimple to be back so soon.

Nonsense. She was a good girl. And a bloke like Pacino was a consummate professional. You didn't mess about with another man's partner, especially not when at work.

The house was uncannily quiet. It disconcerted Scrimple. He walked up the stairs. It was an old house, despite some modern additions to make it fit for its current role, and so the fourth and eighth steps creaked.

Scrimple walked into his bedroom. There was nobody in the bed. He dropped his bag on it and went to check the other bedrooms which all turned out to be empty.

Weird, he thought to himself.

He washed his hands and face in his en suite bathroom and then went back downstairs. There was nobody in the study or any of the other rooms.

At this point he shat himself, not physically but metaphorically.

This was bad. This was wrong. Where the hell was everybody?

Nobody was supposed to leave the house when an interrogation was in progress. They were not supposed to go for a walk in the countryside or pop down to the pub.

So what was going on? He froze for a moment, trying to decide what he should do first. Then he ran to the cubby hole below the stairs, pulled open the door and punched in the code to the gun-safe. He swung open the door and grabbed one of the Glock 17s that lay on the cushioned shelf. There was already a magazine in the semi-automatic pistol. The magazine held 17 x 9mm rounds. Scrimple pulled back the slide and put a round into the breech. There was no safety catch as such on a Glock.

Scrimple turned and walked back through the entire house again, checking each room, looking under the beds, in the cupboards. He found nobody. He crossed the garden and checked the back shed. The entire house was deserted. He held the pistol in his right hand by his thigh. He was sweaty from the exertions and filled with panic.

"What the fuck," he said to himself. Next step, report in.

He went to sit on the garden bench, tucking the Glock in his waistband and pulled out his iPhone. He activated the Ganymede communication app and punched the code for Winchcombe. What was he going to say? They've all gone up in a puff of smoke?

It simply didn't make sense.

The app rang six times. No answer. Then a voicemail came up. "I'm busy, leave a message and I'll get back to you as soon as I can," Winchcombe's voice said. He'd been in the service for a long time. Had worked for both MI6 and MI5 which was unusual and although he could sometimes be a bit pedantic, he'd been a decent guy to work for so far.

"Err," Scrimple began, still flustered, unsure how to explain it all concisely. "This is an emergency. Get back to me right away. I've just got back from London and there's nobody in the house. It's deserted. I don't know what the hell is going on." Scrimple stopped himself there, realising that he was starting to babble. He hit the disconnect button.

Okay, relax. Let's think this through, he told himself.

He went into the kitchen and drank a large glass of water. Then he went into the study and opened the drinks cabinet. He found the bottle of Absolut vodka he'd bought last week and put a few slugs of the clear Swedish liquor into a whisky glass. He sat down in one of the leather armchairs, put the Glock on the side table and sipped the neat vodka slowly while he tried to calm down and make sense of it all.

11

Gavin Hamilton had been running MI5's satellite station in Cambridge for several years now. As he told any visitor from the head shed in London, he loved his job and they would have to drag him out screaming, feet first, if anyone wanted to transfer him back to Thames House.

He was a man in his early sixties but appeared ten years younger since he'd started competing in Iron Man events. He'd lost about forty pounds and had the lean and hungry look of a retired Royal Marines Commando.

His wife had recently passed away from an illness he wouldn't discuss and so he had thrown himself even more into his workouts and his work.

There were two other colleagues who worked with him in the shabby office in Trumpington. They had recently transferred in and he was still training them up, knocking them into shape. Linda Faranger was in her mid-twenties and had studied Spanish and Russian. Wesley Snow was a man of colour, second generation West Indian, in his early thirties and had studied computers at Warwick University.

Much of what they did was boring and routine. Like any office and any job. You sat in front of a screen - in their case in front of four screens - and read or watched stuff.

You wrote reports and assessments and most days left the office at 5 p.m. and went to the pub with your friends.

Hamilton had two friends he drank and trained with, both of whom had no idea what he did for a living and thought he worked for a company that did something in Health & Safety.

"This office is far too hot, mate," Wesley complained. "We've got to get them to give us an air-con." He was sitting at his desk by the window, which was wide open.

"Hasn't bothered me for the last few years," Hamilton said. He was waiting for the computer to tell him if the voice of a student who claimed to be from Malawi matched with the voice of a Nigerian Islamic terrorist target they had on the database. The computer - they all called her 'Gladys' because she could speak and had a bossy, middle-aged woman's voice - was working particularly slowly this morning, as if she too was affected by the charming spring weather and would have preferred to be out on the River Cam in a punt.

"Well you is well hard. Everybody knows that," said Wesley.

His father was a doctor, his mother a paediatric nurse and he'd attended a fee-paying school so nobody took his gangster act seriously.

"What've you got going on this evening?" Hamilton asked as the circle on his screen kept on going round and round telling him that Gladys was still contemplating the facts laid before her.

"Got myself a hot date with a first year biology student," Wesley said. "A real natural blonde."

"Where did you meet her?" Hamilton said, tapping his rollerball pen on his notebook in time to an old Whitesnake riff that was running through his head. He'd met David Coverdale on the tube once before he got famous.

"On Bumble," Wesley said. "She wants a serious relationship with a man who can treat her with respect."

Hamilton glanced over at his colleague and rolled his eyes. "She's come to the right place then. Where are you taking her?"

"That Turkish place Effies. Food's dead good there."

"She'll be impressed," Hamilton said. "Linda, is your boyfriend coming up for the weekend?"

The girl slipped back one side of the headphones she was wearing and said, "I hope so or I might have to start going on Bumble myself."

"What about you then, Gav?" Wesley said. "Got a new woman in your life yet?"

"Not really interested. You get to my stage in life and it's hard to meet anyone new."

"You're a good looking old geezer," Wesley said, grinning. "There'll be loads of MILFs out there who'd want to date you."

Hamilton shook his head with a contumely smile. "At my age you just can't be bothered any more. I'd rather do 60 miles on my bike than go on a date with a stranger."

"That's what you say," Wesley laughed. "But when that perfect lady walks through the door your heart will pound and you will know she's the one."

Gladys the computer spoke up: "There is no match for your sample," she insisted. "Enter a new recording or try again."

"Piss off, Gladys," Hamilton told the software and opened another program to check the week's calendar.

"Wesley, I need you to go along and infiltrate that anti-colonial march that's taking place tomorrow afternoon," Hamilton said. "They reckon someone wants to pull down the statue this time."

"Can I do the march?" Linda asked. "You always get me to do the lesbian biker-chick Nazis. It's getting a bit boring."

"I don't mind," Hamilton said. "You can do the march but I can't send Wesley to do the Nazi lesbians."

"Why not? I love lesbians," Wesley said, perking up. But he knew it made no sense. They wouldn't take him seriously if he accidentally knocked his drink over one of them and then tried to start a conversation. Everybody knew that it had to be horses for courses when it came to undercover work. Hamilton had requested at least two Muslim officers but they were in short supply and they needed them in London, he was always told, and Manchester.

He leant back in his chair and thought about the work-out he was going to do this evening at the gym. He'd have to pick up some chicken and rice from the Waitrose across the road when he left the office. And some more of the whey protein.

Later that evening he'd go and have a drink with a classics don from Pembroke who was one of his long-term assets. The professor had an eye for weird and wonky students whose political views were about to cross the line into radical territory. He enjoyed gossiping over a few pints and never stopped repeating his story about how he'd told Tom Hiddleston that he'd never make it as an actor and should concentrate on being a Latin teacher instead. Tom had got a double-first and then went on to conquer Hollywood. Hamilton's favourite two Pembroke alumni, as he enjoyed telling his professor informant, were Gavin Lyall, a thriller writer from the sixties and Tom Morris, who had put the puppets into 'War Horse'.

It was a tough gig heading up MI5 in Cambridge, he always moaned with a big grin on his face, especially since he'd gone to Balliol College, Oxford where he'd read what the brochure officially called *Literae Humaniores*.

12

There was something uncanny about the situation, Scrimple concluded, after finishing his glass of vodka. An empty house, an open dishwasher, it was like a ghost ship where everyone had been swept off the decks during a mutiny.

He didn't like it at all. He didn't understand it. He held the grip of the Austrian semi-automatic tightly because it seemed the only life-line he had. Was he being set up perhaps? Why hadn't Winchcombe answered or returned his call?

Maybe he's on the crapper? Or driving somewhere.

Scrimple checked his watch. It was nearly fifteen minutes since he'd walked into the silent house. Maybe whoever had come and taken Esmeralda, Pacino, Tchaikovsky and the North Korean would be back for Scrimple?

He came to the conclusion that he had to fall back and regroup. It sounded clever. He had to get out of the house, go somewhere less obvious and continue to get in touch with his contacts. He didn't have any other number for MI5 except Winchcombe's. There was no other hotline that he could call. There was no emergency alarm button.

It seemed a bit stupid but nobody had ever mentioned what to do if Winchcombe wasn't available.

Scrimple had a mobile phone number for Kat Pedder. He punched in her name and it began to ring. *Come on, come on.*

She would know what to do. She'd laugh and tell him that they had been pulled out to another location but hadn't got around to telling Scrimple because he had been in London.

The mobile rang out at eight rings and a voicemail came on: "Hi, this is Kat. I'm out of the country on a long holiday so just send me an email."

Scrimple stared at the screen of his phone. Unbelievable. Where the fuck was everyone.

Okay, calm down. Check the safe, get some clothes, get out of here.

He went back into the house, cautiously in case someone had come in while he was in the garden. He checked the rooms again quickly and then went to the safe that was at the back of the cupboard in his bedroom. He punched in the code, used the key that he had on his key ring and opened the heavy door.

There wasn't much in the safe. There was a Pelican R20 Ruck case, about 7 inches long, 3 inches deep which was water-proof and orange in colour. He opened the front snap and found that it contained 12 USB memory sticks lying loose inside. Scrimple had no way of knowing if that was one day or one week's worth of recordings but it was good that they were still here. Then there was a stack of cash in the safe: about £2000 in twenties and tenners. They used it for petty cash and it was topped up every time when a set of guests left and before a new one arrived. He grabbed the money, managed to fit it into the Pelican case on top of the memory sticks, closed it and then locked the safe again.

On the top shelf of the cupboard was a North Face duffel bag. He packed enough clothes for a few days, put the Pelican case in as well then transferred his wash-bag. Finally he went to the gun cupboard under the stairs. He took the other Glock 17 and packed it.

He stared at the two L119A2 assault rifles. Should he take them both? They both had the shortened 10.5 inch barrel and were equipped with what he'd heard his instructor call a Magpul buttstock which was a triangle of reinforced polymer that could be adjusted. They would easily fit into his duffel bag.

He decided to take them both and all the 5.56 mm ammunition. No point in leaving any of this kit here. He could always return it once he'd got to the bottom of this mystery.

Five minutes later, having locked up the house properly he was driving down the main road and wondering where to hide out.

Roland's farm house was up on the hill, about three miles drive. Scrimple entered through an open gate across a cattle grid, then drove along a tarmac road for a mile and came to an imposing stone house which had views in all directions. There was a barn around the back and a modern garage complex that could house five cars. Roland's Land Rover Discovery was there which was a good sign. Next to it stood his classic Porsche 911 - one of the air-cooled ones - an old Volvo estate and a battered Golf.

Scrimple knew that Roland's wife had left him last year which was why he spent a lot of time in the pub. Sitting up here in this large, imposing house must be lonely.

The front door opened as he pulled up the Polo near the garage. Roland, dressed in his usual pullover and scruffy cords said: "What are you doing up here?"

His tone was curious but friendly. Scrimple had never been at the house before although Roland had described it to him a few times and even invited him to go pheasant shooting in the past. Scrimple had never taken him up on the offer because his work schedule had always been unpredictable.

"I'm really sorry to drop by like this," Scrimple said, trying to put a smile on his face. "Are you busy with anything?"

"Watching the football and having a whisky. Come on in."

"Roland, I've got a problem. My Mrs. has kicked me out of the house. We had an argument about nothing. You know how it goes."

"You need a place to stay for the night?" the wealthy farmer said with a knowing grin.

"If it's not too much of an inconvenience? I could check into a hotel or a B & B but I thought I'd ask you first."

"I've got seven bedrooms so you can take your pick." Roland turned to go back into the house. "On second thoughts you'd better use my daughter's old room. She was just here a few days ago. The other ones don't get dusted that often." He laughed and watched as Scrimple took his duffel bag out from the car. He wouldn't be laughing, Scrimple thought, if he knew the bag contained two assault rifles normally issued to the SAS and enough ammunition to withstand an embassy siege.

"I'll show you the room, drop your bag there and come and have a drink and tell me the whole sordid tale," Roland said, leading the way through a long hallway that smelt of dog and damp Barbour jackets, then going up the stairs. There had been two black labradors but the ex-wife had taken them, Scrimple remembered.

"Here you go," the farmer said. "Sorry about the pink wall paper."

Scrimple knew that Roland's daughter worked in London and since her mother had left Roland she made a point of coming to stay every second or third weekend.

A while later they were ensconced in the lounge. Roland had a vast flat screen TV and the football was on at a low volume. It was very much a man's room. A tray stood on the table in the corner with the remains of what had been lunch. A half empty bottle of Macallan and a jug of water were on a side table.

"It's not bad here," Scrimple complimented the farmer.

"Too big for me. If I had any sense I'd sell up, take the money and go and live in my place in Spain." He let out a grunt of irritation. "Can't get myself to do it. My son and daughter would kill me. This land has been in the family for five hundred years."

"Right," Scrimple said because they'd had this conversation before a few times in the pub, usually after the third pint.

"So what did you do to make the little lady so angry?" Roland wanted to know. He placed an empty glass in front of Scrimple and held up the bottle of Scotch. Scrimple nodded. Roland filled his glass half full and pointed at the jug of water.

"Who knows," Scrimple said and felt a bit guilty. Esmeralda didn't deserve to be lied about like this but he had to make his story convincing. Roland had met her a few times in the pub. "I couldn't get it up. Even the little blue pills didn't work so she accused me of having it off with another woman. It just got a bit out of hand and I said some things that you shouldn't say to your girlfriend."

The farmer nodded sagely. "I've been there before. Especially once you've had a drink or two you've got to be careful what comes out of your mouth. Women will never let you forget." He took a sip of his Scotch and stared into the distance. "She just went and found herself another bloke. Told me I had been nasty to her for over a decade. I had no bloody idea."

"That's women for you," Scrimple said. "I just need to make a phone call. Can I use your toilet while I'm at it?"

Roland told him there was one next to the kitchen and Scrimple went off. He was praying fervently that this time Winchcombe would answer. He'd also try one more time in case he could get more than voicemail from Kat. There had to be someone who could tell him what to do, what was going on.

But nobody came to the phone. Scrimple, speaking in a low voice and covering his mouth with his hand as he stood in the toilet left a similar message for Winchcombe as last time and also tapped out a short message in the encrypted Ganymede app. For Kat he didn't bother. He didn't have her email address so he wasn't going to send her an email.

There was a mirror over the Victorian-style wash basin. Scrimple stared at his face and asked himself: "What the fuck is going on?"

For now, he was sure, he was safe in this remote location. He had some time to take stock and decide what he should do next.

As he walked past the coat rack where he'd hung his waterproof jacket, he felt the inside pocket and touched the reassuring hardness of the Glock pistol. The other one was in the duffel bag upstairs with the assault rifles.

"Did you apologise to her?" Roland grinned when Scrimple came back into the lounge.

"No answer."

"You've got to let them get it out of their system," Roland said. "Not that I know bugger all about women. I was going to put a steak on the grill. I've got a few more in the freezer. Fancy a steak?"

Scrimple nodded. Last night's steak and the mellow evening with McAlistair felt like a very long time ago.

13

Bohumir drove the Mercedes C-Class to an address in Slough. It was a red-brick terraced house and he parked the car on the drive.

He went to ring the doorbell but the door was opened before he reached it. A bullet-headed Albanian in a bomber jacket told him in English to follow and they walked down the hallway into the kitchen.

"How did it go?" Bohumir asked one of the other two Albanians sitting at the kitchen table playing cards. He was the boss, as evidenced by the gold rings on his fingers and the gold Rolex on his wrist.

"No problem," said the boss, whose name was Spahiu.

"What about the soldier? Did he put up a fight?"

Spahiu shook his head. "Bardhi here hit him from behind before he had a chance to pull his gun. They were all sleeping. The woman tried to scream but once we told her she would be raped, she shut up."

"Where are they now?" Bohumir asked.

"We've got them in the cellar. It's a bit damp but not too bad." The Albanian pointed up at the ceiling and added, "The Korean is upstairs. We gave him some diazepam so he fell asleep."

Bohumir took out a fat envelope from the inside pocket of his black suit jacket and placed it on the table. "Count it. It should all be there."

Spahiu, the boss, nodded at Bardhi to put the cards down and check the money. They were crisp £50 notes featuring the faces of two grumpy Victorian men. Bardhi confirmed that there were 200 of the notes as had been agreed.

"What do you want us to do with the prisoners?" Spahiu asked. He had a gold tooth at the top of his mouth and he enjoyed showing it off.

"Keep them for three days and then let them go. Blindfold them and set them free somewhere in the countryside."

"We can kill them, it's always cleaner."

"Did any of them see your faces?" Bohumir asked.

"We wore ski masks all the time," Spahiu said. He winked at the Slovak. "We are fucking professionals, you know."

"What weapons did they have?"

"The soldier had a Sig Sauer, that was it. I've kept it for myself. They are not cheap and as the English say, a nice piece of kit."

"There should have been more weapons in the house. We were told there were two assault rifles in a gun cupboard."

"Nobody used them. So we did not find them."

Bohumir shrugged. "It doesn't matter. Can you get the Korean and I'll take him away."

Spahiu waved at the bullet-headed man who'd opened the door and he walked down the hallway to go upstairs.

"Don't kill the prisoners, Spahiu. It's part of our deal that you keep them alive."

"I don't care. We'll give them sandwiches and water and then kick them out of the van. What are you doing with the Korean?"

"We're going to send him back to Asia."

"Back to Korea?"

"No, he's going to China. We have some work for him to do."

"If he's from North Korea why couldn't you bring him across the border from there into China? Why does he have to come all the way to the UK first?"

"It's impossible for people to escape from North Korea. This was a much easier solution."

"What does he do that's so special, this Korean?"

"He's some professor," Bohumir said evenly, but his tone implied that he didn't want to provide any more information. "He does professor shit and it's important for my principals."

"You work for the Chinese?"

"Not exactly." Bohumir gave the Albanian a dry laugh. "It's been good doing business with you. I'm sure we will have some more work for you in a few months."

"*Mirupafshim*," said Spahiu and gave the Slovak a slow, ironic wave good-bye. The bullet-headed man appeared in the doorway with the North Korean man who was blinking rapidly. He looked as if he'd been woken up from a deep sleep and was confused what exactly was going on.

"Hello, Mr. Park, I work for Mr. Guo and I've been sent to bring you to him," said Bohumir and shook the Asian man's hand.

"What is happening?" the Korean said, looking from one face to the next.

"Come with me," Bohumir said and gently pushed him towards the front door. He threw a quick *"Dovidenia"* over his shoulder which was Slovakian for good-bye.

It was getting dark by the time they reached the big house in Belgravia and Bohumir parked the black C-Class in the underground garage next to the Bentley. Mr. Park had fallen asleep after ten minutes - the drugs were still working through his system - but woke up when Bohumir shook him and told him they had arrived.

They took the service elevator up to the fourth floor and Bohumir showed him into a pleasant room decorated with blue wallpaper. There was an en suite bathroom with a marble floor and a shower. It was one of the smaller guest rooms.

Bohumir pointed to an alarm clock on the bedside table next to the king size bed. "If you have a shower and freshen up Mr. Guo is expecting you for dinner in half an hour. There should be clothes that fit you in the cupboard."

The Korean bowed slightly and said thank you. He was starting to understand what was happening. After all, this had been planned for many weeks between him and a go-between who worked for Mr. Guo.

"Now, we are in London?" he asked.

"Yes, Mr. Park. You are in Mr. Guo's house."

"That is very fine. I think I am hungry."

"Mr. Guo has an excellent chef."

The butler left the Korean to freshen up and took the lift back down to the ground floor where he found Mr. Guo sitting in his wing-backed armchair squinting at his iPad. Bohumir reported all that had happened and what had been arranged for the other prisoners.

As they were finishing their conversation, Guo's mobile rang.

"That's fine, that's fine. Excellent work," he said waving the butler away. "It's the girl, I need to talk with her." He stood up and walked to the window. "*Ni hao*, Jing Jing, how are you today?"

The girl at the other end of the line sounded as if she had been crying.

"I'm so sorry to trouble you, Felix."

"What is it?"

"My boss, the lady boss, she has fired me."

"Why did she do that?"

"She thinks I might have an affair with the master when he comes to England next week."

"Is that what she said?" Guo asked, liking the way this conversation was going. He was starting to think of himself already as a knight in shining armour riding to the rescue.

The girl said, "She did not say exactly like that but one of the other servants told me. She is jealous that I'm young and attractive."

"I can understand that."

"You said you could be my friend, Felix. I have nowhere to go. They gave me some money and I must leave by tomorrow morning."

"That is so quick," Guo said and found himself grinning. "What will you do?"

"I don't know. They also gave me a ticket to fly back to Shanghai but it is only for next week so I have nowhere to stay. I need to find a hotel."

Guo said, "Of course you don't need to go and stay in a hotel. You will come and stay in my house. I have many beautiful guest bedrooms. You will be my guest."

"Felix, that is so kind," Jing Jing purred down the phone line. "You are a good hearted man."

"We are friends. That is what friends are for," said Guo. "You pack all your things and I will send my driver to pick you up in an hour. How is that?"

"That would be so wonderful."

14

It was about three in the morning when Scrimple woke up. He didn't know what had woken him but he slipped out of the bed in Roland's spare room and limped barefoot to the window. There was a niggle at the back of his head because they'd finished the bottle of whisky between the two of them.

Scrimple pushed aside the curtain gently and saw a car in the moonlight without its headlights on. The car had just come to a stop about fifty metres from the house. The front doors opened and two dark figures stepped out of the car. There was no sound from the car doors closing. They walked carefully along the edge of the barn using what shadow was available to them. They paused briefly by Scrimple's Polo, studied it, and then moved on until they disappeared by the side of the farm house.

By now Scrimple was awake, his heart was pounding and his blood pressure must have been through the roof. He ducked back to the bed and pulled on his trousers, jacket, socks and shoes. He reached down into the duffel bag and took out one of the L119A2 assault rifles. It already had a magazine fitted. He removed the magazine from the other one and tucked it into the back of his trousers. Under his pillow was the Glock. He grabbed it and stuck it into the front of his waistband.

He had no idea who these men were. He assumed they were men. Once they had come closer to the farm house, he had been able to make out that they were dressed entirely in black, appeared slim and slight in stature, and moved with feline precision. Everything he saw spoke of professionalism and warned of danger.

Scrimple turned the key in his bedroom door and opened it, slipping as silently as he could onto the landing at the top of the staircase. The loud snoring coming from Roland's bedroom made it difficult to hear any other noises. Scrimple waited, listening to the galloping of his heartbeat. He tried to remember some of the things he'd been taught nearly thirty years ago. Breathe slowly in through the nose and out through the mouth in order to calm yourself down.

Then he heard the 'snick-snack' that could have been the front door being opened. If they were professionals they would know how to use a lock pick rake. Scrimple had asked Roland if there was a straight bolt on the inside of the heavy oak door but the farmer had only laughed and asked what was the point, there was nothing worth stealing.

Scrimple wanted to move to get a better vantage point but he knew that if he took a step forward and a floorboard creaked the only advantage he currently had would be lost. He felt the sweat on the palms of his hands as he gripped the L119A2. The weapon weighed about 3 kilograms and the magazine held 30 rounds. Scrimple had clicked the safety forward but could not remember if he was on 'semi-auto' or 'full-auto'.

He made out the rustle of fabric as someone moved and the trouser legs rubbed against each other. They were definitely in the house. An old piece of timber flooring creaked. For a few seconds there was complete silence as the intruders froze. Scrimple concentrated on his calming breathing techniques. His left knee ached and he realised that he wanted to have a pee. That would have to wait.

There was a tall window over the staircase and moonlight streamed in onto the small landing that was between the ground and first floor. That was a good thing, Scrimple told himself. He was in shadow but the intruders had to pass through the light.

And then they appeared, the two black-clad figures, both now holding semi-automatic pistols in their hands, their fists clenched together ready to fire at any threat. The second man was three steps behind the first one.

Scrimple was oddly calm now. He had thought this through as he waited for them to come up. Two camouflaged intruders, coming silently in the night, holding guns. There was no doubt this was a credible threat and to counter it aggressively was acceptable and appropriate. But he had been a policeman for so many years of his life that he had to be fair. He had to give them the benefit of the doubt.

When both intruders were silhouetted by the moonlight on the small landing below him, Scrimple shouted: "Drop your weapons or I will fire."

He wasn't sure what he had expected. Did he really think they would simply drop the guns and put up their hands?

Both intruders reacted instantly to Scrimple's warning. They snapped up their weapons and shifted into firing stances. But Scrimple's finger had been on the trigger and the men had been in his sights. All he had to do was apply that tiny pressure and the assault rifle exploded in a chatter of full automatic fire, cutting down the two black figures, tearing chunks of plaster and wood out of the wall, shattering the hall window.

"Fuck me," Scrimple said, astonished at his own actions. The two men lay twitching on the stairs. A cold wind blew in through the jagged remains of the window. Scrimple did as he had been trained: he flicked the fire selector switch to what he hoped was the safe position and replaced the empty magazine with a new one, tapping it in, hearing the satisfying click. He tugged it to make sure it was in.

There was a light switch outside Roland's bedroom and as Scrimple got there and turned on the first floor hall lights, the farmer stumbled to his door and pulled it open.

"What the hell..." he said and fell into an astonished silence. He stared at Scrimple, holding the vicious-looking carbine. He stared at the figures dying on his stairs.

"Sorry, Roland, I didn't expect this to happen. They were armed and they were coming after us."

"What sort of gun is that?" Roland stammered. He was only wearing pyjama bottoms and his gut hung over the top of them.

Scrimple advanced down the stairs keeping the muzzle on the two intruders and the stock in his shoulder. There might be others that he hadn't noticed. There might still be another threat coming from somewhere else in the house.

"Go back to your room, Roland, and close the door, there might be more of them."

The farmer didn't move, just kept on staring and trying to process what was happening in his house. Scrimple listened but all seemed to be silent. He'd only seen two arrive in the car so it was probably safe now.

Scrimple got to the first man and he surveyed the carnage that a full auto explosion could create. The 5.65 mm rounds had torn flesh and ripped off body parts. Both men were now dead. In the bright light of the single bulb that hung directly above the bodies, Scrimple could make out one important fact. Both of the men were Asian. They looked to be in their early thirties but one couldn't always be sure. They had closely cut hair and their faces had been blacked-out with camouflage cream.

It made no real sense to Scrimple but it had something to do with his safe house being raided. Had they come for the Korean man? Were they North Koreans? And why would they have tracked Scrimple down somehow and followed him here to the farm house?

Maybe they weren't Korean but Chinese? Scrimple squinted at the men's faces but they were so badly damaged he couldn't distinguish the subtle differences that might tell him which race they had been.

"I'm going to call the police," Roland said, suddenly coming out of his daze.

"Don't do that, Roland. These men were after me. I need to get away from here, *then* you can call the police."

"Why are they after you?" Roland asked, shaking his head, as if it might refocus the picture he was staring at. "Where do you get an assault rifle like that? I thought you were a retired policeman?"

Scrimple came back up the stairs. He'd have to check the rest of the house but he had to calm down the farmer first.

"I was a policeman and I now work for the Security Services. I can't explain any more than that." He took a deep breath and put a hand on Roland's shoulder. "These men are either Korean or Chinese. I have no idea. I also don't know why they are after me. That's why I have to go now. Before more of them turn up."

"More of them?"

"I have no idea what's going on, mate. Believe me."

"You just come to my house and drink my whisky and shoot up a bunch of people on my staircase?"

"Roland, get a grip. I'm sorry. Now sit down on your bed or I'll have to shoot you too." Scrimple felt guilty saying the words but he needed a few minutes to get himself sorted and the last thing he wanted was the farmer on the phone to the Hampshire Constabulary who'd come blundering along and slap cuffs on him. That was probably expecting too much. If he called 999 now it would take 40 minutes for a police car to show up. That's what everyone at the pub always moaned about. There had been such drastic cut-backs in the police force over the last ten years there were hardly any coppers to cover the large county at night.

These things went idly through his head as he tossed his stuff into the duffel bag and then emerged from his room.

Roland was standing in the doorway of his bedroom, glaring at Scrimple.

"I told you to sit down and not move," Scrimple said, putting a harshness into his voice that made him feel guilty. He raised the muzzle of his assault rifle so that it pointed at the farmer's belly button. The man walked backwards.

"Just sit there and wait for ten minutes and then you can call the police. I need to call this in to my bosses." He sounded more confident than he was. "They will sort things out with the police."

"You're Special Branch or something are you?" Roland said with a nod that indicated more understanding now.

"Yes, something like that. I'm on an undercover operation and things have gone a bit wrong so I need to get in touch with the head shed for instructions."

"Do you want to take my Porsche?" Roland said, suddenly helpful.

Scrimple gave a laugh tinged with nervous tension. "No, mate, you're all right. I'll be fine in my Polo." He indicated with his head. "Sorry about the mess."

"Fucking burglars," Roland said. "Got what they deserved."

15

At about 6 a.m. on Sunday Gavin Hamilton was woken up by a phone call from the Deputy Director General of MI5. The DDG was in charge of Counter-Terrorism, Counter-Espionage and all operational activities of the Security Service. Her name was Sara Dodwell and she was a woman with many years' experience and a fearsome reputation. On weekends she generally rode a Harley Davidson, wore a leather jacket, ripped Levis and cowboy boots, but today she was obviously working.

"Hamilton, are you awake yet?"

"I'm getting there, Sara. I was hoping for another two hours' sleep."

"What were your plans for the rest of the day?" she asked.

"I was going to go for a ten-mile run and sit in the garden contemplating man's inhumanity to man."

"It's not going to happen. The run, I mean. But I'll give you plenty of new material for your philosophical ruminations."

"I'm not liking the sound of this," Hamilton said and rolled out of bed, pulling open the curtains.

"You remember that ex-Hong Kong policeman Scrimple? You met him a few times with Kat Pedder."

"Of course."

"We took him on to work for us and run a safe house in Hampshire."

"I heard about that."

"It seems he's gone and shot up two unidentified Asian men and the safe house is empty. We can't get hold of Winchcombe who is his only contact and cut-out. So that's three very weird and worrying things to get on with."

Hamilton looked out of the window into his garden and pondered the cluster of apple trees. He lived in a five bedroom house that, these days, was too big for him since his children were grown up and his wife had died.

"Forgive me, Sara but what does that have to do with Cambridge Station?"

"I thought you'd ask me that question and so I prepared a succinct answer," the DDG said, with a dry laugh at the other end of the line. "Kat Pedder and her team are on a sensitive project overseas. She won't be back for weeks. Everyone else is flat out dealing with all this chatter we are getting about a potential bombing of a big public venue. So I thought that you, having dealt with this Scrimple bloke before, are the perfect senior officer to try and get to the bottom of things."

"I understand," Hamilton said. He realised that he didn't mind. It sounded like an interesting mystery and a bit of a change from a routine Sunday hanging out at the gym. "You want me to get onto this right this minute?"

"Yes, Gavin. If you can. The shooting happened on a farm near our safe house, not far from Andover. The farmer knows Scrimple. Apparently they drink together in the pub. Scrimple's disappeared, the police are all over the place, so it needs shutting down and repackaging for the media."

"Can we put a DSMA Notice on it?"

"I'd rather not. That makes the news agencies really curious. No, we want to spin it into something like: neighbours have an argument and shoot each other with their shotguns. But the really worrying thing is, we had an interrogation going on at the safe house and the guests are all missing."

"Have the police been to the house then?" Hamilton asked. He'd already pulled out a shirt and trousers from his cupboard and was reaching for his underpants drawer.

"Yes, they went looking for Scrimple there. Of course they don't know it's an MI5 safe house. They just thought it was his home. Before you get to Andover you need to drop by and check up on Winchcombe. He's not answering any communications and that's bad. So I'm going to send you two guys from E Squadron in case this is a proactive hostile operation. Because that's what it feels like. How Scrimple fits into this, you'll have to figure out."

"Have we tried calling Scrimple?"

"The police have tried but it seems he destroyed his phone and left it at the scene of the shooting. Then he headed off in his car."

"So we could pick him up on ANPR?"

"You'll have to activate that. I've emailed you all the details we have so far from the police and all the addresses. Major Tom Rieve and one of his men will meet you at Winchcombe's house. I've just got him out of bed."

"I've not worked with him before. I've heard he's very effective."

"He is. Don't let the fact that he's posher than Prince William fool you. He has more than a passing acquaintance with casual violence in the service of Queen and country."

"I'll be getting into the shower now," Hamilton said.

"Keep me posted using this Ganymede number. I need hourly updates if you can. I have a very bad feeling about this."

The DDG disconnected and Hamilton got himself ready to leave within twenty minutes. He packed a bag with enough clothes for a few days just to be on the safe side. He only checked the first address because he wanted to get on the road as quickly as possible. Before he set off, he roused Wesley Snow from his sleep and told him to be in the office within an hour so he could coordinate computer searches and other aspects from there. Searching for Scrimple's car registration number on the number plate recognition system was top priority.

Wesley wasn't too impressed but got the message that cow dung had hit the fan and this would not be a normal day.

Hamilton's car was a red Maxda MX-5 convertible. It wasn't designed to do long motorway drives but there was no choice in the matter. He punched Winchcombe's address in West London into the Tom-Tom attached to the windscreen and found that it would take an hour and a half to get there.

When he pulled up outside the terraced house he found two men in black jeans and black wind cheaters lounging on the front garden wall. They both had closely cropped hair and sharp angular faces that hinted at low body fat and high levels of aerobic fitness.

"Major Rieve?" Hamilton asked.

"Call me Tom. This here's Rickman," the taller of the two men said in an officer's voice that hinted at a private education.

"Have you been inside?" Hamilton asked.

"No bodies, nothing suspicious except that half of his wardrobe is empty, no suitcases or toothbrushes to be found. My guess is he's scarpered or someone is trying to make it look like that."

Hamilton checked his watch. The faster they got down to Andover and in front of the police the better. "Will you take me through the house quickly but if that's your professional opinion then I'm happy to accept it."

Major Rieve and Hamilton spent fifteen minutes checking all the rooms in the house. The front door had been locked but the soldier had opened it with a manual lock pick when he arrived.

"No phones, no computer," Hamilton said as they came back out of the front, "feels like he's gone off to the Costa del Sol on an unauthorised holiday."

Rieve nodded. "He could be lying six foot under in the nearest woods. As Ms. Dodwell suggested, it smells of a proactive hostile operation."

"What's your transport?" Hamilton asked.

Rieve pointed at a black SUV parked further down the road. "Standard unit issue BMW X5, three litre diesel, nought to sixty in 5.3 seconds."

"Have you got blue light?"

"We have," the Major said with a grin. Sometimes they had to accompany VIPs in convoys and provide armed support to other units.

"I'm going to leave my little sportster here and come with you."

It didn't take them long to get on the motorway and then Corporal Rickman cranked up the speed to a steady 90 miles an hour, cars getting swiftly out of their way as they saw what appeared like an unmarked police car heading somewhere in a hurry.

"This empty safe house is really upsetting me," Rieve said. He was sitting in the front passenger seat and had turned to speak with Hamilton in the back. "One of our troop was working there providing security. His nickname is Pacino, as in the actor from Scarface. He's a good man and I don't like the fact that he's missing."

"What weapons are you carrying?" Hamilton asked, indicating over his shoulder with his thumb.

"We both use the Sig Sauer P228. In the back we've got two more and four L119A2 assault carbines, Kevlar body armour and other toys that go bang."

Hamilton said, "We should be in good shape then, in case we encounter some angry hostiles."

"Are you comfortable with firing weapons, Gavin?"

"Give me one of the pistols. I'll stay away from carbines."

"So what about this Scrimple bloke then?" Rieve said.

Hamilton shrugged. "He's a funny fellow. Spent time as a Detective Inspector with the Hong Kong Police. Then he became a civilian, did something in business and somehow got involved in one of our operations last year. Kat Pedder was tracking him for months."

"We like Miss Pedder, don't we Rickman?" Major Rieve said.

"She's a good egg," the driver confirmed. "Why isn't she handling this?"

"I've no idea," Hamilton said. "She's overseas on a long term job, apparently."

"Canteen gossip has it," said Rieve, "she's heading up that new Department ADT. The one nobody knows anything about." He raised his eyebrows to see if Hamilton had anything he was willing to share.

He said, "Don't ask me. I work in Cambridge. Nobody ever tells me anything."

"What does ADT stand for then, sir?" Rickman asked, as he nudged the needle past 100 mph to overtake a Porsche Cayenne.

Hamilton said, "I may be mistaken but my understanding is that it's an acronym for Adrestia."

"Sounds like a nice place to go and take your summer holidays, sir."

Major Rieve laughed. "Greek isn't it?"

"Did you have a classical education?" Hamilton asked.

"I did Latin up to GCSE at Uppingham. That was about it. What about you?"

"Yes, I did classics at university. Adrestia is the Greek goddess of vengeance, another name for Nemesis. As in the Agatha Christie book."

"Vengeance? Sounds like our sort of work," Rieve said. "So the rumours might be true that Department ADT is working on sanctioned assassinations?"

"I sincerely doubt it," said Hamilton. "We're not Israelis."

"Yes, they've got their Kidon teams. Vicious bastards. We did some training with them in Syria once." Major Rieve frowned and was silent for a moment then said: "There is this rumour that Kat found some old bloke who used to be a professional assassin working for the Singaporean SID and he's now doing some work for us."

"Are you jealous, Major Rieve?" Hamilton chuckled with sudden enlightenment.

"To be honest, I am. It's E Squadron's job to go around plinking people. Most of the time we aren't allowed to, but sometimes they shoot first and then we're allowed to shoot back."

"Best not to worry about it too much, Tom. Cry havoc and let slip the dogs of war."

"What does that mean then, sir?" asked Corporal Rickman.

"It's Shakespeare," explained Major Rieve, "Mark Antony promises vengeance on the murderers of Julius Caesar. You and I are the dogs of war, unleashed on the enemies of our land."

"Sounds a bit poncey to me," said Corporal Rickman.

16

Scrimple understood that number plates could be tracked via the network of traffic cameras that existed across the country. He also knew that phones could be tracked and had experienced this before, to his detriment. So he had stamped on his iPhone until it was a shattered, bent remnant of its former self and he'd taken off down the farm track in his Polo.

It was still the middle of the night and the farm was well away from its closest neighbours so the gunfire might not have been heard or reported. Roland would call the police, but by the time they arrived Scrimple hoped he'd be miles away.

He parked the car in a public car park in Andover and then walked across town to the railway station, trying to avoid CCTV cameras and hiding his face underneath a baseball cap. By the time he got to the station it was shortly after 5 a.m. and the first commuters were arriving for the early trains to London and in the other direction.

Scrimple tried calling Winchcombe and Kat again without any luck from the red public phone box outside the station. It smelt of urine and there was a suspicious puddle on the floor because that was probably the only thing it was used for these days. Then he called Bob

Kenworthy, the landlord of the George pub in Girton, Cambridge. They had been mates in the Hong Kong police and for many years had drunk, partied and holidayed together.

"What is the matter with you, Scrimple?" Kenworthy said once he'd realised what time it was on a Sunday morning.

"I'm in a bit of bother."

"This had better be good."

"I can't talk about it in detail. But you know I'm working for MI5. Things have gone really weird." He explained briefly what had happened and his dilemma in not being able to reach anyone he knew in his organisation. He didn't want to hand himself over to the police until he knew what was going on. He needed Kenworthy to help him track down a guy called Gavin Hamilton who sometimes came to the pub. He worked with Kat Pedder and would know what to do.

"Haven't you got this bloke's contact details then?" Kenworthy asked.

"No, he's like the MI5 Cambridge office. Completely different department. I've just met him once or twice, that time you got shot."

"I don't have a number for him. He's not on our pub quiz team. He only comes in occasionally," Kenworthy grumbled. "Look, why don't you get your arse up here and then we can sort it out."

Scrimple said, "I don't want to do that. I don't want to drag you into this. Whoever is after me might know that we are old mates and they might be looking for me at your place."

"Okay, so what are you going to do now?"

"I'm just going to keep my head down. I've got a plan. I'll call you later in the day. But in the meantime, don't believe any crap they might say on the news about me being a mad killer. Try and get hold of Hamilton for me."

"I'll ask around once people wake up and the pub opens. I can't promise. If he's a spook he's going to be a bit careful about that sort of thing. I've no idea where he lives. He might be miles out."

"You used to be a detective, figure it out," Scrimple said wryly.

"So who do you think it is?" Kenworthy asked.

"No idea, might be Koreans, might be Chinese. They've come after the guests in my safe house, I guess."

"Why would they want to come chasing after you then?"

"If I knew that…"

"It's that Wendy Shen bitch. She's after you."

"I'm not that important to her. Why would she care? It's been ages."

"You messed up whatever she was working on last year. She didn't seem to me to be the sort of bird who forgives and forgets."

Scrimple groaned. "I'd thought about it. Anyway, I've got some personal protection with me. So I can shoot back if they come after me again."

"Turn yourself in to the police," Kenworthy said.

"I will, but not right away. This is just too weird to be normal. I have to get in touch with someone from the head shed."

"Can't you just drive up to London and ring the doorbell?"

"I've no idea even where the office is."

"Google it."

"Locate that Hamilton guy and that would sort things out."

Scrimple hung up and stepped over the puddle of piss and bought a ticket from the machine to Sherborne. Most of the commuters were half asleep, staring at their mobiles. The Costa Coffee hadn't even opened yet. There was a CCTV camera at one end of the platform and another one at the other end. Scrimple made sure he stood behind one of the pillars.

Finally the train came. The journey took about an hour. Sherborne was a pleasant Dorset market town that existed on the income of several private schools. It also had a large community of retired folk. It had a pleasant high street with the usual shops. There was a Waitrose at the top, a Sainsbury's at the bottom and a Boots in the middle. By the time he arrived the Costa Coffee on Cheap Street was open and he huddled in the corner with an extra-large latte and pastries.

A year ago Scrimple had attended a social gathering of the Royal Hong Kong Police Association in London at the Army & Navy Club's Ribbon Bar. About forty old codgers had turned up and told each other war stories over plenty of drink. Scrimple had caught up with a guy he hadn't seen for ages called Hayden Watts. They were in the same company in the Police Tactical Unit and had spent 9 months training and then on regional attachment.

Hayden had left the Force in 1997 and trained to become a teacher. He now taught History at Sherborne School and lived in a tiny Grade II listed terraced house at the top of the hill. Scrimple had come to visit him once and they'd had a meal, a laugh and more than five pints of beer each in a pub called the Digby Tap. Hayden was divorced and so Scrimple had an idea that if he turned up unannounced and asked for a bed for a few nights it would not cause any domestic strife.

At about 8 a.m. he knocked on Hayden's pale-green door on Greenhill and the man himself answered holding a piece of toast with black gunge on it that looked suspiciously like Marmite.

"There's a sight for sore eyes," Hayden said. "Lost your razor blade did you?"

"That's the least of my worries, not shaving," Scrimple said as Hayden waved him in.

"I see you've brought your overnight bag so I guess you haven't popped over just for a cup of tea," the teacher said. The living room was only large enough to contain two small sofas set at right angles, an open fireplace and a flat screen TV above the mantelpiece. On the floor was an oriental carpet covering traditional flagstones and an oak staircase led upstairs to two bedrooms and a bathroom. At the back was a bachelor-size kitchen and a small courtyard ideal for sitting in the sun and having a sly cigarette.

"I got your message but it didn't make much sense to me," Hayden said. "Cup of Yorkshire tea? Still got one left in the pot. My first class is at nine but it's only a five minute walk."

Scrimple nodded and plonked himself into the two-seater sofa by the window.

"So you need a place to stay for a few days?" Hayden said, handing Scrimple a mug. He was a large man, about the same size now as Scrimple, dressed in jeans and a tweed jacket. In their time they had been slimmer and fitter. Hayden was a few years older than Scrimple, so might have already hit the big six-oh.

"I need to lay low until some things are cleared up. Kenworthy in Cambridge is helping me find someone who works in the Security Service with me and whom I trust." He explained as much as he felt appropriate about the mess he had found himself in on returning from London.

Hayden asked the obvious question: "Why don't you have any contact details for anyone else apart from this Winchcombe bloke?"

"Security cut-off. Something like that. What I do is totally boring and unimportant. I'm not even an official employee or civil servant. So all I have to do is run what is basically a bed & breakfast. I don't need to interact with anyone else except my direct boss, as it were. He seems to have dropped off the face of the earth, or he's keeled over dead. Maybe he's just in hospital with an ingrowing toenail but it feels more complicated than that. Otherwise they wouldn't have sent two killers after me in the middle of the night."

"Who were they?"

"Fuck knows. I guess they are North Koreans who've come to grab back their defector. That's what makes most sense. But then I don't know why they would want to bother with me. How did they even track me down at this farm house where I went? Must have been the car or the phone."

"Right," Hayden said. "You keep your head down here. All the Sky Channels are available on that thing," he pointed at the flat screen TV screwed into the wall. "Don't make any phone calls. I'll pick up some food and be back for lunchtime."

"I need a cheap mobile phone with a few pay-as-you-go SIM cards," Scrimple said.

Hayden nodded and checked his watch. "Fine, I can pick those up at the supermarket." He pointed upstairs. "You know which is the guest bedroom. I've put a towel on the bed if you want to freshen up."

"You're a solid bloke," Scrimple said and buried his face in his hands. He needed a long, hot shower and a few hours kip and then he'd try and figure out one more time what was really going on.

"Could you pick up some WD-40 from somewhere as well," he added. "I don't suppose they sell Hoppe's gun cleaner at Waitrose, do they?"

17

Tradition, Mr. Guo liked to expound, was all the English had left these days. They had no money, they had no expertise and they had no honour, but the old traditions still existed in the right places. It pleased Mr. Guo to honour those old traditions, unless, like the golf club, they made no business sense and they had to be scrapped.

Having a full English breakfast on a Sunday morning was one of those pleasant affectations that he maintained. The buffet table was laid out with Cumberland sausages, streaky bacon, eggs - fried, poached and scrambled - black pudding, toast - white and brown - Cooper's marmalade... there was no end to the culinary ecstasy.

"You want a fresh orange juice, Anthony?" Guo asked the man in the pin-striped suit who was standing at one end of the buffet holding a plate. The reason he was wearing a pin-striped suit and Bengal-striped shirt and tie on a Sunday morning was that he was a lawyer. He was Anthony Peppard-Mills and he understood that when your biggest client was a Chinese billionaire you worked every day the good Lord gave you including the one that is supposed to be for rest.

"My Chef makes the orange juice with special oranges," Guo explained. "He can only buy them in Borough Market. From Japan, they are Shiranui."

"The scrambled eggs look delicious," the lawyer said and filled half his plate from the pan that was sitting on a warming tray.

The door to the dining room opened cautiously and Jing Jing poked her face through it.

Guo waved to her enthusiastically. "This is my friend Jing Jing. She has been working as a nanny in England for only a short time. Come, come. This is Mr. Anthony."

The girl was dressed in tight fitting jeans and a flowery blouse and had applied just enough make-up for a casual Sunday.

The lawyer and the girl shook hands and Guo explained to her what finery was available. "Did you sleep well? It is a new mattress. They are hand-made, by Savoir. Very nice, Number Four model."

"*Xie-xie*, Felix, very lovely sleep," Jing Jing replied. Peppard-Mills gave her a warm smile and went to sit at the far end of the table next to where Guo had been sitting.

There was a hesitant knock and Mr. Park came into the room. Guo introduced him to the others: "This is our friend Mr. Park. He is from Korea. He is a professor, very smart man in the field of virology and epidemiology."

"How do you do?" the lawyer said, standing up so his napkin fell to the floor and shaking hands.

"I am sorry, my English not so perfect."

"My Korean is not up to scratch either, so don't worry about that, old boy."

Guo said, "Mr. Park will help me to re-organise the efficiency of the new laboratories we are buying in Porton Down and then he will go back to work in our China operation. You have completed the sale and purchase agreement, Anthony?"

"Yes, the draft is there in my briefcase. All quite standard. As I understand they need the money desperately or they can't pay salaries next month so I hope their lawyers won't put up any fuss."

"You British lawyers are all so clever," Guo said and stuffed a slice of sausage into his mouth. "Jing Jing, you must eat more. That is not enough. You need some energy for today. We are going shopping."

Jing Jing giggled pleasantly.

"It's a terrible matter," Guo continued. "The employer of Jing Jing, also a Chinese family, the wife fired her with no reason. Only one day's notice. It is very tough. Maybe we should sue them for unfair dismissal. Is that what they can call it in the UK?"

"Yes, that's certainly a legal matter," the lawyer said.

"Felix, I don't have a contract," Jing Jing said quietly. "My aunt arranged the job and it is all done just by handshake."

"Terrible, you must always have a contract," Guo said loudly. "Everything must be done by lawyers. Everything must be water-tight, always. Am I right, Anthony?"

"Absolutely, Mr. Guo."

"Now, I want them to sign this contract next week. Not later than Friday. Mr. Park here is waiting to start work and we can only do that once we have full control of their facility and access to the test data on a new drug called

Gomeldovir. Mr. Park wants to check how effective it is, so we can move quickly to clinical trials."

Peppard-Mills glanced up from buttering his toast and gave a sad smile. "Not all lawyers in the UK work as fast as I do."

"We must put a fire under their asses," Guo said. "This is business. We can't screw around. You know my idea on this. You are all so half asleep in this country. Not you, not you. Everything moves slowly like.... Like... how is that song... a slow boat to China." Guo struck the table lightly with his palm so the crockery rattled. "We don't have any slow boat, we only have speedboat *from* China, in this days."

"I've tried to make the contract as straightforward as possible. There is very little to negotiate on, their lawyer would only be going through the motions."

"Very good, very good. This man, Jing Jing, he's the best lawyer in all of England. Mr. Park, you like the poached eggs? You must try the orange juice from Japanese oranges. The sweetest in the world."

"Where will you bring Miss Jing Jing shopping?" the lawyer asked politely.

Guo beamed. "You know she told me last week, she had never been to Harrods. Today we will go to Harrods and Liberty and Selfridges and House of Fraser. That's why you must eat," he waved at the girl. "For energy." He turned back to Peppard-Mills. "Tomorrow morning me and Professor Park we will drive down to Porton Down and start due diligence. I will put the draft sales and purchase agreement on the table of Professor Whyte and tell him, sign by Friday or no deal. He can chase for another investor."

The lawyer nodded gravely. "Placing the proverbial gun to his chest?"

"No need for gun. Only money. People need money. I think they have done some very good innovation but no money, no honey. You go bankrupt. Mr Park will tell me if what they have is good. It is part of our due diligence. If Mr. Park tells me it is shit, then we won't sign on Wednesday."

"But you believe that what they have is effective?" Peppard-Mills said.

"We read all the research papers and checked the data. It's looking very good. Mr. Park, he's the expert. That's why we need him to come all the way from Korea."

"Do you live in Seoul?" the lawyer enquired.

Park appeared confused for a second, as if he didn't understand the question, then he quickly nodded and said, "Seoul, Seoul, yes, very beautiful city."

"I enjoy Korean food very much. I have a penchant for Kimchi."

"Yes, yes. Kimchi, famous Korean food," Mr. Park agreed and got up from the table to help himself to some more English food.

"Will you be re-negotiating the price if you find anything unexpected tomorrow?" the lawyer asked Guo.

"Maybe, but it is a reasonable price and I don't want to squeeze too hard. Professor Whyte is already suffering high blood pressure. If all is good we can make so much money it will be crazy."

"A huge amount of money?" Peppard-Mills asked.

"Billions and billions. You do not believe me now but if we have another outbreak like SARS or MERS and it goes global then everyone will need to have our medicine. We prepare now," Guo's eyes twinkled with excitement, "to get rich in two or three years' time."

"That's sounds like a good plan."

"They will call me the Elon Musk of the pharmaceutical industry. A visionary. A thought leader, is that not the expression?"

"It certainly is."

"Jing Jing, have another egg and then we will leave about eleven o'clock."

The girl giggled delightfully and did as she was told.

18

By the time Hamilton and the E Squadron guys arrived at Roland's farmhouse there was only one police car left. A bored WPC in uniform was leaning on the bonnet and flicking through her Facebook messages. She glanced up with a frown as the black BMW X5 with tinted windows pulled up next to her.

"Who are you?" she asked. There was a hint of panic in her eyes as the three men jumped down from their SUV. Hamilton was wearing a blue jacket and a white shirt but Major Rieve and Rickman's choice of clothes had a certain gangster chic to it that could be misinterpreted.

"We're from Counter-Terrorism Command in London. I'm Gavin and this is Tom. Our bosses have informed your Chief Constable that we would be coming." He held up a warrant card that identified him as such.

The WPC shook her head. "I'll have to make a call and find out, sir."

"You weren't expecting us?" Hamilton asked.

"Not that I've been told," she said.

Hamilton gave a gentle smile and waved at the farm house. "Do you often have armed foreigners gunned down with military grade weapons in this part of Hampshire?"

The constable shook her head. "Not really. Ever. Not since I've been a police officer."

"So, surely you'd expect someone from our office in London to turn up and give you a helping hand?"

"Let me make that call to my inspector, sir," the woman said, suddenly flustered.

"Who else is in the house?" Hamilton asked. There was a white van parked closer to the door.

"Those are the crime scene techs, they're still working in there. And the owner of the farm. Could I have another look at your warrant card, sir." She eyed Rieve and Rickman, both of whom also produced laminated cards which identified them as serving in the armed forces.

"These gentlemen are seconded to us from the Army. They are experts in matters of firearms. We understand the victims here were cut down by a sub-machine gun of sorts."

"I don't know about guns, sir, but it looked like something with a lot of fire power."

"It's an L119A2 assault carbine, it's one of our standard weapons. The person who fired the weapon here had two with him, we believe," Rieve said.

The constable nodded and then turned away to make her phone call. After a while she finished her call and gave them a relieved smile. "That's okay now. I've been told to give you all the help and courtesy we can. The Superintendent would like to see you in Andover Police Station once you're done here."

Hamilton said, "Yes, we need to talk to him. This is a matter of national security and we need to keep a lid on what happened here for a few days. It's part of an ongoing investigation."

"Who are these dead Chinese then? And who shot them? The farmer said it was a bloke call Scrimple who's a retired Hong Kong policeman who lives in St. Mary Bourne?"

"That's about right," Hamilton said. "We can't talk about it but we know Scrimple. Why he was here and why he shot these two intruders is unclear." By now the constable was leading them towards the front door of the farmhouse.

"I have to warn you. It's pretty nasty in there. You can't go in without Tyvek suits."

"We can just pop our heads in the door. Can we talk to the farmer?"

Five minutes later they were standing outside with Roland who had a glass of whisky in his hand. He'd spent a few hours earlier in the morning at the police station but was back home now waiting for the crime scene team to finish and allow him upstairs.

"We are colleagues of Scrimple's and would like to ask you a few questions," Hamilton said, leading Roland away from the WPC.

"He's trying to get hold of you lot," Roland said.

"Is he?"

"Have you spoken to him?" Roland asked.

"We don't know how to get hold of him. He destroyed his phone."

"Did he now?"

"Tell us what happened, right from the beginning," Hamilton said, lowering his voice to create empathy.

"I think those two Chinese blokes were after Scrimple. He's on an undercover mission or something, isn't he? He turned up here with his duffel bag and he must have had that machine gun in there."

"Start at the beginning, Roland," Hamilton reminded him. "How do you know Scrimple?"

"He pops into the pub. We usually have a pint and a chat. The way you do, you know."

"I know." Hamilton took the farmer through his statement slowly and steadily - unknown to the man - recording it all on a small Sony recorder that he had tucked in his jacket breast pocket.

"Do you have any idea where he might have gone now, Roland? Did he say anything to you as he was leaving?"

"Only that he had to get in touch with the head shed, with you guys."

"Umm, yes, that's the problem," Hamilton said, smiling ruefully and sharing something confidential by way of thanking the farmer for his help, "he doesn't know how to get hold of us."

"He certainly knew how to handle that machine gun."

"Did he indeed?" Hamilton replied, nodding thoughtfully.

Fifteen minutes later they were at the safe house in St. Mary Bourne. The email Hamilton had received from the DDG gave him instructions on where to find the hidden key safe. He punched in a code and retrieved the front door key. The police had come earlier but used a locksmith to get into the house and then closed the door again.

They spent some time walking the house. They found the Burton Safe empty in the bedroom. They found all the weapons gone from the gun cupboard. There was no sign of a struggle, no blood, no damage. Everything was mysteriously quiet and peaceful.

"So what do we reckon happened here?" Hamilton asked letting himself fall into one of the leather armchairs in the study. Major Rieve stood by the window and looked at the garden, a grim expression on his face. It was his default face when he wasn't smiling. Corporal Rickman leaned against the door jamb and absently tapped the butt of his Sig Sauer on his belt.

"Our lad Pacino is no fool. He would have put up a fight if the chances were good but if four or five men came, all properly armed, he'd surrender and wait for the next best opportunity."

"So we're thinking a team came here, and lifted all the guests, took them to another location. But Scrimple wasn't here. He was away in London on a day off." Hamilton nodded, liking the story. "So he comes back, finds everyone gone."

"First thing he'd do is call Winchcombe and report in," Rieve prompted.

"Right. But Winchcombe isn't answering the phone. He's been lifted or he's dead."

"Who would Scrimple call next?"

"Winchcombe is his cut-out. He's doesn't have any other number. What would you do in his position?"

"Grab all the guns and as much ammo as you can carry," said Rieve, "and go somewhere safe and keep trying to reach someone you know."

"He goes to Roland, tells him a tale about being kicked out by his girlfriend. For some reason the team also wants Scrimple. They follow him and break into the farmhouse."

"But Scrimple is waiting for them. Gives them a full mag on full auto."

"Really?"

"Yes, he was on full auto. He's not familiar with that weapon."

"So they're Chinese or they're North Koreans?"

"The defector being interrogated was North Korean. I'd say he was someone really important, more important than we knew, and his countrymen wanted him back. They found Winchcombe and he told them about the safe house."

"Why did they need to come back for Scrimple? He's just the innkeeper," Hamilton said, staring at the recording machine on the table next to him. "Makes no sense. Scrimple isn't important. I could see they took everyone initially. Then they either kill them later or they set them free."

"Pacino isn't easy to kill," Rickman said from the doorway. His eyes had a hard, angry sheen to them. Pacino was his troop mate. They'd fought shoulder to shoulder in nasty places all over the world for ten years.

"What weapons did they find on the dead intruders?" Major Rieve asked.

Hamilton said, "Chinese-made Norinco NP-22s, according to the preliminary police report."

"Clone of the Sig Sauer P226. That doesn't tell us much, because the North Koreans get most of their arms from China."

"We'd better go and see this Superintendent and make sure the press are given a boring story of feuding farmers." He stood up and tapped the wooden desk for luck. "Hopefully Scrimple gets in touch with someone soon. He knows Kat Pedder but she's on an operation and won't be answering her personal phone. Who else does he know?"

19

"I got some minced beef and spaghetti for this evening and there's some cheese, ham and farmhouse bread for sandwiches," Hayden said. "And because I thought you might be missing Thailand I brought some Chang beer." There were eight of the golden-green cans with the Elephant logo on the kitchen sideboard.

"Haven't had Chang beer for years," Scrimple said.

"Waitrose was doing a promotion so I thought we'd treat ourselves. You can start drinking now if you want but I still need to teach a class on the Battle of Hastings and then coordinate a discussion with sixth formers on the evils of alcohol."

"That will be a tough one," Scrimple said, leaning in the doorway of the kitchen. He'd had a few hours' kip, a shower, a shave and felt a bit calmer about things.

"Kids these days don't really care about drinking alcohol. It's too boring, they'd rather be on social media talking shit with each other or taking all the weird and wonderful pills that are out there these days."

"In Hong Kong it was always ketamine," Scrimple said, "when I was still in the Force."

"They've moved on from horse tranquillisers. Who knows what they are throwing down their throats when they go to some festival like Glastonbury. Glad my kids are grown up and flapping about mortgages and childcare by now."

"So what are they like, the boys you teach here?" Scrimple asked. He'd started to make a rudimentary sandwich using the sliced Cheddar cheese Hayden had pulled out of the shopping bag.

"Cup of tea?"

"Absolutely," Scrimple said.

"Boys are generally good," Hayden said, pouring the hot water from the kettle that had just boiled. "They mostly come from decent families where the parents have worked hard to make enough money to pay the ridiculously expensive school fees here."

"How much does it cost?"

"£40,000 a year plus plus."

"That's a shit load of money. You must be on a massive salary."

"Yes, I wish." Hayden reached down to the small fridge to get the milk out. "I'm not complaining, it's a decent wage but I think most of the money goes on paying for the heating and making sure the roof doesn't collapse."

"So are there any really crazy rich parents?"

"There are a few Hong Kong Chinese but they're all really pleasant and normal. If they've got a billion or two tucked away they don't let on. They turn up in a nice Lexus or Mercedes SUV and have a pad in London somewhere flash but otherwise you wouldn't know."

"What about the British parents? Any of them turn up in helicopters?"

"No, that's the Russians and they don't send their kids here. They mostly go to London schools like Harrow and Westminster."

"So will you do this until you retire?" Scrimple asked. The sandwiches and the cups of tea were ready and they went back into the diminutive living room to eat. It was very much a bachelor's house: compact, convenient and with character. It was over 300 years old but Scrimple had noticed the kitchen and the bathroom were full of German appliances.

"What sort of mortgage do you have on this place?"

"Bought it for £140,000, spent £30,000 doing it up and costs me under £500 a month, so I can't complain." Hayden reached into his tweed jacket pocket and dumped a deck of SIM cards on the coffee table next to them. He then placed two black Alcatel phones on the table with sleek chargers. They were the old style phones without a touch screen, about 10 cm long. "I thought I'd get you two of these, £17 each. Can't complain about the price."

"Perfect," Scrimple said, picking up one of the phones and turning it over in his hand. "They're a bit like the old Nokias."

"Battery life is probably three weeks," Hayden said. He glanced at his watch. "Have to be off in ten minutes."

"Can I use a computer, I've got these USB sticks with recordings on them and I want to see if I can find out anything from what they were talking about."

Hayden nodded, put down his cup of tea and went upstairs to get his laptop. He tossed a MacBook Air on the sofa next to Scrimple.

"You won't find any dodgy porn on there. It's an old laptop I don't use any more. So knock yourself out. There's no password. It'll pick up the WiFi automatically."

"Brilliant," Scrimple said.

When they'd finished their basic lunch and Hayden had gone back to work, Scrimple booted up the MacBook and found the BBC News website first. There was no mention of any dead bodies or shoot-outs near St. Mary Bourne. He checked other news websites and even found the Andover Advertiser online but there was nothing about what had happened on Roland's farm. He wondered if it was being covered up or if Roland had not called the police. That seemed unlikely.

He logged into his Gmail account and checked some of his messages but it was only bland stuff and junk mail. Nobody from work had emailed him there. He wasn't even sure if anyone would have his personal email. He emailed Winchcombe to the address he had and told him he was trying to contact him and would call again on the number he normally used or any other number Winchcombe could send him.

Scrimple had to try and make some calls again. He had to be careful about this. He opened the first of the SIM card packets. It was a pay-as-you-go and had £20 on it. He slotted the SIM card into the Alcatel phone but didn't turn it on. Then he got ready to go, grabbing a hat that Hayden had hanging on a hook on the back of the door. It was a white cricket hat with a wide brim and should shade Scrimple's face from any street cameras that might exist around Sherborne.

Hayden had given him a spare key, so he locked the front door and walked for about ten minutes until he came to a thoroughfare called Bradford Road. Walking ahead of him, there were girls in sports uniform with short skirts carrying hockey sticks. Scrimple stopped at the next junction and turned on the mobile phone. It took a minute for the signal to lock on to the nearest tower. He had to do some things to complete set up and then he could make his calls. He tried the numbers he had for Winchcombe and Kat Pedder with no more luck than the last few times. He called Kenworthy who answered after five rings.

"Where are you at?" the man said.

"I can't fucking tell you, can I?" Scrimple replied.

"Are you in a safe place?"

"I think it's good. I'm far away from where you are but I could get into London easily if I had to."

"What's this number?"

"It's a throwaway SIM card that I've got. Don't call me because I'll turn it off and take it out. I'll have to call you. Any luck finding Gavin Hamilton for me?"

"No, nobody knows where he lives. They reckon maybe in one of the villages around the area. Someone heard him say once that he had a five bedroom house and a big garden and lived by himself and was thinking of moving."

"Fucking spooks, why can't they just have their name in the telephone book like normal people," Scrimple commented. He watched another two girls in hockey gear walk past him chattering like birds and ignoring him.

"Nobody has their name in telephone books any more."

"You know what I mean."

"Why don't you just walk into a police station and tell them what's happened and ask them to contact MI5."

"They'll think I'm the town weirdo and send me down to the local looney bin."

"Should be a safe place to hole up."

"Here's the weird bit. I killed two people with a sub-machine gun and there's nothing on any of the news outlets. It's as if it didn't happen."

Kenworthy sighed at the other end of the line. "That's not good. Look, sit tight, keep your head down and call me again in a few hours."

They cut the connection and Scrimple took the SIM card out of the phone. He wasn't really sure how it all worked but he thought if there was no card in the phone and everything was off, then even if someone had this number they could not track him to the nearest cell tower. Even if they did manage to track his phone to a cell tower, that only told anyone who was hunting him that he was in Sherborne somewhere and not precisely which house he was hiding in. He'd probably use one of the other SIM cards next time he called Kenworthy.

He permitted himself a mirthless laugh, after all he had plenty of cash from the safe. He could buy hundreds of SIM cards and toss them each time he made a call. Although, that probably was being overly cautious. Only Kenworthy had his number now and unless someone got hold of him and put a gun to his head he wouldn't be giving up his old mucker Scrimple.

When he got back to Hayden's terraced house and had bolted the door - it had a six-inch solid steel bolt on the back of the 18th century oak door - Scrimple booted up the laptop, inserted the first of the USB memory sticks and began listening to the conversations between Tchaikovsky and Mr. Park, the North Korean defector.

They spoke of his field of expertise and how he had worked for a top-secret research laboratory in Pyongyang under the control of the military. It was a stilted interrogation because the Korean only seemed to understand half of the questions being asked and repeated himself constantly. The interrogator was patient and circled back systematically, firmly and gently on the topics that were of importance.

Scrimple remembered being told that each memory stick could store up to 100 hours of conversation. He fell asleep after the first hour and only woke up when Hayden returned from work.

20

The cellar was dank and dusty. There was one light bulb in the ceiling above them and it was on all the time. There were three camp beds with sleeping bags and three wooden chairs for them to use. If any one of them wanted to go to the toilet they could go behind a screen where a bucket had been placed.

The two men felt sorry for the Filipina woman. Pacino had been trained to put up with imprisonment while Tchaikovsky had spent years in the army and understood how to handle hardship and deprivation. But Esmeralda had not enlisted for this. She was a nurse and a housekeeper and she had not signed up to be involved in what felt like some kind of political game.

They were not being treated badly. They were given sandwiches and apples to eat and plenty of bottled water. For Pacino that was good news. It implied that they might be released at some point. It was obvious to him that it had something to do with the North Korean. He must have been a high-value asset and someone had come after him to free him or take him back home. He'd discussed this with Tchaikovsky at length and he agreed his bosses might have underestimated the importance of Mr. Park. He couldn't be sure what was so special about him because he hadn't got the man to open up properly yet by the time they were abducted.

They had still been in the warm up phase of the interrogation when the four Eastern European men armed with Glocks and Walthers had turned up in the safe house. How they had got in was a mystery. Somehow they must have known the codes or had a key. It was something Pacino was going to pursue when he got out of this place. It felt like there was inside information, maybe a leak. Could it have come from Scrimple? Why would the man leave to go to London on the night before the safe house was compromised? It felt really dodgy to Pacino.

He'd liked the fat ex-Hong Kong copper, he seemed down-to-earth and plain-speaking, and Pacino had thought they might have a good laugh for a few days or weeks while Tchaikovsky got on with his job. Now the finger of suspicion in all their minds pointed firmly at Scrimple.

And if Scrimple had sold them out, for money or any other reason, then he'd really treated his Mrs. in a shoddy, shameful way.

Esmeralda lay on her camp-bed, in the sleeping bag that had been new when they arrived. Every once in a while she could be heard sobbing.

"Don't you worry, lass, we'll get out of this. They'll find us," Pacino said. He wasn't convinced that anyone would find them but he was more hopeful that whoever had contracted the gangsters to come and kidnap them would give the green light soon, and they'd be set free. Probably when the North Korean was back in the place where he belonged.

They were mad bastards, the North Koreans, Pacino knew from his training and his reading. They treated their people like cattle and they were working on a nuclear weapon and the ability to deliver it by intercontinental missile deep into the heart of liberal democracies. Only the Chinese could deal with the North Koreans. They spoke the same language of oppression.

"I hate egg mayonnaise," Tchaikovsky said. "Do you want to eat the rest of this sandwich?"

"No, mate. Save it for later. Hand me that water bottle."

The interrogator tossed the half empty plastic bottle of mineral water over to the soldier.

"They're definitely Albanians," Tchaikovsky said coming back to a topic they'd been kicking around for hours. "You can tell from their accent."

Pacino made a noise of disgust. "They're gangsters and they've had military training. That's all I need to know. If I get half a chance I'll take out the lad who comes and brings us our food."

Esmeralda sat up and brushed the hair from her face. "When do you think they will release us?" she asked.

"Soon, lass. Soon. We just need to be a bit patient."

"Scrimple will come and find us," she said quietly. "He was a police man. He'll work it out and come and rescue us." She looked at the men, first one and then the other. They both nodded to make her feel better.

"Do you want to get back to this chess game then?" Tchaikovsky said. They'd found some chalk in the corner and had drawn a chess board on the brick wall where there was good light. Then they had drawn the pieces on the squares and as they moved them would rub out the abbreviation and make a new mark. A 'K' was a king and 'P' was a pawn. And an 'N' for the Knights, of course.

"Later. I'll do my work out now," Pacino said. He walked to the other end of the cellar and started doing press ups. The interrogator and the woman watched and listened as he counted past 100, then 200 and kept on going without a pause. That's why he was in the SAS, because he could do stuff like that.

Around 1 p.m. the bullet-headed man came downstairs and brought them more food. Their captors were not very imaginative. Every meal was sandwiches and water. Sometimes they threw in a few packets of Walkers crisps and a big chocolate bar of Cadbury's Fruit and Nut. It must be someone's idea of a balanced diet upstairs.

Pacino had initially watched like a hawk how the man delivered the food. Was there any chance to overpower him and attempt to escape? But the Albanian gangsters - if that's what they really were - had thought it out carefully. Perhaps it wasn't the first time they'd kidnapped someone and held them for a few days or weeks for a ransom.

The door of the cellar prison was heavy-duty steel. Set at eye height was a small barred opening, five inches by five inches, so they could check what was happening inside. At the bottom of the stairs going up, at the end of a corridor, was another identical steel door. The bullet-headed man would come downstairs with his plastic bag of groceries and another invisible man would open this door and then lock it again from the outside. The delivery man would tell the captives to go and lie on the ground at the end of the cellar and clasp their hands behind their necks. When he could see that they had all complied he would unlock the door to the cellar, empty his carrier bag on the floor, then lock the door and return to the door at the bottom of the stairs which his colleague would unlock once he'd looked through the opening and confirmed there was no threat.

Even if Pacino could leap up, sprint the ten yards across the cellar before the delivery guy had re-locked the front door, manage to overpower him and make it to the door at the end of the corridor, the man on the outside of that would simply laugh at him. Then they'd come downstairs with their guns and punish Pacino for injuring their brother.

It wasn't going to be that easy to escape.

The bullet-headed Albanian came to the door and yelled at them to move back to the end of the room and lie down as always. The three of them complied and Pacino heard the keys rattling in the door. He heard the door squeak open and the sound of plastic sandwich packets hitting the cement floor. In his head, he counted the seconds 'one Piccadilly, two Piccadilly, three Piccadilly....'

It was seven seconds by the time the keys rattled and the door to their prison had been locked again. That meant he had six seconds to get from a prone position to the door. He'd have to knock the guy out with one blow.

Pacino intended to practise that move, over and over again for the next few hours. It was something to aim for, even if he hadn't figured out yet how to get past the second locked door. If the bullet-headed guy had a gun on him, that might be the answer. But if they were smart they wouldn't let him into the cellar corridor with a weapon.

The guy outside the second door would have the weapon and could poke it through the opening, between the bars, and blow Pacino's brains out.

21

Scrimple was dreaming. He was back in Hong Kong, on that day…

"Wong Tai Sin station transfer burglary case to us just now," Ling-jai said to Scrimple.

"Shit, we were doing so well," Detective Inspector Scrimple said, looking up from reading the South China Morning Post. They were on 'B' shift and so far there had been no crimes reported to his CID Investigation team. "Where's the D-Sergeant?"

"He go out to interview the informant about the underwear burglaries."

"It would be nice to clear that one up. Get one nice number on the board."

Tze Wan Shan was a densely populated residential area made up mostly of public housing estates that sat north of the famed Wong Tai Sin temple. From a policing point of view the division was a sleepy backwater and it had a modern, compact police station run by a Superintendent called Victor Chen who was ambitious and could be intensely irritating. Scrimple was in charge of a team of detectives, mostly seniors who were within five years of their retirement and who tried to avoid as much trouble as they could.

On a busy day, they might get two crimes reported to the Duty Officer in the Report Room who would then come and confer with the Detective Sergeant on whether they would open a CCR, the Crimes Complaint Register and allocate a file number. Scrimple's D-Sergeant was very good at keeping these file numbers low and the detection rate as high as possible, which pleased the bosses.

Scrimple's function as the inspector was to sign off on all the paperwork. He reported to Woman Chief Inspector Maria Sham who was the Assistant Divisional Commander - Crime. She was a pleasant lady who had realised that Scrimple was a remnant of another era, a former way of living and working that in two years' time would be swept away as Hong Kong came to the end of its colonial history. She was punctiliously polite with her expat inspector but essentially ignored him and only dealt with the Chinese D-Sergeant and Detective Constables.

"Where the hell was this burglary?" Scrimple asked Ling-jai, who was his JI, an old acronym that stood for Junior Investigator, a role that had traditionally functioned as secretary cum translator to foreign Detective Inspectors.

"It's on the Chuk Yuen building site, where they are making a big new housing estate."

"What the hell do they have to steal there?"

"The site supervisor said one of the construction huts had been broken into night before last. He reported to Wong Tai Sin station and then they just now transfer to us. It's in our divisional area."

"So they were burgled nearly 24 hours ago?"

"Maybe, boss." Ling-jai was a lean youngster with a gleam of intelligence in his eyes and a university degree under his belt. Working in CID in this role was a good jumping off point to be selected for inspector training.

"What did they nick? Money that was left overnight?"

"They say shovel and picks and some power tools." Ling-jai was reading from the yellow sheet in his hand.

"So basically, just shit."

"Maybe, sir."

"We've got to go and visit the site." Scrimple checked his Timex, it was shortly before 6 p.m. "Last time I didn't attend the underwear burglaries and the DVC found out and bollocked me for half an hour. *All DIs have to attend every burglary scene before they write up the TPM*," he mimicked the Superintendent's voice.

"Yes, sir. I'll radio the D-Sergeant and get him to come back and we quickly go down there. DC Tong will have this case. He's next one on the rota."

"You go and grab him from the *daai-fong* and I'll just get a quick can of Coke from the canteen and then we can pop down there." Scrimple checked the map on the wall and found the big blank space which was going to end up housing fifty thousand people when it was all completed.

He made his way down the stairs to the canteen where they had vending machines and basic Chinese dishes were served by three ancient ladies. Sitting at one of the tables, tucking into a bowl of noodles, moving his chopsticks with great dexterity was Dougie, the expat ADVC Ops. He was in full light-green uniform and on his shoulder were the three pips of a Chief Inspector. Dougie was a decent bloke, in Scrimple's estimation, even though he'd attended some fancy boys' boarding school in Dorset and had a double-barrelled name. They'd been in the same PI squad at Police Training School in Wong Chuk Hang but Scrimple remained two ranks below him. All of the four uniformed patrol sub-units and their commanders reported into Dougie. Normally he worked a 9 - 5 shift but he often came back in the evenings and joined his lads on patrol.

"How's tricks, Scrimple?" Dougie said, putting down his chopsticks.

"Just got a bloody transferred burglary case." He put his coins into the machine and punched up the Coke.

"You should get the paperwork done by end of shift. Your JI is a fast typist."

"I thought today might be an easy day with no crimes reported at all. I wanted to get home early and watch the footie. What are you doing here at this time of the day?"

"Got a new *liu bom-baan*, so I thought I'd come and walk the streets with her and see how she handles herself."

"Is she cute?" Scrimple asked, popping the tab on the can and then taking a swig of the cold, fizzy stuff.

"It's not up to me to comment on that, I'm her boss and I'll treat her in a professional and courteous manner whatever she looks like."

"Umm," Scrimple replied. Intellectually he understood why Dougie was a Chief Inspector and he would never be promoted to that rank, however long he hung on in the Hong Kong Police. They were going to take the 'Royal' away after 1997, was the gossip around the messes. "Did you hear about Gary Crocker? He's flying 747s for Singapore Airlines these days."

"Good on him," Dougie said, standing up with his empty bowl and chopsticks. Crocker had been another one of their intake at training school and left after two contracts to become a pilot. "Got to get downstairs. Have fun investigating your burglary."

"Right," Scrimple said and tossed the empty Coke can into the black bin in the corner.

When he got back to his office, Ling-jai had rounded up the troops. The D-Sergeant would meet them downstairs in the unmarked saloon car they always used and DC Tong stood quietly in the hallway waiting for instructions. He was in his late fifties, spoke no English at all but smiled a lot at his inspector. In his hands was a camera which they'd use to record what the crime scene looked like.

Scrimple went to his desk and unlocked his top drawer and took out his gun. It was the usual snub-nosed Colt Detective .38 issued to all CID personnel and it held six rounds. Once a year Scrimple had to go to the range and train with it, mostly missing the target, but it was usually a fun day out and they always went on for beers and dinner afterwards, paid for by the person with the worst score.

He clipped the gun in its holster to the outside of his trousers over his right kidney and then donned a blue cotton jacket that had been made by Sam the Tailor, who gave coppers a discount when you produced your warrant card.

Ten minutes later they were at the building site. It was a large flat expanse that had been bulldozed ready for the pile drivers to go into action. There was a dusty access road, at the end of which stood a collection of wooden construction huts. It was the first one that had been broken into by smashing the padlock on the door.

On the way down from the station, they had picked up the site manager from his home and he had unlocked the site gates so they could drive in. DC Tong pulled the unmarked car up next to the burgled hut. By now the sky was dark and the stars were out but the ambient light of Kowloon was all around them. The building site sat eerily in half-shadow.

"Let's get on with it," Scrimple said irritably. He had to be able to describe the crime that had been committed here so that if they ever arrested the culprit it could be clearly identified and the case closed. They had brought a fingerprint kit but the site was dusty and, since the burglary the night before, men had been using the hut. Dusting for fingerprints was simply going through the motions. But much of being a detective was exactly that. Recording a crime was the first step in solving the crime.

The D-Sergeant and the detective approached the door of the hut. Ling-jai was standing by the car clarifying something with the site manager, their informant who had originally reported the burglary. Scrimple stood by the bonnet of the car and was admiring the golden hue that was coming off the city that stretched out in front of him. If he stood on tiptoes he could just about see parts of Mong Kok. Behind him rose the mountain range called Fei Ngo Shan.

Suddenly he became aware of a commotion. There was a struggle going on in front of the hut. The Sergeant and the detective were trying to force open the door but someone was inside holding it shut. They were yelling and shoving, attempting to get it open.

Scrimple had a sudden epiphany. The burglar had returned to the site of his crime 24 hours later to try and steal more stuff. How bizarre!

For a minute Scrimple watched as the sergeant, the detective and the JI joined together to shove open the door. Finally it opened and they fell inside. Then there was further scuffling. They couldn't get the burglar down. He must be a heroin addict, off his head, feeling no pain. The JI came staggering out of the hut clutching his nose. He must have been hit in the face.

Scrimple decided it was time for the big white Chief to intervene and show them how it was done. As an inspector he didn't carry handcuffs, but he'd help them subdue the man so they could cuff him.

He waded into the fight which was now entirely inside the darkness of the construction hut. All he could see were moving shadows. The sergeant seemed to slip away and then there was a series of shouts from the outside as if there were other men who had been hiding around the back of the hut. Scrimple found himself alone, all of a sudden, with a dark form who was trying to scratch his eyes out and get away. Scrimple punched the burglar repeatedly in the face but it seemed to have no effect. He threw his entire weight onto the frenzied criminal who kept fighting back, trying to get away.

"*Sau kaau, sau kaau*, Sergie," Scrimple yelled for handcuffs. But there was no-one there to help. He found out later they'd been attacked by three other burglars wielding hatchets.

And then he felt it. He'd forgotten about his revolver. You never used your revolver. It was just something you carried like a pager or your wallet. It was part of the kit.

But the burglar had found it and before Scrimple understood what was happening, the man had flicked open the popper that held the revolver in the holster. Now he was trying to tug the gun out. Scrimple got his hand on the butt of the revolver, but it was too late. The gun was out of its holster and now it was simply a tug of war. They were fighting for possession of the gun.

The burglar was spitting and swearing like a demented Gollum, cursing the police and the entire white race.

"*Diu lei, ham gar charn, sei puk gai, sei gwai lo chai yan...*"

It was a tug of war that could only end badly for Scrimple if he lost. And his arms were tiring. He tried to get his finger into the trigger guard so he could turn the muzzle and shoot the burglar, who was trying to do the exact same thing.

Then with a massive, unexpected kick into Scrimple's balls the burglar managed to pull the Colt out of the policeman's hands. It was completely dark in the construction hut but Scrimple thought he could see the glint of triumph in the man's eyes as he yelled: "*Ngoh hui cheung, mo yuk.*"

Scrimple froze. The burglar had told him he was going to shoot.

For a second it felt as if he were already detached from him body. As if he were floating above it. He had a lucid thought that he was about to be shot in the gut, the ambulance would take too long to arrive, he would bleed out and die here on the dusty floor. He would be the laughing stock of the Police Force.

A calm voice came from the door. It was DC Tong who had his own Colt Detective out and was sighting it at the burglar who was pointing Scrimple's gun at the inspector.

DC Tong spoke gently at the frenzied man and told him in Cantonese that shooting a white inspector would be the worst decision of his life. He'd be hounded to the ends of the earth and if he made it to prison he would forever be looking over his shoulder.

The burglar shifted stance and instead of pointing his gun at Scrimple he pointed it at the detective. They stood there for a minute in a Mexican stand-off until the detective backed away and allowed the burglar to exit the hut and into the night.

"Fuck me," Scrimple said under his breath, holding his groin. He took the four steps to the door and was just in time to see the burglar disappear up a mound of sand still clutching the Colt Detective. Along with the gun, Scrimple saw whatever notion he had of a career as a policeman vanishing over the mound.

For a few seconds the man was still silhouetted against the night sky.

"Shoot him, Tong, shoot him," Scrimple yelled.

"No, sir, not authorise."

"I'm authorising you. It's perfectly legal."

"No, sir."

The only good thing to come out of that night was the ironic fact that the burglar had dropped his wallet during the fight. In his wallet was his ID card and Kowloon Regional Crime Unit III arrested him within two weeks, recovering Scrimple's gun. But Scrimple's reputation would never recover.

He woke up with a shudder. It was 2017. He hated that bloody dream. He always had it when he was under stress. The recordings of Tchaikovsky interviewing Mr. Park were still droning on and it was nearly 6 p.m.

22

Colonel Wendy Shen didn't think of herself as a Communist. She was first and foremost a loyal Chinese citizen, proud of her people, her nation, her motherland and the achievements of the government and its leaders.

She had learnt in kindergarten how the Chinese race had the oldest culture in the world and had invented everything from gunpowder to navigation. While the rest of the world was populated by barbarians cowering in dirty huts, the Chinese had written poetry and created ceramic vases.

Then there had been an age of darkness for two hundred years and now, the Chinese race was coming back to reclaim its rightful place in the world order. The Americans were a spent force. Since the Second World War they had been a superpower but by now they had dissipated much of their might hurling it against the threat of Islam, while allowing China to take over the manufacturing of every product of importance. Even the crowning glory of American invention, the iPhone and the products of Apple were manufactured in the Foxconn facility in China that employed 1.7 million workers.

America was nothing but a *zhilaohu,* in the words of Chairman Mao. Nothing but a paper tiger: in appearance powerful but in reality to unable to withstand the wind and the rain.

As for the British, the French and the Germans - all powerful imperial forces that had brought China to its knees in the 19th Century - they were merely *zǒugǒu* of the Americans. They were pathetic, incompetent running dogs who served their masters in Washington, like a poodle who yaps. Not even a useful dog, not a *guzui* fighting dog who could tear a man to shreds with his bony snout. Just useless yapping running dogs.

Wendy Shen sat at the desk in her bedroom in the house they had rented in Windsor and pondered these matters. Her team had been in the UK for two weeks now working on the Guo operation. It had a code name which was *Liu Bei*, the name of a traitor from ancient history.

There was a knock on the door and the man they all called Baldy came in.

"Shen-boss, Shady Mouse got a report from the police system that you need to see."

"Is it a problem?"

"I'm sorry," Baldy said, nodding. He had worked with Wendy before and gave her all the respect that she was due. They walked back into the living room where a large dining table served as a work bench for several laptops and big monitors. At the centre of the table sat a skinny, pasty-faced Chinese man with thick glasses and a wild growth of black hair that cried out for a trim. His white polo shirt was covered in spots of soya sauce because he always ate hurriedly, never taking his eyes off his screens. This was Shady Mouse, the technical wizard of their Action Unit. He could hack anything that had an electronic signal, or so he claimed. He had recently transferred in from the PLA's cyber warfare team called Unit 61398.

"Wang and Liu are dead," Shady Mouse said as Wendy came to stand behind his high-backed Corsair gaming chair.

"How can they be dead?" Wendy snapped. She didn't want to hear it but she needed to know.

"I've got a confidential report here from Hampshire Police. Two Asian males were found dead at a farm near Andover. They were killed by a man with an assault rifle."

"Scrimple?" Wendy spat the name out with venom.

"It says the police are looking for a man called Scrimple, who the farm owner identified as being the shooter."

"Not possible."

"Computers never lie," Shady Mouse said and popped a Haribo gummy bear into his mouth.

"Shut up, you *zháinán*," she said, calling him a housemale, a pejorative term for a geek. "Send the report and everything you have to my laptop. I need to study this and think."

Baldy said, "I'm sorry, boss. They were good men."

"If they were good men," Wendy barked, "how can that fat idiot have killed them?" She marched into the kitchen and took out a can of Fanta. "They were supposed to observe him, capture him and bring him here. How difficult can that be? The man is an oaf."

"Maybe he's really better than we thought," Baldy suggested.

Wendy shook her head and sighed. "I know, I know. I shouldn't underestimate him. He looks like such a fool and then he always finds a way to beat us."

"He must be one of their best men," Baldy said. "His disguise it three layers thick."

"He's not good. He's just a lucky, bumbling fool," Wendy said. "Inform me when Scruffy gets back and when Jing Jing sends in her latest report. I need to give her instructions." She returned to her room, drank her Fanta and sat in the comfortable armchair with the view of the garden which had a high wooden fence around it.

Scrimple was her personal vendetta but the General had given her permission to pursue it as long as it did not interfere with Operation Liu Bei. They had been watching Guo for some time now and wanted to see where his plans took him. That is why they had placed Jing Jing into his household and that was coming along nicely. They were not sure yet whether what he was doing was going to benefit the motherland or if he was behaving like a traitor. They had watched as he had exchanged messages for weeks with the North Korean defector. This was when they had stumbled across Scrimple, running the safe house that was intended for the North Korean professor. Then they had observed when the abductors came to the safe house and took everybody away. But Scrimple had not been there.

Wendy had instructed Wang and Liu to keep observing and when Scrimple had turned up again at the safe house, all by himself, they had followed him. Wendy had given the order that they should surprise him in the night and bring him back to Windsor. She had been so looking forward to seeing his stupid, fat face and introducing herself to him again.

Yet something had gone wrong. Wang and Liu, like Baldy and Scruffy were the muscle on her Action Unit. They were highly trained and competent with all weapons. How could Scrimple have managed to outwit them and kill them? The police report that Shady Mouse had hacked said nothing about Scrimple being wounded. It simply said he was on the run and they were searching for him, to help with their enquiries.

Damn the man. She should have killed him when she had the chance in Munich, in Hong Kong, in Cambridge. She shook her head with frustration and then shocked herself when she discovered there was a tiny sliver of admiration for him somewhere in her heart. No, curse the man to hell.

Wendy Shen had worked hard to become one of the most feared field commanders in the PLA's Strategic Support Force and the youngest Director of Department 3 in its history. All of her missions, most of them, had been successful, but the ones that had not exactly gone to plan were all tarnished by the appearance of that bastard *xiyang guizi*, that white devil.

She went to her laptop and read the report carefully and thought about it for some time. Then she searched around on the internet and came to a useful conclusion.

"You have his car registration number?" she instructed Shady Mouse back in the living room. "Find the car. Can you get into their ANPR system?"

Shady Mouse turned his head and stared at her. It was like asking Sebastien Vettel if he knew how to drive a manual gear shift.

"I've already found his Volkswagen. It's parked in Andover. He left it and then started walking across town but I lost him on the CCTV cameras. They are not well-positioned. I think, boss, he took a train but can't tell when or where. I can run a program that checks cameras for face recognition at all the stations up and down the line." He pushed his glasses up his nose then scratched his forehead below the hair line. Wendy suspected he was not showering at least twice a day like a normal civilised person.

"How long will that take?" she asked.

The hacker gave her a cheeky smile. "Five minutes or five days. The program will run and keep on looking for him."

"Get on with it."

By now Scruffy, Baldy's oppo, had returned from the grocery run and was sitting on one of the sofas eating a chocolate bar that he'd discovered called a Double Decker. Wendy pointed at them both.

"Remember Cambridge?"

"How can we forget?" Baldy said, making a sad face.

"You two will go back there to the George pub in Girton and find the landlord there. He is called Bob Kenworthy and he is an old friend of Scrimple's from the Hong Kong police. I shot him last time but he survived."

The two soldiers nodded.

"Put a gun up his nose and make him tell you where Scrimple is or where he might be hiding."

"Do we kill him?" Scruffy asked. He was a knifeman and so he preferred that weapon whenever he got the chance.

Wendy said, "You can cut him up and torture him a bit but don't kill him or damage him seriously. Not without my instruction. I am sure Scrimple will have told him where he is going. Or..." Wendy's face was suddenly suffused by an angelic smile, "Scrimple is there hiding with his old friend."

"Do we bring both of them back here if we find him?" Baldy asked.

"I'll decide if that's the case." Wendy pulled out her Huawei phone and checked the time. "Get going now. You can take the Ford van."

"Shady Mouse, any report from Jing Jing yet?" she asked.

"No, boss, but there's a message from Lei Lei saying she has the alternative base set up and connected."

"Fine, we might move there next week. Maybe we can even wrap this one up. I still don't know what Guo's plan really is with the English laboratory but maybe we will know soon. Jing Jing will move on to the next phase this evening."

23

The meeting with the Superintendent had gone well. They'd conferenced in the Chief Constable and everyone was in agreement that the farm shootings would best be kept out of the press, possibly even out of the division's crime figures.

Now Hamilton, Major Rieve and Corporal Rickman were back at the safe house. They'd picked up some microwave meals and provisions from an Asda in Andover and were now brainstorming what they could do next.

Wesley from Cambridge pinged Hamilton as they were sitting down to a congealed mess that masqueraded as shepherd's pie.

"Found Scrimple's car through ANPR. It's parked up at one end of Andover and then I used CCTV to track him walking across town and lost him. I guess he went to the train station but none of the cameras there could find him. Does he know how to avoid face recognition?"

"He might do. He might have had some training on it," Hamilton said in between blowing on his fork to cool down the hot mashed potato. "What else have you come up with?"

"Now this is much better - depends on how you see it, actually it's worse, but it sort of explains —."

"Get to the point, Wesley," his boss said with a hint of impatience.

"I've found Winchcombe on CCTV near the airport. He was working really hard to avoid detection. He had what looked like a fake nose and a wig."

"And face recognition picked that up?" Hamilton marvelled and then risked putting the fork with the food into his mouth.

"I'm not just a sexy supermodel rock god, body-double to Stormzy, you know. I've got a brain as sharp as MoStack's lyrics, man."

"Get on with it."

"I ran the new beta version which hasn't been released yet but a mate of mine gave me the code word to be part of the trial."

"You mean the new 'Trufflehunter' release?"

"Ah-ha, boss. It has more fuzzy logic than a Stefflon Don track."

"Wesley, while your knowledge of the current musical scene might impress the blonde undergraduates, it is of no interest to me," Hamilton said in as avuncular a tone as he could muster.

"So I found Winchcombe sneaking out of the country on a New Zealand passport. But he's alive and well. Or he was when he boarded that plane to Auckland."

Hamilton now adopted the tone of a college lecturer. "And what does all that tell us?"

"Winchcombe wasn't kidnapped, killed or drugged to give up information about the safe house. He took the Big

Bung. The final retirement golden handshake. Someone gave him a serious pay-day and he's done a runner giving the Security Service the great thick middle finger."

Hamilton laughed down the phone. "You may go far in this chosen career of yours, young man." They talked a little bit more and then hung up. Wesley was going to continue scouring the electronic void for any sign of Scrimple. He had to be out there somewhere. Quickly he shared the update with the others who had finished eating and were now cleaning their weapons.

There had been an idea bubbling at the back of his brain. He had a quick google for the phone number and then called the George pub in Cambridge, Girton. The landlord came on after a young woman's voice had first answered.

"This is Gavin Hamilton," he introduced himself.

"You're a hard bastard to track down," Kenworthy said, sounding relieved.

"Have you been trying to find me?"

"Scrimple, remember him, tasked me to get in touch with you. But nobody knows where you live, what you do, where to find you... It's as if you worked for the Secret Intelligence Service."

"Right, let's cut to the chase then. I don't work for MI6 but I work for MI5 and your mate Scrimple did as well, as a junior contractor of sorts and now he's gone AWOL after having killed two Asian blokes."

"Funny, but I actually know all of that."

"Do you know where he is?" Hamilton asked.

"I don't, but he's been in contact and he will be calling me back and he desperately needs help."

Hamilton punched the air in pleasure. "Okay, we're making some progress. Did he tell you who the two guys are that he killed?"

"He has no idea. He is shitting himself because he came back from a night out in London and the safe house was empty and now he's on the run because he doesn't know who he can trust."

"For starters he can trust me," Hamilton said.

"He thinks he can, which is why he asked me to find you. He doesn't have any contact details for anyone except a bloke called Winchcombe who he's been reporting to and who seems to have vanished from the face of the earth."

"Winchcombe *has* vanished. How can I get hold of Scrimple?"

"He won't tell me where he is and he's using burner phones because he's afraid of being tracked. He will call me later in the evening and then I can give him your number and he'll call you."

"That's good. Do you have any idea which part of the country he's in?"

"No idea, but I thought he might be heading into London as it's easier to hide in the crowd there obviously."

"Fine, when he calls," Hamilton instructed, "you tell him that I'm at the safe house in St. Mary Bourne with a team of armed guys. This is my number and this is an alternative number to a Duty Officer that should be able to get him through to our big boss who's keeping a close eye on developments."

"The big boss is involved," Kenworthy said, somehow managing to mix awe and sarcasm. "Listen, Gavin, Scrimple's an old mate of mine. He has this uncanny ability to get himself into the most appalling shit. But he's an innocent. He's just a bloody nightmare on legs. You've got to help him sort this out."

"I get that and it's what I'm working on. Nobody thinks that Scrimple's done anything wrong here. There's something going on, we don't understand it yet but we need Scrimple to come in so we can continue to get to the bottom of it."

"I'll be sure to tell him that. Where the hell is that Kat Pedder woman? She's part of your gang. He's been trying to get hold of her and she never answers her phone either."

"She's overseas somewhere doing something, that's what I've been told."

"You take care of my mate Scrimple or I'll make sure you can't drink in any pub around Cambridge ever again. I know every landlord around town."

"I'm sure you do," Hamilton laughed it off but he heard the mild threat. If Kenworthy blew his cover around town he wouldn't be working in Cambridge again and that was a depressing vision. He hated London like the plague. Even more frightening was the notion of being posted to the new Halifax office they'd just opened. "You tell Scrimple he can trust me and we'll get this sorted."

"You keep your promise and you drink free at the George as long as I'm the landlord here."

Hamilton answered with an agreeable chuckle and they signed off. Next call was to the DDG. He got through to an assistant who told him she'd call back within twenty minutes. In fact it was less than ten.

"Brief me," she said. He gave her a concise version of what they had achieved so far. "Good work," was her reply. "Once you've got hold of Scrimple and you've brought him in, take him to a new safe house here in London. I'll have Cynthia send you details for a vacant one."

"What about the E Squadron lads?"

"Keep them with you. You don't know who else might pop up waving guns."

"Roger to that, Sara."

Hamilton walked over to Major Rieve who had just slotted his Sig Sauer back into its holster. He updated the two soldiers with all the latest developments.

"So what do we do now?" Rieve said. "Sit tight for Scrimple to call?"

"That's what I reckon."

"We could always go to the pub," suggested Rickman.

Hamilton shook his head. "Too high profile. They know Scrimple. People all know each other around here. They'll recognise us as being law enforcement and gossip. Best we just stay here and quaff some of that stuff over there." He pointed at the drinks cabinet which had always been kept extensively stocked by the safe house manager, Scrimple.

"Haven't had Lagavulin for a while," said Major Rieve bending over to check the labels. "Grey Goose, Finlandia, Twisted Nose Watercress Dry Gin from the Winchester Distillery. I think that's the one for me. I hope he's got Fever Tree tonic in the fridge."

24

It was food time soon, Pacino estimated. Their captors had taken away their watches, maybe because they suspected men who worked with the intelligence services might have secret emergency beacons in their kit. Chance would be a fine thing, he sneered. If he had a Benchmade Mini Griptilian knife hidden in his shoe he would be able to take out the man who brought the food more easily. But Pacino had also been trained to kill with his bare hands.

He hadn't really figured it out completely but as the cap badge said: 'Who Dares Wins' and if you just sat on your hands and felt sorry for yourself then you would never win any battles.

"I'm sorry," Tchaikovsky said. He was studying the chess board they had chalked up on the wall. It was the seventh time he'd beaten Pacino and he'd probably come to the conclusion that the man from E Squadron was not the ideal chess opponent.

"Sorry, mate, my mind wasn't really on the game," Pacino said. He was sitting on his chair, watching the door and listening.

"You've got be more careful with your openings. You're always playing the Ruy Lopez and it's predictable."

"That's all my captain taught me," Pacino said with a harsh laugh. He didn't mind a game of chess but he was a man of action and not one to mess about for too long analysing his options and working out different scenarios.

"I'll teach you a few more," Tchaikovsky said.

"Don't bother, we're getting out of here."

"Are you sure about this?" The interrogator gave him a doubtful look. They had talked about it in whispers, in the far corner, for a long time but Pacino's mind was made up.

"They've obviously been told not to kill us. We will be set free when the time comes. Why else are they wearing hoods? We should be patient."

"I can't sit and cool my heels here. It's not right. We must make an effort to escape," the soldier said. "If they've been told not to kill us, all the better. The man with the gun will hesitate and that will give me the edge."

"I don't like it," the interrogator said. He looked over at the Filipina woman who was sitting on her camp bed. Her lips were moving and her eyes were closed. Earlier they'd asked her what she was doing and she'd told them she was praying. Each to his own, Pacino thought. He didn't know if he believed in a God. When he'd had to kill people close up he'd seen a flicker of life vanish from the eyes which one of his colleagues had described as the soul leaving the body. But where did it go? That was all a bit too clever for him. So he didn't spend any time thinking about it. Maybe there was a God and when he died, he'd find out. But on balance he thought that when he killed a man, the man was simply dead. The body stopped working and that was the end of any thoughts in the brain.

End of. In the meantime you led your life as best you could, had fun with your mates and your women and when the great big full stop came, then that was it. He rarely had morbid thoughts because it was just a waste of time.

You killed people because you were ordered to kill them or because you knew they were coming to kill you. It was as simple as that.

He had plenty of respect for anyone who believed in God and who prayed. It simply wasn't his thing. He was a man of the here and now. You got on with your job. And if a bullet came along and stopped you from doing your job, then so be it.

"I've timed it and I know I can do it," he said to the interrogator who sighed and turned back to study the chess board on the wall.

"I'd prefer if you just waited. If they came for the Korean, they only kept us on to give them a chance to transport him safely out of the country. Think about it. Maybe nobody even knows yet that the safe house has been compromised."

"If it was that cunt Scrimple who sold us out then, sure, nobody will know what's happened at the safe house."

Tchaikovsky said: "If you were in his shoes, and you'd taken a big backhander to sell out your colleagues, what would you be doing now? You'd be on a plane to the farthest corner of the earth, probably with a false passport in your pocket and a hundred thousand pounds in a Swiss bank account."

"Swiss bank account," Pacino snorted. The very idea of someone selling out his mates for money was so abhorrent it made him physically ill thinking about it. "Who the fuck has a Swiss bank account?"

"Traitors do," Tchaikovksy said with a twitch of his shoulders.

"Fucking traitor, when I get out of here, I'm going to hunt the man down and string him up."

"We don't know if it was him."

"Who else would have told the bastards the door codes and given them a set of keys?"

They both heard the sound from the end of the cellar's corridor. Their eyes met. Tchaikovsky nodded in resignation and said, "Make it work."

A moment later they heard the footsteps coming closer. There was a banging on the steel door and the same Eastern European voice as always said, "You go lie at the end of the room. Now."

The men and Esmeralda stood up and walked over to the area where they always lay down when food was delivered. They had tried to sweep the dust up here with an old piece of cloth they'd found. All three of them lay down on their bellies and clasped their hands at the back of their necks. Pacino began his countdown as he heard the keys rattling in the door: one second, two seconds and then he catapulted to his feet and threw himself at the door like a springbok who had only one chance to escape the cheetah.

The Albanian was surprised. He must have become complacent by how well the prisoners had behaved themselves. Pacino reached him on the fourth second and had him by the throat, smashing the back of the man's head viciously against the wall. As the man slumped,

Pacino drove a clenched fist into his throat and heard the cartilage crumple. That usually meant death would follow quickly.

The door was wide open. The corridor five yards long. Pacino patted the guard's waist band just in case he did have a weapon but there was none. That took less than a second and then he was bounding down the corridor. He had a sense that Tchaikovsky was right behind him.

The guard on the other side of the steel door leading up the stairs shouted out something. He had heard the commotion and wanted to know what was going on. His head could be seen moving behind the bars of the small window in the door.

Then he did what Pacino had been praying for. He unlocked the door to find out what was happening. He'd have a gun his hand and that was all that Pacino would focus on. The door opened and the masked man's face and shoulders appeared. There was a semi-automatic in his hand and for a split second Pacino recognised it at as his own Sig Sauer that had been confiscated.

Then the weapon spoke: it made its customary crack and Pacino felt as if he'd been kicked in the guts by an angry mule. Then another kick in the chest, and a third one in the face.

Then it was all over for Pacino. Within a minute he was dead and had gone on to the other place.

25

It was time to call Kenworthy so Scrimple walked out of the house in the opposite direction for ten minutes and then dialled his numbers. As usual he first tried Winchcombe and Kat Pedder, without any luck. He really didn't know what to think about the fact that Winchcombe had become a ghost. With Kat he could understand that she might be undercover working on whatever project for which she was now responsible. But with his direct superior it was disconcerting. The man wasn't young anymore so perhaps he'd had a heart attack while walking along the road and knocked his head and was lying in hospital. That might make sense on a normal day; it was too mundane an explanation in the context of what had happened at the safe house.

He called Kenworthy's mobile number and it rang six times. Then it was picked up.

"Have you found that bloke for me yet?" Scrimple asked.

There was no answer from the other end of the line. Scrimple listened and said hello a few times, then assumed that the line had just been disconnected. His cheap Alcatel phone was probably running on 2G and he suspected the old networks were not being supported in the same way as the 4G networks. Who still used a 'dumb' phone these days without a touch screen and internet connection? Probably only drug dealers, terrorists and men on the run like him. He tried dialling again and the phone was answered on the second ring. But still he could hear no sound from the other end.

"Bollocks," he said. The battery was fine, he'd been charging it for the last few hours. The connection seemed fine and was giving him two bars, not perfect but good enough. He began walking back down the hill towards Hayden's house. After a few hundred metres his phone began to vibrate and chirp. It was Kenworthy's number.

"Bob, mate, talk to me," Scrimple yelled into the phone. There was no answer. He cursed the phone network and hit the disconnect button. Maybe he'd try again an hour or two later and then the atmospherics might be better or the great big switchboard in the sky would have fixed itself.

When he let himself into the house Hayden was already back from work. Scrimple told him what he'd been up to.

"So how are your posh kids then? Did they learn anything vital from you?"

"Who knows what they really learn. You try your best," the teacher said and began preparing a spaghetti Bolognese.

"I told you that I discovered I had a son from a long lost girlfriend? He's studying in New York now."

"Is he a nice bloke?"

"He is and clever as well. Studying theology at an advanced level."

"Is he a bible basher then?" Hayden said with a smile to show it was meant in a light-hearted way.

"I can't really tell. He seems totally into it but he doesn't seem to want to become a priest."

"And he's not gay?"

"Do you have to be gay these days to be a priest?" Scrimple said taking a sip from his opened can of Chang beer.

"It helps if you want to be a Bishop in the Church of England I am told. Better still if you're a woman. All the vicars seem to be women these days."

"I think I'll go and visit my son in New York if I can manage to find a way out of this mess," Scrimple said wistfully.

"Never been to New York. Went to Disneyland once," Hayden said and turned the heat down a bit on the cooker.

When the food was ready they sat down in the living room on a sofa each and tucked in.

"Remember that officers' mess we used to have upstairs in the Hermitage. You could get food any time you wanted. And the serving wenches were sweet..." Scrimple chuckled at the memory.

"I hated working C shift," Hayden said, "Going to work at ten o'clock at night and then trying to keep your eyes open sitting in a Land Rover at three in the morning. That was probably the main reason I didn't stay on."

"Yeah, that was all a bit shit. I had a dream earlier when I fell asleep about being back in the Force. It was a bit too vivid." He shook his head to push away the memory of the dream.

"Didn't involve bonking any Cathay Pacific stewardesses from Hot Gossip then, your dream?"

"I never bonked any Cathay Pacific stewardesses," Scrimple said, the corners of his mouth turned down. "Ever."

"Sorry to hear that."

"I can't complain. There were some nice girls. My girlfriend now is lovely. She's got a heart of gold and massive tits. Gives a great blow job and she's a great cook."

Hayden picked up the remote control and flicked it at the flat screen TV above the fire place. "Let's see what's on the news."

There was a story about Brexit as there was every day and Scrimple's eyelids started drooping. He was going to get an early night. Maybe he wouldn't bother calling Kenworthy again. He'd do it first thing in the morning. Hayden was a solid bloke and staying at his place was making Scrimple feel less insecure about everything. He was starting to feel more optimistic that there was a logical explanation and it would all be sorted out soon.

The next story hit him like a hard punch in the solar plexus. The woman newsreader said: "And in Hampshire, police have come across the dead bodies of two men and an Asian woman. They were found in a ditch not far from the village of St. Mary Bourne. Initial reports are that they were all shot several times and then dumped at the site. Police suspect that they may be the victims of a people trafficking gang or some other organised crime gang with access to hand guns."

Scrimple looked at Hayden who was staring at him. Then he gave out a long groan, wracked with anguish and sadness for the loss of Esmeralda. It could not be anyone else.

He turned his attention back to the TV screen; the images were showing the village where he had lived for so many happy months. There was a shot of his local pub, the George Inn and police cars lined up on the side of the road. In the distance a black BMW X5 could be seen pulling up behind one of the police vans and then the story switched to something about underfunding of care homes.

"I have to ask you this," Hayden said, his face pale with shock. "You definitely had nothing to do with those three people being killed?"

"Fuck, no," Scrimple snapped. "They were my guests at my safe house. The two blokes were colleagues. I'd never met them before but they seemed decent enough. And the Asian woman…" he couldn't say it. At least, that part of the mystery was cleared up now. They hadn't been kidnapped for a ransom. They'd just been abducted, then killed later and dumped. No news of the North Korean. Someone had come for the defector and then they'd cleaned up. They'd come after Scrimple because he was a loose end. So that meant Winchcombe was probably dead as well. The room began spinning until Scrimple got a grip and took two deep sips of his third can of beer.

Hayden was still staring at him and from the expression on his face he seemed unsure if he was harbouring a criminal or a victim.

"I think you've got to turn yourself in to the police," Hayden suggested.

"They'll lock me up and throw away the key. It looks as if I killed all those people."

"No, it doesn't. You can explain exactly what happened. You can't run away from this. It will just make it worse."

"I think I loved that woman," Scrimple said, partially to himself. The poor girl. She must have been terrified and Scrimple wasn't there to protect her. She didn't deserve to be involved in all this. All she was doing was helping Scrimple in his job. To be killed for that was so unfair. It was brutal. It was evil. The sadness started to be replaced by an anger. Bit by bit it built up into a rage that he held down and contained. The rage swirled around inside him like a typhoon.

What if it wasn't some Korean snatch team that had come after their man? What if it was a Chinese team? The two men he'd killed could have been mainland Chinese although after he'd shot off their faces there was no way of telling. But what if it were Wendy Shen who was behind all of this?

He thought about it for a little while and decided that notion was farfetched. They'd come after him because he should have been in the safe house during the abduction and he wasn't. They'd tracked him down as a loose end. Koreans, not Chinese. That had a clear logic to it. Wendy Shen was just a bad nightmare like all the others, a spectre from the past he couldn't shake off. But she definitely wasn't part of this.

"You've got to turn yourself in," Hayden said again.

"Let me sleep on it and tomorrow morning I'll make a decision."

His friend nodded. "How about a cognac or two? I've got some nice Hennessy in the cupboard over there."

"Those bastards killed my girlfriend," Scrimple said quietly, "I'm going to find them. That's just not on." He patted the cushion that lay next to him on the sofa. Underneath, hidden from Hayden, was one of the Glock 17s. Having it close by gave Scrimple a small measure of comfort.

26

Wesley had been in touch and told them that the police had found the dead bodies of Pacino, Tchaikovsky and Esmeralda. They jumped into the X5 and drove down the road to the site. It was easy to find from the gaggle of blue lights.

"Do we think Scrimple killed them?" Major Rieve said from the back seat. They were letting Hamilton sit in the front these days as the ranking officer, as such.

"No, I think they were killed shortly after they were abducted. Their bodies just haven't been discovered until now. Then whoever lifted the North Korean came back for Scrimple. They paid off Winchcombe and he's off in the wind, although I wouldn't put much money on his chances of surviving for long."

"He's a traitor, isn't he, sir," Rickman said, pulling up behind one of the police vans. "We should track him down and take care of him."

"Wish it were that simple," Hamilton said and clapped him on the arm. "Maybe in the old days."

Wesley had made contact with the Superintendent they'd met earlier and so they were expected. The policeman was a rangy, lean fellow with a large jaw. He wore a troubled frown. "You lot are just messing up all of my crime figures. We haven't had so many dead bodies in one week, ever." He was still in uniform but had donned Wellington boots to cross the muddy field and view the crime scene.

"We're not pleased about it either. Two of those dead bodies are most likely close friends of these gentlemen here." Hamilton nodded at the two soldiers who were standing together. Their faces were hard and betrayed no emotion. They had seen death before and had friends die in their arms, often in unsung operations, in distant locations, for unfathomable reasons.

The Superintendent walked them to where the dead bodies lay under white sheets. The crime techs were already buzzing around the area like hornets in Tyvek suits.

"What do we know so far?" Hamilton asked.

"Shot at another location, possibly a few hours before they were dumped here. They will work on DNA and other evidence but unlikely it will help us until you identify the killers." The policeman gave them a quizzical look. "Can you identify the killers for us or is it a matter of national security?"

Hamilton shook his head sadly. "We don't know very much more than you do, to be honest. We are working on the assumption that they were a North Korean hit squad who came to grab back a defector we were interrogating in that house. These dead bodies are just collateral damage, I believe. And the man Scrimple is a loose end they tried to clean up but he got away."

"Good on him, and he took two of the bastards out as well." The Superintendent sounded surprisingly vehement in his opinion. "So where is he? Haven't you found him yet?"

"We've spoken to someone who has been in touch with him and any minute now my phone could ring." Hamilton pulled out his phone and stared at it, because it was silent. "So far, no call, unfortunately."

"So this Scrimple bloke, is he one of your top operatives, or whatever you call them?"

Hamilton gave a dry laugh. "Hardly. He's just a regular bloke and he was running what's basically a bed and breakfast for us. We've got hundreds of these. Forget that I told you that. Anyway, you've signed the Official Secrets Act."

"I have," the Superintendent said.

"Now, these two blokes," Hamilton lowered his voice, "and one of those dead men, they are what you might call top operatives. Seconded from the SAS."

The Superintendent nodded knowingly and then they went to the bodies and did the identification. There was no doubt about who they were. Pacino had been shot three times. Tchaikovsky had been shot four times and the Filipina woman had been shot once in the back of the head. *Brutal*, Hamilton thought to himself. An execution.

"We haven't been able to keep this out of the news. Two dog walkers found them and told everyone in the pub before the local patrol car even got here."

"Just go ahead and investigate it as normal and keep liaising with us. When we find out more we'll let you know." Hamilton held up his phone again. "I just wish this bugger would ring soon. If we can bring Scrimple in we should know a lot more."

"Where can we find you? Will you be staying in the house here in St. Mary Bourne?" the policeman asked.

"Yes, for now. It's as good a hotel as any." They shook hands and the MI5 team returned to their BMW. "Back to the ranch," Hamilton said and Rickman nodded.

Half an hour later, Hamilton had lost patience and called Kenworthy on his mobile phone. It rang out and voicemail came on. He tried a few more times and the same thing happened. Hamilton left a terse message simply saying his name and to call him. He then called the pub number and after a few rings a young woman's voice answered.

"This is urgent. I'm with the police. I'm looking for Bob Kenworthy," he said.

"No one's seen him for a few hours. It's really odd. He opened up the pub and was talking to Margaret but then he seems to have disappeared," the barmaid said. "We thought he was downstairs in the cellars sorting out the barrels but we've looked and can't find him."

An alarm bell of mighty proportions began tolling at the back of Hamilton's head. "When exactly was the last time anyone saw him?"

"It was about two hours ago. It's been busy in the pub so we haven't really kept track. Margaret has the keys to the till."

"Right, if he turns up, tell him to call me. This is my number. This is urgent."

"All right," the girl said, sounding more worried than she had been. "Maybe he's just gone down the road or into town to have a chat with a mate."

"Does he do that often?"

"Not really. He'll always tell us where he's going and when he'll be back."

"So this is unusual?"

"I guess so. Yeah."

Hamilton ended the phone call. This didn't feel right. If someone else knew the connection between Scrimple and Kenworthy they would go and have a word with the pub landlord the way Hamilton had. If someone were really keen to find Scrimple they might even grab Kenworthy and smack him around a bit or even do what was done to Pacino and the others. Not a good thought, he decided.

They were back in the living room. He took a bite from a pork pie that was sitting on a plate by his elbow and then tried to get through to the DDG and report. She called back within fifteen minutes.

"This is a serious escalation," she said, referring to the three dead bodies. "An attack on our own people. Someone's brought war to our own back yard."

"Yes, Sara, that's how it feels."

"How are the E Squadron lads? How do they feel about the loss of one of their own?" Sara Dodwell asked.

"Hard as nails. Not showing any emotion. But angry as hell." Hamilton looked up as he said this and Major Rieve's eyes met his. The soldier nodded in confirmation.

"You've got to bring Scrimple in and find out what he knows," the DDG repeated her earlier instructions.

"If the other side has got hold of Kenworthy then Scrimple may not have got my message with my phone numbers. How else can we get him to call in?"

The DDG grunted in affirmation at the other end of the line. "I suspect you have an idea?"

Hamilton smiled. The woman could read most men's minds on a good day. "I was thinking maybe I go on television dressed as a police officer and make an appeal for him to turn himself in and call a special number. He'll recognise me if he sees it and hopefully will call."

"That sounds like a plan," she agreed. "Get hold of your new Superintendent friend and set it up."

"So, I'm authorised to appear in public on television dressed as a policeman?" Hamilton double confirmed.

"You can be dressed as a policewoman for all I care, just bring the silly bugger in from the cold and debrief him. By tomorrow lunch time latest."

27

This was their third mission in the United Kingdom. Baldy and Scruffy had worked with Colonel Wendy once before in Cambridge and so knew the topography. On that mission they'd been sent to assassinate a list of Hong Kong students who had been active and prominent in the Hong Kong democracy movement. The idea was that they would meet with accidents or be the victims of muggings and murder. The police were not supposed to see the patterns but other students with radical political views would get the message, shut up and fall in line.

The mission had gone well initially until a Hong Kong student had identified them to the police. Somehow the man Scrimple had also been involved and after that the mission had fallen apart. However, the big bosses had considered it a partial success because the message had been clearly sent to those young men and women who were not loyal to the motherland. Wendy and the two of them had managed to leave the country without any problems and so, a year later, here they were again, working on foreign soil.

It was of course a bad omen, as Scruffy had said in between mouthfuls of his chocolate bar, that the white devil Scrimple had turned up again and somehow managed to kill two of their comrades in arms.

Baldy was still convinced that Scrimple was a master of disguise. He was like one of those old, fat, drunken Kung Fu masters from the movies who staggered around and then defeated anyone who came to challenge his school or his style.

"We must be extra careful," he had impressed on Scruffy as they drove up to Cambridge. "They look ancient and useless these men, but underneath they are dangerous."

When they arrived at the pub, it was late afternoon. A few men sat at the bar and drank beer and serving them was the man they had come to snatch. He had a heavy belly and three days growth of beard. Wendy Shen had shot him that time but he'd survived.

They knew there was a small car park around the back and an outdoor deck where people went to smoke. This is how they would approach him.

To ensure a quick getaway Scruffy parked on the main road, one tyre up on the kerb behind a few other cars. Then they entered the pub through the front door.

"What can I get you, gentlemen?" the landlord said fixing them with a friendly but inquisitive eye. They knew he'd been a policeman in Hong Kong and that was another reason to be careful.

"We come to do summer course at Girton college," said Baldy, whose English was better than his partner's, although still heavy with the sounds of a native Mandarin speaker, to pre-empt any questions or suspicions.

"You're a month too early," Kenworthy said. "You must be keen."

"Yes, we just come to look and have interview," Baldy explained. "Maybe we have two pint of your best bitter."

"That will be this one," Kenworthy said and tapped one of the pumps. He took down the glasses. "Where are you lads from in China?"

"North of China," Baldy said.

"I used to live in Hong Kong for a very long time," Kenworthy said, with a pleasant smile. Cambridge was full of Chinese students and there was a language school up the road which helped to make the Thai restaurant, which was in the other half of the pub, busy nearly every night.

"Hong Kong very nice. They have good food there," Baldy said. Scruffy had started wandering past the toilets into the back room which led out on to the decking. "We sit in the back. Is nice weather."

"Knock yourself out," the landlord said and took the twenty pound note that Baldy was holding.

"I just go toilet," Baldy said, pointing in the direction where his partner had gone.

"I'll bring the drinks out to you. No worries."

When Baldy stepped out from the toilet, Kenworthy was just setting down the two pint glasses that were filled with Adnam's bitter on the outside table where Scruffy was sitting. Baldy came up fast behind the landlord and pushed the barrel of the Norinco NP-22 semi-automatic into his back.

"This is gun. I will shoot you if you make noise. You must come with us. We will ask you questions."

Kenworthy glanced over his shoulder and he understood what this was about. It would have been foolish to shout or to run. Baldy and Scruffy marched him out of the car park and bundled him into the back of their white Ford van. They took him to a quiet dead-end road which they had located on Google Maps. Then they interrogated him. Even after Scruffy had cut him three times on the face and there was blood all over his shirt, the landlord would not tell them where to find Scrimple. He kept on telling them he didn't know.

Baldy was starting to believe him and was going to call Wendy for further instructions when Kenworthy's mobile began to ring. Baldy grabbed it and hit the answer button. He thought the god of war was smiling on him when he realised it was Scrimple at the other end of the line. Baldy said nothing and Scrimple kept on calling. Then Baldy called back on the same number and Scrimple answered.

Within half an hour Shady Mouse had triangulated the call and narrowed it down to a half mile radius around the local cell phone tower. Within fifteen minutes of that Shady Mouse's cunning algorithms had worked out that there was a former Hong Kong police officer who was a teacher at Sherborne School and he had a terraced house on the main road. That's where Scrimple was hiding.

It took them three hours to drive back to the safe house in Windsor because the traffic on the M25 was slow, a lorry had broken down. They dropped off Kenworthy who was blindfolded, handcuffed and placed in one of the empty bedrooms. Until they had Scrimple, Wendy had instructed, he was their hostage.

Baldy and Scruffy had a bowl of noodles and some cans of Red Bull then they began the three hour drive down the M3 and the A303 to Sherborne. On the way they passed Andover near where their colleagues had been killed. Baldy, who was driving, noticed it but Scruffy was asleep in the passenger seat.

It was their plan to arrive about one in the morning. They stopped off for petrol at an Esso station and Scruffy bought a Double Decker bar. Baldy had another can of Red Bull and something called a Yorkie. They didn't have these chocolate bars at home in China. They drove down a dark windy road for ten miles until they came to the outskirts of Sherborne town. The streets were deserted, it was after midnight. They found a parking space on Marston Road which was close to their target building. They parked the van between a Land Rover and an Audi. Sherborne seemed an affluent town.

Baldy reported in to base. Shady Mouse was awake, he never seemed to sleep.

Scruffy, dressed in dark clothes with a black baseball cap on his head, carried a heavy steel item in one hand. They had decided to go in silently if they could, using an electronic pick rake but if the door was bolted then Scruffy would swing the Enforcer, which was 16 kg of hardened steel and could take out most regular doors. Both of them carried an NP-22, the Chinese clone of the Sig Sauer P226.

They walked past a sign that read Sherborne International School. Shady Mouse had done the research and told them there were many mainland Chinese students studying at several schools around the town so their faces would not draw any attention. A woman with her dog passed them and she nodded at them in a polite way. The Enforcer came in a bag that could be mistaken for a duffel bag. They were just a father and uncle visiting their son and on their way to one of the hotels at the end of Cheap Street. Or perhaps their AirBnB.

The two men identified the house number they'd been given. It was a classic heavy wooden door in lime green. The stone building, part of a long row, appeared to be over 300 years old. Baldy slotted the rake in the Yale key hole and let it whirr. It took four minutes and then all the tumblers had fallen and the door was unlocked. He tried it but it didn't move. Baldy recognised that the door must be bolted from the inside.

He stepped aside and gave Scruffy the signal that it was his turn. The pavement, which was elevated by three metres from the main road, remained deserted although cars passed below them occasionally on the way to the next town.

Scruffy took two deep breaths, got his legs in a firm horse stance and then swung the heavy steel tool so that it went crashing into the door just below the lock.

The door flew open, Scruffy flattened himself so Baldy could rush past him into the living room, sighting his gun into the darkness. Then Scruffy followed immediately. They didn't have much time now, after breaking the door down. The neighbours would be confused. Nobody would be calling the police for at least fifteen minutes but by that time the Chinese men wanted to be back at their van with a compliant Scrimple.

But Scrimple had no intention of being compliant.

Baldy was met by two 9 mm rounds that were fired in rapid succession from a Glock. He stumbled and fell. Scruffy got two rounds in his chest and then a third one entered his eye and exited taking out most of the back of his head. At this close range the Austrian weapon was beyond deadly. Another shot rang out. The bullet entered Baldy's head at the base of his skull and squashed itself on the flagstone floor, bouncing back into his mouth.

28

"I have here the preliminary Sales and Purchase Agreement for 90% of the shares in your company," Mr. Guo said as he slid the document across the conference table.

Professor Whyte's face was pale but Mrs. Block had an expression on her face which could be construed as relief. She knew exactly how short of cash they were and that this document was their only hope of survival.

"You must ask your lawyers to check it carefully and come back to our lawyer with any changes they require but this must be done by Wednesday at five in the afternoon at the latest."

Whyte gasped at the deadline and Mrs. Block looked astonished. Guo said, "I come from China and we do everything fast, you know. I am sorry." But he wasn't sorry at all. He had the bit between his teeth and his master plan was moving forward.

When they had arrived, he had introduced Mr. Park as an important member of his team from Korea. Guo had an idea that everyone in Korea was either called Park, Lee or Kim so there was no need to be clever with fake names. In any case he knew that Asian people all looked the same to foreigners.

"Park here will be doing our due diligence. We want to begin today as we discussed on the phone. I am not talking about the financial aspect. For that we are using a company called Wong & Chan who are our London accountants. Now that you have signed back our Letter of Intent and all the non-disclosure documents then they can come to have a look over your books. They can start tomorrow." Guo turned his beady eyes on Mrs. Block. "But I am sure it will all be perfectly in order. It is England, after all? You do everything by the rules." He gave a low chuckle. "Not like in my country, where we bend the rules and we break the rules and change the rules." He was very pleased with his little cultural exposition.

"The accounts are all up to date," Mrs. Block said, with a dusting of frost over her words.

"If we can agree the final version of the Sales and Purchase Agreement by Thursday I will immediately have £400,000 cash advance transferred to your account." Guo beamed at Mrs. Block. "That will be enough for two months' payroll I am sure and we can complete next week."

The accountant nodded. She realised that he was dangling the lure and it was bright and shiny and Professor Whyte would be insane to ignore it. The business would be dead if they didn't bite.

"Park is very excited about the data he has read on Gomeldovir. He is impressed by its potential."

Professor Whyte perked up at this. "What do you specialise in, Mr. Park?"

"Professor. I am professor and have two doctorates," the Korean man said. He wasn't showing off. He was making an important point. Guo approved. There would be no pulling the wool over their eyes. If Park found anything that wasn't right, that was exaggerated or that appeared dubious Guo was prepared to pull out of the deal at the blink of an eye. Every good negotiator knew that. You did not fall in love with your deal or potential acquisition, ever. You were always prepared to walk away from any deal, even when it was one minute before completion.

What was the fun expression one of his English friends had taught him? It was never over until the fat lady sang. But Mr. Guo felt the fat lady was singing and dancing and clapping with delight on this Gomeldon Advanced Research Laboratory deal. It was only one half of the equation, but like Yin and Yang both halves made up the whole.

"Can we now go and have a closer look at the facilities," Guo suggested. "Maybe Mrs. Block can send the agreement to the lawyers already." Guo glanced at his Vacheron Constantin Patrimony. It was one of his favourites because the blue bezel in rose gold was impossible to purchase these days. "It is eleven twenty. So they have nearly three days to make their comments. Plenty of time."

They all got up and the Managing Director led them off to get changed into lab coats and other protective equipment. Guo was in a particularly good mood this Monday morning, not simply because he was moving his new project forward rapidly but because last night Jing Jing had come to his room.

On the drive down from London he'd had a dreamy expression on his face as he listened to the Carpenters and recalled every tiny detail of the sexual encounter that had occurred.

They'd had a nice dinner at a Japanese restaurant. Jing Jing had been delighted. She had tasted sushi before but nothing like the fresh fare that was flown in for this restaurant every morning from Tokyo. The *Otoro* tuna was so fatty it simply melted in their mouths. Guo had enticed her to drink chilled sake and her face had flushed quickly and her giggling had increased in frequency.

She was such a delightful creature. He could understand why her female boss would have been jealous, feared that the husband's eyes would stray sooner or later, and pre-empted this by banishing Jing Jing from her job.

Then, after a nightcap, Guo had shown her his collection of rare vases which were stored in a sealed room in the basement. He only had four but they were so exquisite that any woman's heart would melt at their beauty, the delicacy of their workmanship.

Later, after he had showered and gone to bed, there had been a gentle tapping on his bedroom door. He had been surprised and intrigued. When he opened the door he found her standing outside in her pink Juicy Couture tracksuit, the one he'd bought her at Selfridges.

She appeared embarrassed but her eyes had the brazen glaze that came from the alcohol and something else.

"Felix, you have been so kind to me," she said. "You are taking care of me in my time of trouble. I feel guilty that I have nothing to offer you in return."

Guo nodded sagely. "It is my pleasure. You did not deserve to be treated so badly by your boss." He was wearing his silk, burgundy pyjamas and he'd cut all his nose hairs and trimmed his eyebrows after his shower.

"I am just a poor country girl with no education and my parents are farmers. I have nothing to offer you in return for your kindness."

"You have something that you could offer me. But only if you wished so yourself. I have no expectation. I do not force you." Guo made things clear.

The girl had nodded, then giving him a guileless smile. "I wish to but I ask you to respect me. I have no experience. I have not done anything with a man before."

Guo was astonished and didn't know what to say. He stepped back and opened the door fully so she could enter his bed chamber. He reached for her face, its alabaster hue soft and warm and pleasing to the touch. The girl smelt of rose petals. He had kissed her and she had responded.

Later he'd been awestruck, almost unbelieving, that Jing Jing was still a virgin. She gave her special treasure to him.

"Boss, need to talk to you," Bohumir said and woke Guo from his reveries. They had just arrived at the GART facility in Porton Down and Bohumir, sitting at the front of the car had been on the phone.

"What is it?" Guo demanded. He'd been miles away, not for a long time had he been so happy and excited about a woman.

"We've got a small problem. The Albanians who were watching the safe house people screwed up."

"How screw up?" Guo snapped. He didn't like to hear this phrase. He paid good money to people who worked for him so that they did not ever screw up.

"It seems that one of the men, the soldier, tried to escape and during the escape attempt they all got killed."

Guo sat up with astonishment. "They all got killed? Are they crazy? This is not good."

"They gave me a courtesy call and have packed up and disappeared," Bohumir said grimly.

"What about the dead bodies?" Guo wanted to know.

"They took them back near the safe house and dumped them. Made it look as if they had been killed there a few days ago."

"That's stupid," Guo said. They had always planned that things would be kept as low key as possible. "Why can't they just bury them or make them disappear in acid?"

"They are stupid. They are effective but they are mainly stupid gangsters," Bohumir said, shaking his head.

"You told me your friend had used them before and they were good."

"My friend said they were competent, they did not cheat him but that they were not so smart."

"Will it come back to us?" Guo asked.

Bohumir shook his head. "Nobody knows you. Nobody knows me except my face. But I look like any one of half a million Eastern Europeans in London. It will be fine. I have told them that if they appear again I will personally kill them."

"Arrrgh," was the noise Guo made to show his displeasure. Then he waved it away, as if he were flicking off a fly. Sometimes people got hurt. Sometimes they died. You could not make an omelette without breaking the skin of the egg. If you wanted to be rich you had to walk over the bodies of the poor.

29

"They're both dead," Hayden said, crouching over the two men on his living room floor. "Did you have to kill them?"

Scrimple, somewhat in a daze, simply shrugged. The Glock was still in his hands.

"For my money, they're Chinese," Hayden said, standing back up and closing the broken front door as best as he could. That stopped the cold air coming in. Sooner or later the neighbours would be standing there wanting to know what all the strange noises were about. The police would be here in ten or fifteen minutes. "Not Canto-pop, they look more like Northerners. Jiangsu or Shandong province."

"You don't reckon they're Koreans then?"

"No, they're Bong-heads," Hayden insisted, using an expression that Scrimple hadn't heard for decades.

"Fuck me, maybe it is Wendy Shen after all," Scrimple said to himself. *What was he going to do now?* He didn't want to get Hayden into trouble. He had to bug out fast. This was Dorset where everything moved in slow motion, his friend had been telling him earlier in the night over cognacs, so he had a window of opportunity.

They will have come in a car. He grabbed the first man roughly and rolled him over, searched his pockets. He found a set of car keys with the Ford logo on the fob and also a wallet and a phone. On the second body he also found a wallet and a phone. Scrimple ran upstairs and brought down his duffel bag. Everything had been packed and he'd gone to bed wearing his clothes and shoes in case something like this might happen. He hadn't expected it to happen, didn't imagine it would happen, but when it had happened he'd been ready and the two Chinese intruders hadn't. They were dressed in exactly the same way as the two at Roland's farm and they had the same two semi-automatic pistols. Scrimple threw all his loot from the bodies into the duffel bag.

He turned to Hayden who'd been standing in the middle of the room in front of the fireplace with a bemused expression on his face. "I'm really sorry about messing up your house like this."

"At least you're alive. They were armed and dangerous."

Scrimple thrust half of the wadge of cash that he'd taken from the safe at home into Hayden's hand. "That's for the dry cleaning. Really sorry about the carpet. Is it antique or something?"

"Who gives a shit," his old copper friend said with a shake of his head. "Just stay here and turn yourself in to the police. They should be here in the next twenty minutes." There was a timid knock on the front door and they both looked over but didn't answer it.

"This is manslaughter. I just killed two more people," Scrimple said, pointing at the two bodies with the muzzle of his Glock. "No, I'm off. Tell the police everything that you know. Tell them it wasn't my fault. I've got to move on until I can get in touch with the bosses in London and find out what's really going on."

"The police will sort it out, mate," said Hayden. "I'll make us a cup of tea."

"No way. These guys came in a car and they must have parked it close by. I'm going to find it and then I'm driving off."

Hayden nodded in resignation. "Suit yourself. Better go now before the neighbours lynch you for disturbing the peace and spoiling their beauty sleep. This will make me famous around town. Might even get a free haircut down at the barbers on Cheap Street."

"Take care, son," Scrimple said and they shook hands. "I'll see you if I survive the next few days."

"Turn yourself in, for goodness sake." Hayden tried one more time.

Scrimple shook his head firmly and tugged open the door, then barged through the crowd of five or six people that had gathered in dressing gowns. The fact that he was still holding the Austrian handgun parted the crowd rapidly. He'd decided to turn left. There were more places to park cars down there he'd noticed the previous afternoon when making his phone calls. *And how the hell had the bastards tracked him down again this time?*

He marched rapidly downhill and every ten seconds tried clicking the door-opening button on the set of car keys he'd acquired. It was when he got to the bottom of Marston Road that a Ford van greeted him with flashing lights. That was his new found friend. He turned into the road and walked past a sign for Sherborne International School, slowing down as he came closer to the van. There might be a driver or someone else, but then the doors would not have been locked. He approached cautiously, searching for any movement or shadows from inside the van. It all seemed silent. In the distance he heard a police siren. He'd better get a crack on. That was faster than expected.

Scrimple pulled open the door of the van. It smelt vaguely of sweat. But not the sweat of Western men. There was a different character to it. His subconscious recognised it. It reminded him of prison cells and unwashed Asian men behind bars. He tossed his duffel bag on the passenger seat, started up the engine, noticed it was an automatic and that the petrol tank was nearly full.

Within five minutes he was pulling out and driving in the direction of Yeovil. His bet was that the police cars were coming from the bigger county town and if he headed towards them it might be counter-intuitive. He had no idea where he was going. For the moment he was safe because nobody knew about this van or its number plates. The police out here were not going to be able to throw up road-blocks in sufficient time to catch him in a net. In Hong Kong the police could toss down a cordon in fifteen minutes flat. Out here, they probably had never done the training. They were just country coppers and chances were they only had two patrol cars working night shift with one harassed bobby in each. Thank you George Osborne for austerity and cuts to the police budget.

He drove at a steady sixty miles an hour with the lights on at full beam. There was hardly any traffic on the road at this time of the night. The dashboard clock told him it was coming up for 2 a.m. Good job he'd caught up on some sleep in the afternoon.

Scrimple had no idea where he was heading now. He simply had to put as many miles between himself and the scene of the shooting. Then he could feel a bit safer and give it some more measured thought.

First thing he'd do is call Kenworthy. He hadn't got around to that earlier.

He passed the Yeovil Golf Club and then turned right, driving through a trading estate. Eventually he turned onto a road that led in the direction of Mudford. If he headed North he should hit the A303 at some point. Then he could decide to go West to Exeter or East to London. If he kept on heading North he should get closer to Bristol. That seemed a useful thought. Hold on to that one, he told himself. It was a big city and he could dump the van and hide up in a cheap hotel where they were happy to accept cash. Thousands of students lived in Bristol and there was a big population of immigrants. That could be a good place to try and duck down.

Eventually, after Shepton Mallet, he pulled up into a dark lay-by and closed his eyes for a few minutes. A face appeared in the darkness and it was the face of the man he'd known as William. The spectre seemed to be grinning at him. He shook it away and thought about Wendy Shen.

So perhaps she was behind all of this. She'd tracked him down after all this time and sent men to the safe house. They'd found everyone there but not Scrimple. So they'd killed them all and then come back for Scrimple. Now he was on the run. He reached over and patted his duffel bag. He gave a grim chuckle. So far he wasn't doing badly in building his arsenal. Two Canadian assault rifles, two Austrian semi-automatic pistols and two Chinese copies of the Sig Sauer. He couldn't remember which one it was a copy of but they weren't bad. Bring it on, you fat bitch. I'll kill all your men, he thought.

Wendy wasn't really fat. She was fleshy, in a sexy way and he'd bonked her once before he knew who she really was. That had been an eternity ago.

His Alcatel burner phone rang, it was Kenworthy's number.

"What's up? Have you found that Hamilton bloke?"

"Scrimple. Where are you?" The voice of Wendy Shen came dancing hauntingly down the line.

"Who is this?" he yelled, although of course he knew damn well.

"Your friend Wendy. Do you forget me already?"

"Fuck off, fuck you, bitch, fuck you." Scrimple ranted.

"Why are you so angry?" Her voice was soft and low. She was teasing him, he understood that, so he hit back.

"Both your guys are dead. Just like the ones I killed at Roland's farm."

There was a sharp intake of breath from the Chinese woman. "You killed Baldy and Scruffy?"

"Yeah, whatever their fucking names were," Scrimple yelled down the phone triumphantly.

"That cannot be right," Wendy said but he could hear the doubt and the displeasure in her voice.

"You'd better believe it, you Chinese cunt."

"Where are you now, Scrimple?" she asked softly.

"As if I would tell you."

"My computer technician can tell me exactly where you are. We could even see where you are standing using one of our satellites."

"Bollocks, you can. Why did you kill my girlfriend and the other guys?"

There was a moment of hesitation from her. Then she spoke with a puzzled note in her voice. "We didn't kill your girlfriend or anyone. That has nothing to do with us."

"I don't believe you. Why do you keep sending these men after me?"

"I miss you," she said, "and I asked them to bring you to me so we can have a nice conversation again, like we did the first time we met."

"Just leave me alone," he snapped, although it was a useless request. He knew that.

"That is not possible. You must come to me," the Chinese woman said firmly.

"Why would I do that?"

"Because I have here, your friend Kenworthy, and I will torture him and kill him if you don't come to me. You must come immediately."

Scrimple sat in the van and waited for his head to stop spinning. The woman had left him no choice. He tried to calm himself.

How could he get hold of someone to help him? Where the hell was the Reliable Man? So many times the man had helped him out of a tight spot. Or where even were his colleagues from MI5?

Suddenly he had a thought. Maybe there was someone at the safe house? Or they had diverted the phone to the head office in case Scrimple called? It was worth a try.

30

The phone rang shortly after 4 a.m. and Hamilton rolled over and answered. He was using Scrimple's bedroom in the safe house.

"Wesley, this had better be good," he said.

"I think you'll like this. We've got two more dead Chinese blokes."

"How is that good?" Hamilton said, sitting up and turning the bedside light on.

"Your man Scrimple is a one man killing machine," Wesley said, not trying hard to disguise the awe in his voice.

"In case you had forgotten, going around shooting people is not something that we condone in MI5."

"The man's obviously on a mission."

"The man is out of control and on the run, as far as I can tell." Hamilton placed his bare feet on the carpet. "Right where was it then, and when?"

"Happened about two hours ago in a town called Sherborne. Scrimple was staying with an old Hong Kong police friend who is a teacher there. Two unidentified Chinese males burst through the door with guns. Scrimple took them down. No other casualties."

"They must teach them different police tactics in Hong Kong," Hamilton muttered. "I assume he's in the wind again and wasn't arrested by the local constabulary?"

"That's right. Last seen running down the street carrying a holdall which apparently is full of guns and ammo."

"He's probably still got those assault rifles with him. Did he use that one again?"

"No, the police report says several rounds were fired from a 9 mm pistol."

"Okay, so he used one of the Glocks that he has." Hamilton laughed. He had to admit, he too was starting to admire the man's style. It was wrong, it was wild but it made sense. "I'll grab the lads and we'll get on the road ASAP. Now, I want you to get over to the pub in Girton as soon as it's decent, say nine o'clock, and go banging on the door. Find out if the landlord Kenworthy turned up again and what's going on there. There's something not right about him disappearing. Might be nothing but turn up and tell them you're from the police."

"Right, boss. I didn't get much sleep last night," Wesley said.

"What do you want, a gold medal?"

"I wasn't complaining."

"It sounded like it," Hamilton said. "I'll call you later when we're on the road. Send me the address and the local police contacts. See if you can pick Scrimple up on any of the street cameras."

"Ahead of you on that one. Nothing so far. They're a bit poor down there and can't afford CCTV. Or they don't have any crime."

"Probably not much crime. Not until the one man crime wave called Scrimple turned up in town. So the guy he was staying with is unharmed and we could interview him?"

"I guess so," Wesley replied. They cut the connection.

Hamilton woke up Rieves and Rickman and told them fifteen minutes so they had time to brush their teeth and throw their kit together. Being soldiers they were probably always packed, ready to bug out any second. Wasn't that something they were taught in the army? It had been over forty-five years since Hamilton marched up and down a parade ground in his school's cadet corps.

As he was turning off the bedroom light and was about to walk downstairs he heard the phone ring in the living room. That was odd. It was the landline and the phone stood on one of the occasional tables. It was a classic black GPO 746 model with a rotary dial, that had been around since the 1970s.

"Hello?" Hamilton answered cautiously on the fifth ring.

"Who's that?" a man's voice asked.

"My name's Gavin. Who are you?"

"Are you Hamilton?"

"Yes, are you Scrimple?"

"Fuck me, am I glad to hear your voice. I'm in big shit."

Hamilton laughed with relief. "I know but we're just on our way to dig you out the shit."

"Do you know what's happened? Did you get my message from Kenworthy?"

"We didn't get any message from Kenworthy. He seems to have disappeared."

"Oh, that fucking bitch," Scrimple said at the other end of the line.

"We've been trying to find you. We know you've been hunted by some Asian operatives and that you managed to escape them."

There was a near hysterical bark of laughter at the other end of the phone. "You can say that again. Chog bastards. Wendy Shen sent them. I've just had her on the phone. She's kidnapped Kenworthy and is holding him for ransom, demanding that I come to her."

"What's her involvement with the North Korean guy?"

"I've no idea but she's obviously behind all of this and she killed my girlfriend and Pacino, and Tchaikovsky."

"She did? This is the same Wendy Shen that I trashed my car chasing the last time? The one who caused all the carnage in Cambridge?"

"That's the one," Scrimple confirmed.

"Do you know where she is?"

"She wouldn't tell me except to start driving towards London but she said she'd call back and give me instructions on how to find her. If I didn't come, she'd kill Kenworthy."

Hamilton processed the new information rapidly. "Right, mate. I'm here at your house with two guys from E Squadron. Pacino's boss in fact. So we've got firepower. Can you get back here soon? I guess you're outside Sherborne somewhere but in which direction?"

There was a brief pause while Scrimple probably considered what he was being told. "I think I can get back to St. Mary Bourne by six or seven."

Hamilton picked up on the hesitation. "You do trust me on this? I'm one of the good guys. It sounds like this whole operation is another one of Wendy Shen's black ops. We need to mobilise all of our resources. So I need you back here, back on the team."

"You and Kat Pedder are the only ones I trust. I don't know what the hell happened to Winchcombe. Is he dead too?"

"We think he's the one who sold you lot out. He was probably given a big pay-off and we know he's left the country on a false passport."

Scrimple didn't say anything at the other end. There was just a sigh.

"Get your arse over here. Corporal Rickman will rustle you up a full English breakfast and a massive coffee and then we'll take it from here."

"What do I do about Wendy?" Scrimple asked.

"If she calls, tell her you're on the way. Get more details from her. When you get here, we'll work things out. I need to wake up the DDG from her beauty sleep. I might wait until 6 a.m. for that one."

31

On returning from their visit to Porton Down, the butler, Bohumir, excused himself saying he had to run some errands around the shops. He took the tube and changed trains several times until he exited at High Street Kensington, then made his way to the Muffin Man Tea Shop. He ordered a Lapsang Souchong tea and two hot buttered crumpets.

The shop was half full of ladies who were busy sharing confidences with each other and moaning about their husbands.

It was ten minutes before Bohumir was joined by the other man who spoke to him in a harsh New York accent.

"How ya been?"

"It's coming along," Bohumir replied. The other man, who was wearing a well cut dark suit but no tie - he sported a heavy gold chain around his neck - ordered a regular coffee from the waitress. He was bald, except for a halo of hair around his ears and he had a powerful nose and small, fierce eyes. He looked like a man who made garments for a living but sold them to customers at gun point.

"This frigging country. When will they discover air conditioning?" he said. Bohumir did not know his real name but everyone called him Abe.

"As the man said, if you don't like it then go back to your own country," Bohumir said with a smile that was meant to show he was just pulling Abe's leg.

"What is my own country? That's the question I need to answer first." Abe took a sip from the coffee that had been delivered. "Frigging dishwater. They don't know how to make real coffee. You should be able to stand up your spoon in it."

"This is a place you come to drink tea."

"Whatever. So tell me what's going on."

Bohumir leant forward and in a low voice reported quickly and efficiently what had been happening in the Guo household over the last few days.

"So did he fuck her?" Abe asked.

"It was noisy when I walked past the bedroom door."

"And she's pretty?"

"Pretty, if you like the skinny Asian ones."

"You mean she's like a stick insect?" Abe wanted to know.

"No, she's got some shape to her. Lovely eyes." Bohumir shook his head and pursed his lips. "It just doesn't feel right."

"You mean a fat old slime-ball like him with a young cute chick?"

Bohumir shook his head again. "No, that happens all the time. It's just all a bit too slick and easy. He meets her at his son's school. They go for dinner, she loses her job. It feels engineered."

"These modern Chinese chicks, they're smooth operators. She's got a pussy and she wants to get on in life. She meets a guy with plenty of bling bling and she moves fast."

"It's too fast."

"Maybe you need to find yourself a girl again. You must have forgotten how it works."

Bohumir gave a sniff of irritation. "It feels staged. Someone has placed her there."

"The Chinese?" Abe said.

"Probably."

"Why would they be interested? He's just going about his regular business. Why do they need to place an asset close to him?"

"Same reason you've placed me close to him."

Abe wasn't entirely convinced. "Maybe. Then keep a close eye on her. He might be telling her his darkest secrets as she's sucking his teeny weeny cock. That's no danger to us at the moment." His phone gave a small burp and he checked the message that had popped up. "Do you think she's smart?"

"She comes across pretty dizzy. That's another reason I don't trust her," Bohumir said.

"Lots of pretty girls are a bit dizzy. They don't need to work with the bit up here so much," he tapped the side of his head, "if they've got the other features."

"She's not right. That's my gut feel." Bohumir concluded the matter.

"How's the deal going? Is the Professor the real thing?"

"I heard them talking and he says they had already weaponised several zoonotic viruses at the lab outside Pyong Yang. They were focusing on the coronaviruses from bats and civets as being the most effective. But he was specialising in pangolins."

"What kind of animal is that?" Abe said, his eyebrows shucking together.

"Some kind of scaled mammal that eats ants and termites, common in Asia."

"They can't weaponise this kind of stuff unless they have vaccines and antidotes," Abe said.

Bohumir shrugged. "According to Professor Park that wasn't such a big consideration with his military bosses. They just wanted something that could make North Korea powerful and wipe out any enemies."

"So do they think this Gomeldovir will be effective as an antidote to whatever virus they'd be launching?"

"You've got to know how the virus works exactly, map the DNA and then target the antiviral perfectly."

"And Guo believes his Professor Park will be able to do that?"

"Along with Professor Whyte and his team. They won't be allowed to know the big picture."

Abe summarised: "Guo makes a targeted Coronavirus. They launch it in various countries around the world. Say Africa, the Middle East and then along comes Guogene and saves the day and saves the world and Guo adds a few more billion to his bank account."

Bohumir nodded. "It's a simple plan."

"The problem is that Africa is too close to Israel. We can't let this get out of hand."

"And not if the Chinese are aware of it and have placed that girl in the house."

"We were on a conference call with some of the top people at TEVA yesterday," Abe said, "and they say this is risky business. They have nothing developed yet that is effective against SARS, MERS or Avian flu. They don't like what we've told them so far."

"The easiest solution is for them to buy the Gomeldovir lab before Wednesday," Bohumir said, pushing his empty plate away from him. However unpalatable the subject was, the crumpets had been excellent as always. "Then we could take out the North Korean and maybe even Guo."

"The problem with us Jews is that you can never tell us what we *must* do. We are a stubborn minded people," Abe said shaking his head with a mild air of frustration. "It says so in Exodus."

"I'll take them both out this evening, if you give me the green light," Bohumir said. He'd been a member of Mossad's Kidon unit for eleven years now and nobody was asked to join that elite squad if it was thought they had a soft heart.

Abe gave a growl of irritation. "I don't think we'll get authorisation that fast. And it's always difficult when it's London. They never authorise London. You can kill half of Dubai, they don't care but London is sacred ground." He stood up abruptly. "I've got an idea how we could get it done in an oblique way."

"I'll take care of the bill," Bohumir said. Abe gave him the semblance of a salute and returned to his office at the embassy.

32

There is a pleasant town in the Burgundy wine region called Beaune. It has an ancient defensive wall and, under the cobbled streets, it has hundreds of kilometres of caverns and tunnels where for centuries some of the finest wine in the world has been stored.

Bill Jedburgh had come to Beaune to hunt and kill a man called Mustafa Rulaysah al-Masri. The target had been allocated the codename of 'Gwyddgrug'. Jedburgh wondered if other people found it amusing that some computer program was randomly allocating names of Welsh villages to enemies of the state.

"Are you going to have the garlicky snails then?" Kat Pedder said as she stared at him over the top of her menu. They were in an intimate restaurant with ten tables and the owner took the orders and his wife did the cooking. It had been recommended as one of the best in town by the manager of their hotel. Jedburgh and Kat were posing as a couple on holiday. The manager had not blinked when they checked in. Jedburgh was a handsome, fit man in his fifties while Kat was a compact thirty year old blonde with short hair. Their age gap hinted at trophy wife or boss marries Personal Assistant. This was the legend they had agreed on. Their passports identified them as Mr. and Mrs. David Somersytt.

"I will be having the garlicky snails followed by a garlicky chicken stew and then a cognac-laced mousse au chocolat," Jedburgh said. He was studying the wine list and unsurprisingly all the wines, white and red, were from the region. "How about a La Tache?" he suggested.

"Is that a good one?" she asked.

"If you like Pinot Noir, that one should hit the spot."

"Can we afford it? I suspect from the twinkle in your eye that it might be a Grand Cru or something?"

Jedburgh lowered the wine list. The table was small and rickety, the folding chairs uncomfortable, but that was all part of the charm. "It's rare. They only have 5 hectares from what I can remember. I went on a course in London once."

"You didn't answer my question," Kat said with an indulgent smile. She had started to get used to him by now, Jedburgh suspected. At first she'd been both frightened and irritated by his style. Now she was starting to become pleasant company and appeared more relaxed. She was one of these Millennials that thought they carried burdens on their shoulders that other young people had not done in their time.

Jedburgh had been in the army, then joined the Royal Hong Kong Police in his twenties and, in retrospect, they had not always been easy years. Then later his life had changed and although it had become harsher at times, it had become more rewarding.

"Let me tell you a story that you cannot ever repeat to anyone," he said, waiting for her to acknowledge this bond of secrecy.

She rolled her eyes and said, "Cross my heart and hope to die."

He nodded in acceptance. "You don't need to say that but just promise me that it will remain our little secret, forever."

"I bet you say that to all the girls."

"Not exactly. You may know by now I don't share much information with anyone. As a rule."

"Get on with it. You're starting to make me slightly interested."

"Fine." He languidly glanced around the room. There were two other couples but they were nowhere near earshot. The owner was pouring wine at one of the tables. "In the 1990s I was tasked to kill a drug dealer by the Singaporean SID. He was running a drug manufacturing plant out of a toy factory in Vietnam."

Kat had sat up and there was a glint of real interest in her eyes.   Jedburgh continued: "It was all very messy and nearly went completely pear-shaped but in the end I killed him. This man had an obsession with diamonds and he'd just acquired one of the rarest of diamonds in the world. Something called a fancy red."

"Go on," Kat said. She really wanted to hear the whole story now right from the beginning, you could tell from her demeanour.

"Somehow in the course of these events I came into possession of this fancy red diamond and since nobody else claimed it, I kept it." He smiled and waved over the owner so he could tell him about the wine they'd chosen.

When the owner had moved back to his counter, Kat said: "And what was the point of that story exactly?"

"My point is, we don't need to be worrying about the MI5 expense account on this mission. We can treat ourselves. As one of my old bosses once said: 'we must do what we can to mitigate the rigours of life'."

Kat shook her head irritably. "Tell me again about this diamond. So have you still got it?"

"No, I haven't."

"So where is it?"

"I sold it last year to a man in Antwerp."

"And what's he done with it?"

"Locked it up in a vault for the next twenty years perhaps, like I did."

"How much did you sell it for?" the girl asked.

"I sold it for 22 million US dollars."

There was a sharp intake of breath. Her face showed shock. She would have assumed that the diamond was worth a lot of money but that sort of money was mind-blowing.

"It was a 5 carat cranberry coloured diamond and there has never been another one like it, since it was found in the early nineties in Brazil," Jedburgh said.

"Who did you sell it to?" Kat asked.

"A rich Jewish man who was not too particular about its provenance. He recognised it immediately as the lost Red Teardrop."

"Wow," was all the girl said next.

"So let's not worry about paying 900 Euros for a bottle of wine."

This time the girl said nothing at all. She shook her head.

Jedburgh said, "We won't be eating out when Mustafa comes into town and we'll have to move really fast so let's enjoy this while we can. Working for Queen and country should have its moments of indulgence. You didn't take a vow of frugality when you joined the Service, did you?"

"No, it's just that my annual salary at the moment still doesn't stretch to getting a mortgage on a property in London."

"You're still young. You'll figure it out. I'm sure the big boss, the DDG, has a nice pad in London. That will be you by the time you're her age."

"Maybe," Kat said, sounding unconvinced, and then they called over the owner to order their food.

When Jedburgh was on his seventh snail, digging out the little slimy creature from its shell, Kat Pedder came back to the story. She must have been mulling it over all the while.

"How does that work? Does someone just write you a cheque for 22 million dollars and you deposit it at the bank? Or do they give you a suitcase full of cash?"

Jedburgh smiled and took a calculated sip from his glass of wine. "Do you know how much one million US dollars weighs?"

"Of course not."

"About 10 kilograms. The largest American bank note is only $100 so you would need 10 suitcases if you were paid in cash. Not practical."

"Oh," she said. "Then how do you do it?"

"You sell the valuable item through a reputable diamond broker. Someone like Christie's but more specialised. In fact you use two brokers, one for the seller and one for the buyer. They both write a document of provenance. In this case the documents stated the diamond had been given to the seller for a business transaction in lieu of payment. The seller had no idea how unique the diamond was and kept it for a long time but has now decided to sell it. The buyer has offered the agreed price and all experts involved feel that is the diamond's current market value. It's like buying and selling a house."

Kat nodded. She'd stopped chewing her food. This was a world she simply did not know.

Jedburgh glanced around the room again. It was something he did all the time, not nervously, but like an owl that was always aware of its surroundings.

"What do you know about Labuan?" he asked the girl.

"Nothing, some friends of mine went scuba diving there once."

"It's an island off the coast of Sabah in East Malaysia. It's an international banking centre. What the popular press in England might call a tax haven. No capital gains tax and no tax on dividends. Just like Hong Kong."

He grabbed the final shell with the pincers and began digging for the snail. "So the buyer, shall we call him Mr. Goldberg, and the seller, both happen to have bank accounts with the same private bank. The bank's compliance department does its due diligence. It has both of the provenance letters. All that seems in order. No drug or terrorist money. The US and EU authorities have nothing to worry about. It's all transparent, it's a regular business deal and then they transfer the funds from Mr. Goldberg's account to the seller's account. He gets an email the next day telling him it's done."

"That's you," Kat stated.

Jedburgh nodded sagely.

"What do you do with that sort of money?" she asked.

"I spent half of it on buying myself a new home," Jedburgh said.

"And the rest?"

"The bank invests in whatever instruments tickle their fancy and they give me an income of 8%. That's the money I am forced to spend on nice wine and comfortable hotel rooms."

"You are forced to?"

"I don't have any family. I don't have anyone who will inherit."

"Oh. You never had any kids?"

"We're not going there," he said firmly, closing off any further questions.

"That's a lot of money for one man," Kat decided.

"I've got a lot more than just that," he said and gave her a wink. "So we might have to risk another nice bottle for dinner this evening."

33

"Here's a cup of coffee for starters," Hamilton said when Scrimple arrived and they'd shaken hands and introduced the lads from E Squadron.

"I could do with ten hours sleep," Scrimple said getting his lips around the mug. Esmeralda had bought it for him and it said 'Be wild and be free' on the side. A choking feeling welled up inside of him as he thought of the Filipina. She'd been special and she'd been good to him.

"I only stopped for one pee break. I could do with about ten hours sleep." He repeated himself.

Hamilton was sitting opposite him and the two soldiers were on the other chair and sofa. They were all looking at him with some curiosity.

"You've done well to get here," Hamilton said. He clapped Scrimple on the shoulder. "Welcome home."

"It's never going to feel like home again, after what happened to them," Scrimple said and took another deep sip of the hot brew.

"Are you hungry?" Major Rieves asked.

"A bacon roll or two would go down well. With lashings of HP sauce," Scrimple said. Rickman jumped up and said he'd get it sorted.

"Did Wendy call you on the way?" Hamilton asked.

"She sent me a text message with instructions." Scrimple put down his coffee and pulled out the cheap Alcatel phone. He passed it over to Hamilton who read it out aloud.

"Drive to Legoland car park, Windsor SL4 4AY. Call me after you park car. We pick you up. Be alone or your friend die." Hamilton shrugged. "That's pretty clear. Anyone been to Legoland?"

None of them had been to the kids' amusement park but they checked Google Maps and found it had a large public car park. It would be busy and it would be a good place to hide behind other people.

"So they've got a base somewhere in the Windsor area," Major Rieve commented. "It's a good location. Easy to get into or out of London on the M4. Touristy enough so nobody remarks on the foreign faces. Close to the airport."

"So what's the plan?" Scrimple asked. The smell of frying bacon came wafting out from the kitchen and he realised how hungry he was. Being on the run took it out of you.

"In my opinion, you should have your bacon sarnie and go upstairs, have a long hot shower and then get your head down for an hour. Have a power-nap. You look exhausted but you'll need to have your wits about you. We'll do some planning while you're getting some kip."

"What do I do about the text from Wendy?" Scrimple asked.

"You send her a reply now. Say you are stuck in a traffic jam on the M4 and it will be a few more hours before you get to Legoland," Hamilton said. "She's been chasing you for days. She won't mind waiting a few hours longer. Gives us time to get prepared."

"What do you have in mind?" Scrimple wanted to know.

"We need to let them pick you up. You need to lead us to their base so that we can raid it and grab the lot of them. Right, Tom?"

"I can whistle up another two troops of lads if we need to do a full assault," Major Rieve said. "They're all in the barracks in town."

"We're going to have to assume Wendy doesn't just want to grab you and kill you. She's got something else in mind," Hamilton said walking over to the window and sitting on the window ledge as Rickman came out of the kitchen with two bacon sandwiches on a plate.

Scrimple shrugged. "How the hell do I know what the crazy bitch even wants?"

"But you're prepared to go in there by yourself, knowing that we'll be close behind you?"

"What choice do I have? If I don't turn up she'll murder my mate Kenworthy."

"Do you think she might be planning to take you off to China along with the North Korean?" Hamilton suggested.

"What would she want with me in China?"

"Put you on trial for being a spy or enemy of the motherland? Send you to some labour camp in Shenyang?"

Scrimple stared at the MI5 man with an expression of abject horror. Hamilton shrugged. "We've got to think it through. What's this really all about?"

"I shagged her once," Scrimple said, then bit into his sandwich. A piece of bacon got stuck between his front teeth but it all tasted exactly like comfort food should taste.

"What are them oriental ladies like, sir?" Rickman asked, sitting on the arm of one of the chairs dangling one of his legs.

Scrimple gave a low, mirthless laugh. "A friend of mine once said they taste like sugar and spice and everything that's nice." He took another bite from his sandwich. "But this woman tastes as bitter as hemlock and is twice as deadly."

"So how did you get to have sex with her then?" the Corporal asked.

"She thought I was some kind of enemy agent and then came along to seduce me and find out more about me." He finished off his food then added: "Can't seem to shake her off now. Like a dog turd on my shoe. The ugly smell just won't go away. She won't get out of my life."

Rickman nodded knowingly. "I know what you mean, sir. One of my ex-wives was like that. Just wouldn't leave me alone. Kept on turning up at the pub even though I was married to another woman."

"How many ex-wives have you got then?" Hamilton asked, a sly look of curiosity in his eyes.

The soldier held up his hand and hid his thumb. "I'm footloose and fancy free these days. The last Mrs. R went off with a Polish dustbin man. Said he had a better property portfolio than I did." He shook his head sadly. "I told her I had a gold-plated pension and an eight inch cock but that didn't persuade her to hang around."

Major Rieve laughed grimly and said, "In Rickman's defence he was only home for three weeks last year so you can understand why it's hard to hang on to a wife."

The Corporal shrugged, took the plate and brought it back to the kitchen.

"What we're going to do is put a tracker device on you, Scrimple," Hamilton said. "The Major has a box of them in the back of his car, don't you?"

Rieve nodded and added: "We've got one that can transmit up to a distance of two miles and pick up everything you say. It goes into your ear and even if they strip you naked and give you new clothes nobody will find it. Unless they know what they're looking for."

"We need to give you a weapon of sorts," Hamilton went on. "You don't want to go in there completely unarmed. What are your thoughts on that, Tom?"

The Major suggested: "We can go old school. Give you a belt that has a push dagger built into the buckle. Have you ever used one of them?"

Scrimple shook his head.

"It's a short-bladed dagger with a T-shaped handle. The blade protrudes from the front of your fist between your index and middle finger. You punch at the Adam's apple with it."

"Right," Scrimple said with a frown. "I quite liked the assault carbine I used on the bastards up at Roland's farm. No arguing with that one."

"What else could we give him?" Hamilton prompted. He was busy texting on his phone, probably providing some update to the powers that be.

"Yes, we like the C8," Rieve said with a grim laugh. It was the original name for the assault carbine, preferred by the Regiment, since it was less of a mouthful. "Here's another thought. We've got a pair of glasses in our kit box where if you twist them a small charge goes off six seconds later. It's used for blowing out the lock on a door, or like a mini-grenade that can shake things up a bit and give you the chance to run for it."

"I'll take it," Scrimple said.

"Same idea with that one. Even if they strip you down, most likely they'll leave a bloke his glasses."

"I wear contact lenses these days," Scrimple said.

Hamilton checked his watch and said, "Why don't you get a shower, mate. Get some kip. I'll wake you in an hour. We'll prepare the stuff and do an online recce and line up the extra troops."

Scrimple nodded. In truth, he was going to skip the shower and just crash out. His brain was starting to shut down from the stress and the driving.

34

The DoubleTree Hilton near Lambeth Bridge has 464 rooms over 14 floors. MI5 kept eight rooms permanently in the hotel for its use. One of the benefits of a large anonymous hotel is that one can have a discrete meeting without being seen in a coffee shop. It was not always appropriate to have meetings in someone's office. Not a lot of people liked to be seen coming through any of the public entrances to Thames House, where MI5 was based. A neutral venue was convenient and there were many entrances and exits in a large hotel.

It took the DDG five minutes to walk from her office to the DoubleTree. She wore a long coat and a hat so her face was obscured and took the elevator to the twelfth floor where she used a key card she'd been given by an MI5 assistant to let herself into what the hotel described as a deluxe room. There was no bed in this room. The space was taken by two comfortable beige sofas and two more armchairs. Drinks and biscuits were laid out by the minibar. She poured herself a glass of mineral water and gazed out at the river from behind the blinds. She sat down, pulled out her mobile and read some emails while she waited.

Ten minutes later there was a gentle knock on the door and she opened it.

"We're going to have to stop meeting like this," Abe Berenson said with what he thought was a smile but came out more as a leer.

"Abe, I haven't seen you for eight months," Dodwell said drily and waved him to sit on the sofa next to the arm chair she had taken.

"Has it been that long, doll?"

"Does patronising women come to you naturally or do you have to go to night school to learn it?" the DDG said, but she tempered the sarcasm with a smile. They'd known each other for a long time and fencing a bit was always part of the show. "Would you like a coffee or a grape juice?"

"I'm all good, Sara." He shucked up his trouser leg because he was a fussy dresser. The gold chain was around his neck as usual. "Now, you sure you're not Jewish with a name like that?"

"Why do you always ask me that?" Dodwell said.

The man from Mossad gave a cheeky laugh. "It's because I always ask you that question. Then you know it's really me, not somebody who's taken over my body to deceive you."

"Nice to see you too, Abe. What have you been up to?"

"You know, this secret stuff and that secret stuff. Say, we're getting a lot of intel about some jihadis wanting to blow up a stadium somewhere in the UK. Are you hearing this?"

"We're all over it," Dodwell said. "Is that what you wanted to talk to me about?"

The man from New York by way of Tel Aviv waved his hands from side to side. "No, no, that's just by the by. I got something really sensitive that I want to run by you. Say, it's hot in this room. Why don't you have air conditioning in your hotels?"

"It's never that warm for long enough, you know that," Dodwell said, "you've been in London for five years now."

"Is it five years? Feels like a life sentence."

"Where are they going to send you next?"

"Miami, I was hoping. The beaches are nice and the terrorists are pretty."

"A bomb is always ugly," Dodwell said firmly. She fixed him with her steely eyes waiting for him to get on with it.

"So, here's the thing, we've got this little operation that we've been running. I've got a person in deep cover and we're keeping an eye on this Chinese businessman who we think is trying to manufacture some weaponised viruses." He paused to gauge the DDG's reaction. Her eyebrows had shot up and her eyes registered strong interest.

Abe went on: "It's political but it's also business. You know TEVA is one the biggest pharmaceutical companies in the world, and we look out for our own."

"You do," Dodwell nodded in confirmation.

"We think this is real nasty stuff. It's come out of North Korea, and we all know how crazy cuckoo those guys are. So what we know is that this Chinese businessman he's hoping to step up into the big leagues, not just a few billion but ten times that. Who knows. He wants to manufacture a cure for a virus and then unleash the virus on some poor countries. And then he can clean up with the cure for the virus."

Dodwell put her hand up to stop him. "Tell me about the North Korean angle again."

Abe nodded and looked sheepish. "This is the bit where it comes into your backyard." He started nodding his head, not saying anything more yet.

"We've lost a North Korean professor from a debriefing session in one of our safe houses," Dodwell said tersely. "But then you know that already."

"Yeah, I do. This Chinese billionaire bribed someone in your organisation and then had the North Korean guy lifted."

"Three people were found dead near our safe house."

"I don't know nothing about that, Sara, trust me."

Dodwell nodded, not because she trusted him but to indicate that he should continue.

"So there is this lab in Porton Down, the Chinese guy reckons they've got the cure, or they've been working on the cure, that matches with the disease that the North Korean has been working on."

"Ah-ha," Dodwell said. She wanted to know where this was leading. Abe needed something from her or he would not have asked for the meet. The Israelis always played everything close to their chest. They shared only what they wanted to share. They trusted nobody and every step they took was in the furtherance of their own advantage.

"Look, Sara, we've know each other a long time. You know I always level with you. Don't mention the Russians last year, I had no idea about that. But if I know things I'm totally honest with you. That's true, right? What I'm saying is: I'm really uncomfortable about this virus stuff. This could be some real nasty shit, an epidemic, a pandemic. Who knows." He tweaked his nose between his thumb and forefinger, and sniffed, then brushed the tip of his nose with the back of his hand. "I want to just take out this Chinese guy, this North Korean guy and burn down the lab in Porton Down." He stopped there and stared at her with anticipation.

"Are you asking my permission or giving me a heads up?" the DDG asked.

"I don't think my bosses are going to give me permission to clean this up the way I want to." He shifted uncomfortably in his seat, which was unusual for the voluble New Yorker who always exuded a cloud of confidence. "I wanna ask you if you can arrange it at your end. This could be a whole bunch of bad for the United Kingdom as well as the rest of the world if we don't stop this thing now."

"My dear Abe," Dodwell stood up and walked over to the desk in the corner on which stood an electronic device of sorts which had blinking red and yellow lights on the front. It was the jammer which made sure that the room could never be bugged, any conversations were entirely private. "You cannot be seriously asking me to authorise an extra-judicial execution on British soil?"

"I'm gonna say, we do it all the time, so what's *your* problem?"

"Your organisation does it all the time but in the UK we call that murder."

"Murder, shmurder," Abe tried to make light of things, "if they're bad people and they're going to do bad things to good people, then how can it be wrong?"

"It against the law, and you know that." Dodwell opened a bottle of grape juice and poured the contents into a glass. "That's not the reason you are here though, is it?"

Abe gave a little shrug. "My bosses, the committee that sanctions the work of the Kidon units, will never give me permission to do this in London. They don't want to rock the boat. Or even anywhere in England. Nobody cares about Scotland."

"What about the Somali last year in Sunderland?"

"Who the hell cares about that one? Isn't that part of Scotland?"

"What is your point?" she said sharply.

"If you can tell them that you're okay with this. Then I can swing it somehow. But I need your help on this."

"Are you completely mad, Abe? You want me to write a memo to your boss in Tel Aviv saying: hey it's fine that your boys gun down some foreigners on British soil?"

"I'm trying to save the world here, Sara. You've gotta see the big picture."

35

The man codenamed 'Gwyddgrug' - although Jedburgh preferred calling him by his proper name, Mustafa - was coming into Beaune to pick up a shipment of explosives.

The vast majority of terrorist bombings were done using something called TATP, triacetone triperoxide, because it could be put together using common household ingredients. The downside was that it required extensive training to handle safely since it could be highly unstable.

MI5 and its sister services had received information that Mustafa, a wealthy Muslim idealist who based himself in Paris, had acquired a large shipment of Semtex 90H, the most practical of all explosives: a mixture of PETN and RDX which could be split and shaped. Mustafa had not bought the Semtex directly from the Czech manufacturer - imaginatively called Explosia - but had acquired it from a Lebanese arms dealer who was based in the Ukraine.

The Semtex was going to arrive in Beaune that evening where it would be packed into hidden cavities that had been built into ordinary wine boxes. The shipment was intended for a prestigious importer of fine wine, based in Manchester, called Rhotbart Ltd. Why the shipment was going to Manchester instead of London had not yet been determined. It was believed that someone at Rhotbart had been radicalised or bribed to create the order in their system and it would never arrive in their warehouses.

The British love French wines and are its second biggest consumer in the world after the United States. The traffic between France and the United Kingdom was so regular and so obvious that customs officials rarely bothered examining any truck that came from the famous wine regions such as Burgundy, Champagne or Bordeaux. There was a calculated risk for Mustafa and his fellow jihadis that the unique shipment would not move smoothly through customs but it was a tiny risk. You did not need very much Semtex to blow up buildings and cause maximum destruction.

All this was known to the intelligence services because encrypted communications had been intercepted and decoded. There was a misapprehension - a deliberate *ignis fatuus* - that GCHQ could not read everyone's emails and instant messages. The fact was that they could, when they wanted to, nearly all the time, provided sufficient energy and effort was invested. The trick was to know where to look and what to read, because there was simply far too much data swirling around the electronic void.

Kat and Jedburgh - who had once been known as the Reliable Man, a name now long forgotten - were staying at the L'Abbaye de Maizieres, a hotel in the heart of town that had been a Cistercian abbey in the 13th Century. Mustafa was in the same hotel, in the comfortable Clairvaux suite. The terrorist had already taken delivery of the Renault *Trafic* van which was decked out in the livery of Rhotbart Ltd and filled with the deadly boxes and their sumptuous camouflage. The van was parked around the corner and Mustafa would be setting off early in the morning to drive to Calais where a man called Arnold Whelp would bring the van across the Channel in the belief he was smuggling bottles of Hungarian wine as part of a tax dodge. Whelp would drive it all the way up to Manchester. Who was receiving the van up North had not yet been established but the computers were whirring away, thinking about it, probing, prodding and paring the bytes they were being fed.

The plan was for Kat to stay in her room and for Jedburgh to kill Mustafa, get his keys and for them to drive away the van and hand it over to a woman from MI6 who would bring it to a secure location.

"How do you that?" Kat asked Jedburgh. He was wearing a pig-skin jacket that extended down to the top of his thighs.

"Do what?" he asked with a frown.

"How are you so calm before you go and do what you do?" She was sitting in an uncomfortable armchair pretending to read a promotional tourist magazine.

He shrugged. "You do something often enough and for long enough, it's like blowing your nose."

"Blowing your nose?" Kat repeated. She was wearing white jeans and a purple blouse. There was a hint of make-up on her face, not too much and her hair was still damp from the shower she'd taken earlier. The first night sharing the room had been mildly awkward. But it had two Queen-sized beds so that bit had been simple. She had worn a set of stripy pyjamas from Marks & Spencer when she went to bed and Jedburgh had worn a decent pair of baggy shorts and a Rugby shirt. By now they'd got used to each other and there was only a tiny bit of tension in the air. Jedburgh recognised it for what it was, while Kat pretended that it didn't exist.

There was a small radio on the desk by the window and it had just squawked to tell them that Mustafa was back in his room. It was shortly before midnight.

"Sure you don't want to come along?" Jedburgh said. "Watch and learn?"

"You must be mad. I can't even believe that I am doing this."

"You're not. I'm doing it. You are supervising. You are the boss," he said with a wink. "Relax, watch some television. I'm sure they have 'Friends' in French on one of the channels."

"Piss off, you patronising old man," she said without rancour.

"I am all of those and much, much worse," he replied and picked up a chunky fountain pen that had been lying next to the radio. It was a Waterman Carene model in glossy red. It was capable of signing contracts but that was not its intended function. Jedburgh hooked it into the breast pocket of his shirt.

"A friend of mine used to say that in this world there is always danger for those who are afraid of it." He opened the door, turned and gave her a little wave with his fingers. "Remember, I used to do this for a living, now it's just for the pleasure of your boss."

Jedburgh walked down the staircase, crossed a corridor to another part of the building and began walking up a spiral staircase. The walls were stone and had been holding up the roof for 700 years. He ran his fingers along the rough texture.

When he had killed a man in front of Kat Pedder over a year ago it had been a sub-conscious decision on his part to close one chapter in his life and move on to the next one. Emotionally it had been difficult. He had loved Poppy very much. As much as a man can love who has spent a lifetime dealing in death. His heart was hard, but it had never turned to stone. But once he had been identified as the Reliable Man it was time to duck out and hide again. Kat had brokered a deal with her boss Sara Dodwell to cover up everything. The DDG knew she had Jedburgh's balls in a vice once he had willingly stepped out from the shadows. It had never been her intention, when they were hunting him, to bring him to justice. All along it had been her ambition to capture him and burnish him into a secret weapon that could strike stealthily at the heart of the terrorist menace.

And that was what he had become. Once again. Working as an assassin for the intelligence services. Only three people in the organisation knew who he was and what he did. Part of their deal had been that he would vanish, find a new place to live, and when Kat called with instructions from her boss he would make himself available, appear and practise his deadly art. In return they would protect him, forget his chequered past and not bother him too often.

He had found a pretty new place to make his home. He smiled when he thought about it, then knocked on the door of Mustafa's room.

"*Qui est là?*" the terrorist asked from inside.

"*C'est moi, le patron. Il y a un petit problème avec votre voiture en bas,*" Jedburgh said, frightening the man with the thought that perhaps someone had stolen his van. The door was flung open. He was a swarthy man with handsome features. His father had made his money in trading garments and the son had inherited wealth at a young age. He was in his dressing gown and there was a toothbrush in his hand.

Jedburgh pushed him hard in the chest, grabbed the front of the dressing gown firmly then swept Mustafa's legs away from under him. Kicking the door shut behind him, Jedburgh turned the younger man onto his front even as he struggled to get free, still shocked by the sudden violence.

Jedburgh got both his knees onto Mustafa's back, holding him down with the weight of a man who still spent two hours every day in the gym. The assassin pulled the Waterman fountain pen from his shirt pocket, twisted the cap which made a needle appear. It was the same principle as an Epipen auto-injector. Jedburgh plunged the needle into the back of Mustafa's neck, just above the upper-most vertebrae. A lethal dose of a drug cocktail based on pancuronium bromide was injected into the terrorist's neck.

He was dead within four minutes.

The Reliable Man arranged the body in bed under the sheets, which would confuse the police for a short time in the morning. He replaced the toothbrush in the mug on the shelf above the sink. Eventually the medical examiner would discover the puncture mark and they would understand what had happened. By then the van and the team from MI5 would be back in Britain.

36

Legoland was busy. Young and old kids were parking their cars, going off to have a day of fun in the sunshine.

Scrimple sat in the van he'd appropriated in Sherborne and made the call. The car park was already three quarters full so he'd taken time to find a slot and was wedged between a Mazda and a Golf.

A Chinese man's voice answered the phone then passed him on to Wendy.

"Are you in Legoland car park?" she said sharply.

"I'm here."

"Which row you are?" she wanted to know.

He told her and confirmed the registration of the van. There was an irritable intake of breath as she noted that it was one of her team's vehicles.

They shouldn't have come after him in the night with guns, Scrimple thought with some satisfaction. He was feeling nervous despite the fact that he was no longer alone. It was good to know that there was a team out there now keeping an eye on him but they were not here with him in this van and none of them truly understood how devious and dangerous Wendy Shen could be.

"Can you see the dark red column which has a big letter A on top?" Wendy instructed. "The letter A lying sideways."

It took him a while to identify the column. He'd locked the van and began walking.

Wendy told him to stand next to the column and wait.

He waited for five minutes. His conversation on the phone would have been picked up by the communication device he was wearing in his ear. At least he hoped that the tech was still working. It had been fine when they tested it earlier.

During their preparations the men from E Squadron had identified St. Leonard's Road which appeared to run near to the main car park but did not join up. Closer examination however showed that there was a footpath which did join the road to the car park and so they put this down as a possible exit route when Scrimple was picked up. St. Leonard's Road met up with the B3022 which could take them rapidly to Windsor or down to Ascot. Appropriate arrangements were made.

Scrimple stood and watched the world around him. Happy people, with no worries apart from paying their bills and their mortgages and whether their children would grow up and get jobs as plumbers or bankers. Happy people who were already planning their summer holidays and which festivals they would be attending once the party season began.

That had been him, only a few days ago. Not a care in the world apart from the football scores and what Esmeralda was going to dish up for dinner.

Then Wendy had come and driven a tank through his boring, measured life. If he had the chance he would kill her, as he had already killed her colleagues. But would she even give him half a chance? She was too smart for that. He fingered the belt buckle that contained the short push dagger he'd been given. Major Rieve had shown him how to use it and they'd practised for about ten minutes.

"Nothing fancy about it," Rieve had said. He had studied Scrimple thoughtfully for a while as he weighed up the triangular dagger in the palm of his hand. "The most important thing is to be aggressive. Be as aggressive as you can. Summon up all the anger that you have ever felt in your life and put it into this one single punch. Hit with all your body weight and imagine that your fist has to come out the other end of the neck. You only get one punch. It has to be a killer punch."

Scrimple had nodded nervously.

"We know you have the killer instinct," Rieve had said reassuringly. "You've already demonstrated that. Now you need to channel that into one monster punch instead of the pull of a trigger."

It was five minutes before a silver Mercedes A class pulled up and a young, slim Chinese girl leapt out. Scrimple was confused. The girl bundled him into the backseat of the car. She was pretty, she looked like the girl he'd seen in the restaurant that night with McAlistair, Scrimple thought, while the next instant he took note of the small pistol in her hand.

"You shut up or I kill you," the girl said tersely with a strong Shanghai accent. Her mouth and her porcelain features were too pretty to use such violent, dirty words.

"Hello, Simple," Wendy said from the driver's seat in front of him, using her nickname for him that turned his surname into an insult by dropping the 'C' and the 'R'. She floored the accelerator and the car shot back around the access road. They were not using the St. Leonard's Road trick it seemed.

The girl told Scrimple to put on a hood and he complied quickly as she prodded him in the stomach with her semi-automatic. Any friend of Wendy's would be as nasty and brutal as her boss, however pretty the outside packaging appeared.

The windows of the car were tinted so nobody could look inside and be surprised by the strange sight of a person with a black cotton hood over his head.

The drive took twenty minutes and they went around corners and sat at numerous traffic lights. That much Scrimple could make out. The girl next to him smelt of a floral perfume and it distracted him. She had one hand on his shoulder to ensure his head did not slam into the window as the car turned sharply, while the other hand kept the gun pushed into the folds of his ample gut.

Finally they arrived somewhere. The sound of electric gates opening and closing could be heard and then the girl told him to get of the car as she pulled off his hood. He blinked trying to get used to the sudden light again. They were in a paved courtyard of a luxury house. There was a garage block in front of them which had space for five cars. It felt like the sort of house that a moderately successful banker would be able to afford before he moved on and bought himself an estate in Surrey or Buckinghamshire.

Wendy stood with her hands on her hips and stared at him malevolently. She hadn't changed much since he'd seen her last in Cambridge over a year ago. Her face was neither old, nor young, the skin still smooth like any Chinese woman under sixty. The mouth was small, the hair raven black and cut short. She wore a dark grey pair of leggings, that sat tightly on her trim thighs, white running shoes and a navy-blue hoodie with the words 'Givenchy' printed on the front.

Her eyes were hidden behind the yellow tint of a large pair of sunglasses that she wore. Scrimple had an idea that the glasses were not purely to protect her pupils from the sun. Hamilton had told him during the briefings that they now knew the Chinese had a defeat technology that could stop them being detected by the surveillance cameras that MI5 and the police controlled all over the country.

Scrimple glanced back at the girl who had grabbed him. She was dressed in a similar outfit to Wendy, although she was taller by a head, and leaner. Her hoodie was yellow and had the words 'Gymshark' printed across her generous chest. That was odd, he thought, a Northern girl with large breasts. They must be weaning them on milk from Australian cows these days.

Whereas Wendy could be called moderately attractive, the girl was a stunner. She was drop-dead, knock-out, cat-walk, lip-trembling gorgeous.

"Simple, this is Lei Lei," Wendy introduced them, pointing at the girl holding the gun. "She study under me. She will kill you if you do anything stupid."

"Coming here, that was pretty damn stupid."

"Maybe you care for your friend Kenworthy." Wendy turned and walked up the five steps that led to the wide oak door of the house. Two fake stone hounds on either side guarded the entrance. She entered and Scrimple followed with Lei Lei prodding him in the back.

They walked through the hallway and into a high-ceilinged living room. In the middle of the room was a dining table, loaded with computer screens and equipment. A pale-faced Chinese lad with greasy hair and bottle-top glasses sat in a vast gaming armchair.

"This is Shady Mouse," Wendy waved at the hacker. "He can track your phone everywhere. That is how we find you."

"Where is Kenworthy?" Scrimple said. Wendy turned and gave him a cold smile. For a second he wondered if this might be the right moment to attack her with the push dagger but he could smell Lei Lei's perfume and realised how close behind him she was with her pistol. There might be other armed men around the house. Better to understand the lie of the land first and make sure Bob was all right.

"We lock him in one of the storage room behind the kitchen," Wendy said.

"I want to see him."

"Sit in that chair," Wendy ordered, ignoring his demand. Scrimple felt acutely that he might have been duped. They had Kenworthy's phone but there was no guarantee that he hadn't been murdered and dumped like Esmeralda and the others.

But he did as he was told. It was a wooden dining chair. Lei Lei came and snapped a pair of plasticuffs on his wrists and tied his ankles to the legs. He didn't have a choice. The only thing he could do was communicate.

"Why are you tying me to this chair with handcuffs?" he said for the benefit of his hidden audience. At least he hoped sincerely that they were out there somewhere listening to his every breath.

"I want to be sure Kenworthy is still alive," he demanded.

"He was alive when we left one hour ago," Wendy teased him. She disappeared from his line of sight and then came back sipping from a can of Fanta that she must have got from the kitchen. She spoke rapidly in Mandarin to the girl and Scrimple got the gist of it. Lei Lei went off to fetch his friend.

"What is this all about?" Scrimple said, shifting his buttocks uncomfortably on the wooden seat. "What do you want with me?"

"There is an easy answer to your second question," Wendy said. She went and stood directly in front of him and if his hands had not been firmly tied this would have been the chance to stab her. But he was trussed like poultry awaiting slaughter.

"In Hong Kong, in Cambridge," Wendy said, pointing her pinkie finger at him as she held her can of soda, "you have screw up my operation. Always you come and screw me up."

"I never did it on purpose," Scrimple said, overcome by a wave of frustration at what she was telling him.

"Here we are on a new mission in England. And you kill my people. You again. Always you," the last words she spat at him, seething with venom.

"I was defending myself. They came after me with guns," he said, unhappy that he could hear a whine in his voice as if he had to justify himself to her.

"My team has four men. They are there to protect me. You killed all four of them." Wendy glared at him. Her eyes glistened and her cheeks were flushed with fury.

Shady Mouse said in English, "Boss, I am getting some interference signal, maybe he has a tracker on him."

Wendy glanced irritably at the computer nerd. The next moment Lei Lei appeared with Bob Kenworthy. He was unshaven, although that was common with him, and he looked tired, but he cracked a smile when he saw Scrimple.

"There's a sight for sore eyes," Kenworthy said. "This woman just can't leave you alone, can she?" He was barefoot and his hands were tied behind his back. Taped across his left cheek was a bandage and his right eye had a shiner.

"Kenworthy, I'm glad that you are alright," Scrimple said dramatically for his hidden listeners. An odd glint of suspicion appeared in Kenworthy's eyes.

"If being kidnapped, smacked in the eye and then tortured with a knife can be classed as all right, then I'm as happy as a dog with two tails."

"You're alive, that's what I meant."

"Who's dead then?" Kenworthy picked up on the tone.

"My girlfriend for one," Scrimple said.

"Shit," Kenworthy said. He'd been pushed into another chair and Lei Lei had the muzzle of her NP-22 in the back of his neck. "I'm sorry to see you here. I didn't tell them anything."

Scrimple nodded. "They tracked me through your phone. I called you and that was it. That little geek worked it out somehow."

"Clever little choggies, aren't they?" Kenworthy said ruefully. "Although this one is as pretty as a primrose path." He rolled his eyes in the direction of Lei Lei. "Not quite filled with the milk of human kindness though."

By now Shady Mouse had jumped up and was whispering rapidly into Wendy's ear. Her face had taken on an angry turn as she listened. She nodded tersely which had Shady Mouse scurrying off to his dining table where he rummaged around in a pile of cables and then found what he was looking for.

He plugged in a small box with red and yellow lights and then ran an extension cable so he could bring it closer to where Scrimple was sitting.

"What are you doing with that electronic device, Shady Mouse?" Scrimple said clumsily.

"I check you," the hacker said. He was twiddling with the buttons on the device, then suddenly a look of triumph crossed his bland features. He grabbed Scrimple by the chin and dug his index finger into Scrimple's ear until he found the tiny, skin-coloured device and managed to pull it out like a snail from its shell.

Shady Mouse held it up triumphantly so Wendy could see it. The device was the size of a peanut. He then dropped it on the carpet and crushed it under the heel of his shoe.

37

The DDG punched up Kat Pedder's name on her Ganymede app. The phone rang a few times then was answered.

"Are you with him?" she asked.

"I assume you mean Thanatos?" It was a codename Jedburgh had suggested wryly and the DDG had liked it. Kat had needed to look it up online.

"Of course," the DDG snapped. "I got a signal that the mission went well. The van is already in Folkestone."

"Yes, all done and dusted."

"What about the French?"

"No noise so far, Sara. Maybe they haven't even realised that is wasn't a natural death. Thanatos left a little twist of dodgy cocaine on the bedside table. If they're not too clever they might have already signed off on him as a drug overdose."

"Hope so, I don't need that bloke François bleating down the phone at me in case they did get suspicious. But you covered all your tracks?"

"We are confident," Kat said.

"Where are you now?" her boss asked.

"We are in Rheims." Kat sounded a bit wary having provided the answer.

"What are you doing in Rheims?"

"Thanatos wanted to show me the cathedral."

"I'm going to pretend that I believe you," the DDG said. "Where is he?"

"Sitting opposite me in a cafe drinking a glass of Champagne."

"I need both of you back in the UK now."

"But he was supposed to be on leave after this mission for a few weeks."

"Cancel his leave," the DDG said. "I've got a situation developing and I want Thanatos and his special skills close at hand."

"I'm not sure he's going to like that. He's planned to go cave diving in Florida for a week."

"The caves will be there for another million years. Mankind might not be if we screw this up."

Kat sat up with a sharp intake of breath. "I think I misunderstood you, the line is not so good. Did you say mankind might not —-."

"Yes, yes, girl. I did say that and I'm probably exaggerating massively but I need you to bring the man here to London and put him on stand-by."

"What's it all about?" Kat asked. She gave Jedburgh a smile and nodded. He began pouring her another glass from the bottle of Mumm they had cracked.

"What do you know about the Spanish Flu epidemic in 1918?" the DDG asked.

"Never heard of it," Kat said.

"Right, you smart Millennial, google or bing or bong it and then you'll have an idea of a possible worst-case scenario. All the rest I'll explain when you are back in the office." The DDG disconnected the encrypted call.

"Sounded ominous," Jedburgh said. He popped a few tiny salted pretzels into his mouth.

"She wants us back in London pronto."

He shook his head. "No can do. I've got a flight from Paris to Atlanta this evening and then I'm heading down to Suwannee County to spend a week with John Orlowski."

"Who's John Orlowski?"

"He's the man they sent down to recover Sheck Exley's body from the Zacaton Cenote."

Kat shook her head in irritation. The man was smiling at her with a stubborn expression on his face. He wasn't going to make this easy.

"Okay, fine, and who was Sheck Exley?"

"World's greatest cave diver. He died on a 300 metre dive."

"That sounds very deep," she said, humouring him.

"Only 11 men have ever dived deeper than 240 metres."

"Have you?" she asked, mildly interested now.

Jedburgh laughed. "Of course not. I dived with John Bennett in Puerto Galera and Mark Ellyatt in Phuket but I always bottle out at about 70 metres." Jedburgh glanced away and his face became sad for a moment remembering something tragic perhaps. It sounded like a dangerous sport.

"I'm sorry," Kat said, "you can't go cave diving with your mate. She was really adamant about that. She needs us back in London."

"I really like Peacock Springs when the water temperature is perfect at this time of the year," he said and emptied the Champagne bottle into both of their glasses. He held up his hand waving the bill that the waiter had left on the table earlier. "John Orlowski will be very angry if I blow him out. He is a bit of a redneck and always keeps a Glock under the seat of his pick up truck." Jedburgh sipped from his Champagne glass. "You have to book him four months in advance for one-on-one training. His IANTD Instructor Number is 2."

"And Number 1 is dead?" Kat said.

Jedburgh shrugged. "Tom Mount is still alive but doesn't teach anymore."

"You have to cancel your trip."

"I'm flying First Class to Atlanta and the diving is $1200 a day," he said, his face giving nothing away.

"You are the most annoying man I've ever met," she said.

"It's a matter of principle. Nobody said anything about two jobs back-to-back and I've paid for my holiday."

"Five will pay all of the costs and reimburse you for all the money you will lose for cancelling."

"John will still be upset," Jedburgh said and paid the waiter with Euros from his wallet, adding a tip that was large enough to make the Frenchman offer a grudging '*Merci, M'sieu*'.

Kat said, "You don't need any of the money anyway. You've got plenty."

"That's not the point. It's my money and I've earned it and I can spend it as I wish. Her Majesty's Government is currently running a £1.8 trillion overdraft, it can afford to pay for my inconvenience."

"That's irrelevant. It comes out of Five's budget."

"The Single Intelligence Account budget this year is £3.2 billion. What am I asking for? Let's round it down. How about £20,000 for the inconvenience of me cancelling my North Central Florida vacation."

"Fine," Kat snarled.

"And if I have to actually work then it's the usual fee we've agreed with your boss."

"She's also your boss."

Jedburgh nodded in acceptance of the reality of his current existence. For protection one had to pay. "You'd better get on the phone and get me a seat on your Air France flight back to London. And I'm not flying Economy. I'll cancel my flight to Atlanta."

Kat rolled her eyes with relief. The man was just a common killer, why did she allow him to get under her skin so easily?

38

"Simple," Wendy yelled at him. Their eyes met and her fury was obvious. She stepped up to him and smacked him in the face, hard, three times. His cheeks stung and tears ran down them.

Wendy gave a rapid set of instructions to Shady Mouse and Lei Lei. She must have realised immediately that if Scrimple had a tracking and listening device their base was blown and they could expect visitors soon. There was not a second to lose.

The girl ran out of the front door to prepare the cars and act as a look out. The hacker began packing gear into a set of large Pelican boxes. Wendy disappeared upstairs in the direction of the bedrooms.

"You've really put the cat amongst the pigeons," Kenworthy said with a smirk. "What was that thing?"

"It was a tracker that someone gave me so they could find us," he said quietly.

"You're really getting the hang of this spook stuff, aren't you?" his old friend said, not without a note of admiration in his voice.

Scrimple said: "I just hope they don't shoot us before help arrives."

"She really hates you that Wendy woman. I've no idea what she has in store for you but it's not just a few slaps in the face. I think she is planning to send you back to China. Both of us now for that matter."

They watched Shady Mouse as he kept on unplugging cables and tossing keyboards and screens into the cushioned hard polypropylene travel cases. He was concentrating and it was obvious that this bug-out drill had been practised before.

"How soon can the cavalry get here?" Kenworthy asked in a low voice.

"I've no idea. I don't even know if they were listening. There might have been some blocking device and they don't know where we actually are."

"That makes me feel really confident," Kenworthy said. "So your team of SAS men might be driving around the neighbourhood completely lost unable to find us."

"Of course not," Scrimple said, trying to sound confident. "They'll have heard that the device was discovered and they'll be here any minute now."

"It is a troop of SAS we are expecting?" Kenworthy said and gave him a searching look.

"Two or three troops from what they were telling me. I didn't see them. I had to set off before they had got them over from central London."

"I really hope that bitch doesn't kill us just to be spiteful. Now she's got you, mate, she can let me go. Nothing to do with me, your vendetta with her." He nodded hopefully.

"You tried to clock her with a golf club," Scrimple reminded him.

"But then she shot me so we're sort of even on that score. But apparently you've killed four of her best lads. She's seething." Kenworthy leant forward to get a better look at what Shady Mouse was doing. The dining table was nearly cleared now apart from the biggest monitor. Maybe he was going to abandon that one. The hacker had some wet wipes in his hand and was wiping down the table and then the arms of his gaming chair.

"Clean lad isn't he?" Kenworthy commented.

"He's rubbing it all down with bleach to remove DNA and fingerprints," Scrimple said authoritatively.

"I knew that."

"Sorry," said Scrimple.

"No use, I will remember the little prat's face and his stupid name."

Wendy was coming down the stairs with two long duffel bags slung on each shoulder. They were probably heavy judging by the way she was walking but her face was determined and the clock was ticking.

"Listen, Bob. I've got another device on me. If I get the chance and they free up my hands, I'm going to yell 'get down' and you've got to get behind that big sofa."

"What is it?" Kenworthy said, lowering his voice some more. "Some sort of a flash bang?"

"Something like that. I've no idea how big the explosion will be but better we get behind something."

Lei Lei ran through the front door and picked up the two duffle bags Wendy had dumped at the foot of the stairs. Shady Mouse's gear was now all packed in four Pelican cases and he paused to take a breath and give the two Englishmen a pernicious glare.

The girl ran in again and picked up two of the cases and started hauling them out to where the cars were parked.

"She's fit, isn't she?" Kenworthy commented. "Wouldn't mind bending her over my bar at the George and giving her ten inches of Bob's best."

Scrimple stared at him and rolled his eyes. Was that all the man could think of, or was it his way of dealing with the stress of their uncertain situation?

Kenworthy said quietly, "Where the fuck is your SAS team? Perhaps they forgot to put a new battery in your tracker."

"It was working fine when we tested it."

"Reminds me of that time we did a raid in Shap Pat Heung on an illegal gambling den and we didn't bother to test the radios. All comms were down and the gamblers got away."

"They'll be here soon."

"Scrimple's famous last words."

Wendy approached them as they sat on their two wooden dining chairs, hands tied behind their backs. "You both come with us. We have another place. Shady Mouse put up an electronic wall so your friends will never know which house you were in." There was a tone of triumph in her voice but also a tinge of uncertainty. Her best laid plans were coming awry and the way she was staring at him, Scrimple knew she had it in for him.

Lei Lei came back into the house and handed Wendy the car keys. Wendy pulled a semi-automatic pistol from the back of her waistband and pointed it at Scrimple as the girl cut the plasticuffs from the back of the chair so that they could move him.

"Don't be stupid, Simple. I am happy to shoot you but I don't want you to die too easily," Wendy made clear. Scrimple stood up and massaged his wrists as Lei Lei cut loose his legs. She then went to do the same with Kenworthy while Wendy watched like a hawk. Shady Mouse had come out of the kitchen and was standing by the front door. He had a laptop bag slung over his shoulder and a baseball cap on his head now.

"We will walk out to the SUV and all get into that one," Wendy instructed. Lei Lei had produced a set of regular metal handcuffs and was about to clamp them around his wrists when Scrimple reached up to remove his glasses. It was an innocuous gesture, as if he wanted to rub his eyes or wipe the perspiration off his brow. But he held the spectacles in both his hands and twisted them so that the nose piece gave off an audible crack and one lens came to rest facing in the opposite direction from normal. He knew he had six seconds and he started counting them in his head as he tossed the glasses at Shady Mouse.

The hacker looked confused, then, as anyone would do, he tried to catch the glasses. He managed to hold on to them even as Wendy shouted an angry warning in Mandarin.

Scrimple yelled at Kenworthy to get down and they both threw themselves at the nearby sofa, rolling over the top and around the side as the explosion ripped through the room. The sound was intense and Scrimple felt disorientated. He tried to catch his breath but an acrid, sharp smell stung his nostrils and he began coughing, desperately trying to get oxygen into his lungs.

He had a sense that the same thing was happening to Kenworthy. "Kitchen," he yelled and staggered forward until he got to where he wanted without any bullets smashing into his back. The smoke must be blinding Wendy.

His old mate was close behind him and they stumbled into the kitchen slamming the door shut behind them. Scrimple grabbed one of the chairs and rammed it under the door knob. Two rounds smashed through the kitchen door and took out the glass pane of the window. Then there was silence.

A few moments later Scrimple could hear the revving of a powerful diesel engine and the screech of tyres. Were those his guys arriving or Wendy leaving?

Next there was silence and the smoke that had followed them from the living room cleared. Kenworthy was still retching his guts out but nothing came out of his mouth.

"Are you alright?" Scrimple asked.

"Right as rain," Kenworthy said in between coughs. "That was more than a flash bang."

"They're designed to blow the hinges and locks off doors," Scrimple explained.

"I think you blew the hinges off poor old Shady Wanker out there."

There was more silence and they waited. Nobody had come to their rescue but they thought Wendy and her team had bolted. They sat for another fifteen minutes to be sure. Kenworthy had ransacked the cutlery drawer and found two seriously large kitchen knives with sharp edges. They sat on the floor holding on to their weapons in case Wendy was still in the house.

Then they heard an English voice outside: "Hello, anyone here? This is the police. Scrimple? Anyone?"

Scrimple's knees ached as he pulled himself to his feet and opened the kitchen door.

Corporal Rickman was standing in the living room flanked by three other men in black overalls. They were all holding assault rifles, the same type he'd been using.

"Just two of us, we're all fine," Scrimple yelled because his ears still felt as if they were full of cotton wool. He stared at the floor where Shady Mouse was sprawled. It was obvious he was dead because there was a hole the size of a football in his chest. The wall behind him was covered in bloody flesh and debris.

"Did you get Wendy and the girl?" Scrimple asked.

"We just got here," Rickman said, shaking his head. "Are you all right?"

"We're good," Scrimple said. At that moment Major Rieve appeared in the doorway, dressed in the same overalls. He looked relieved to see them.

"Poor fucker," Kenworthy said, with no real remorse in his voice, nodding at the hacker's crumpled body. "No more Shady Twat."

39

It was a few hours later that Wendy turned up at Mr. Guo's house.

Jing Jing knocked lightly on the door of Guo's study where he was deep in conversation with Professor Park. They were both speaking English because it was the only language they had in common. Stacks of documents, research papers and test results, were spread out over the antique partner's desk with the leather surface.

"Felix, I am sorry to disturb," Jing Jing said, "I want to introduce my auntie who has come to visit."

Guo leapt up from the high-backed leather coachman's chair in which he'd been lounging. He told Park to get himself a drink and he'd be back in a while.

"My auntie," Jing Jing explained, as Guo came out into the hallway, "she is my mother's second cousin. She was visiting London on a business trip and wanted to take me for lunch tomorrow. She just dropped by to say hello."

Wendy was standing in the other reception room and pretending to admire the Picasso charcoal sketch of a bullfighter that was hanging over the mantelpiece.

"So nice to meet you, Auntie," Guo said respectfully in Mandarin and shook Wendy's hand as they were introduced. Of course he was older than her but it was a nice touch.

"My niece told me how kind you have been when her employer treated her so badly. You are a good man. My cousin asked me if I could help and check up on her, she is still so young," Wendy did not indicate by anything in her voice that the age gap between Guo and Jing Jing was nearly thirty years. He was obviously a man of wealth and any genuine family member would respect what a fine catch he could be for the girl.

"My wife passed away a few years ago," Guo said. "A man dedicates himself to working and making money all the time, we forget how nice it is to have beauty in the house."

"You already have much beauty in this house, Jing Jing was telling me." Wendy indicated the miniature Picasso. The painter had done countless pictures of bulls and bullfighters. This was a minor work but had still cost Guo a few million when the American owner needed cash fast in 2008.

"Yes, I am an admirer of all things that are beautiful," Guo said unctuously and beamed at Jing Jing. "Where are you staying Shen *Tai Tai*?"

"My company has put me in a Hilton Hotel near the Big Ben building," Wendy said.

"Why don't you come to stay here for a few days? We have many spare rooms," Guo offered.

Wendy thanked him politely but said they had a telecommunications conference - she worked for one of the big component suppliers to Huawei - and her colleagues were all in the hotel so it was better she remained there.

"Shall we have dinner this evening together?" Guo suggested. He was working hard on impressing Jing Jing's relative. He didn't want to comment but wondered about the red burn mark that Jing Jing's aunt had on her face. It looked like a bright red rash. Perhaps it was an allergy. She must have put some cream on it as it had an oily sheen.

"So sorry, Guo *Saang* but my company has a function this evening so I can't have dinner with you tonight but perhaps tomorrow would be available?"

"Yes, tomorrow is good. We might have an occasion to celebrate. I am hoping to close on an exciting deal soon and waiting to hear news. We should know by tomorrow, then we must drink the most expensive Champagne from France."

"That sounds very exciting," Wendy replied with a polite smile nodding. "May I spend some time speaking with my niece?"

"Of course, I must go back to my business discussion. Tomorrow and tomorrow and tomorrow we will celebrate." Guo grinned happily at both the women and left them to return to his study. In the corridor he passed Bohumir who was talking with one of the cleaning staff about the bedrooms.

"Jing Jing has an auntie who is visiting London," Guo told his butler. "They are in the reception room. Ask them if they want some tea or snacks."

The butler nodded and told the maid that he'd speak to her later.

Guo went back to his desk. Park was studying a stack of papers that were mostly numbers with test data. He'd been explaining some of what he had found earlier and he was still positive that the work being done in Professor Whyte's lab was going to be of great value.

Guo reached for his mobile and punched up the name of his lawyer, Anthony Peppard-Mills.

"How is the contract going?" Guo asked the fellow once he got through on his mobile. "Do the other lawyers come back with any problem?"

"It's coming along, Felix. They don't like some of the warranties I've put into our SPA but that means they know they have nothing of substance to contest. Sometimes lawyers screw up acquisitions because we try to be too clever or make ourselves too important. I'm trying to avoid any of that happening."

"You make clear to them that if GART goes bankrupt we can still offer to buy up all their client's research from the administrators and transfer over key employees. Even cheaper that way."

"They understand that, but they are lawyers. They have to make simple things complicated."

"You are a lawyer. You don't make it complicated."

"A long time ago, Felix, I discovered that if I keep things simple I can be more successful than anyone else in my profession."

"Ha ha," Guo said. "You my good man. You're the best lawyer in London. You push them harder. I want to finish the financial due diligence quickly and start working. Professor Park is very excited. He wants to be in the lab."

Guo looked over and caught the North Korean's eye, giving him a thumbs up. The professor nodded back enthusiastically.

"You fix this contract. I want to celebrate soon and then we can move faster."

They hung up and Guo flicked through some emails on his computer. The members of the golf club were calling an extraordinary meeting to complain about the new management. Guo decided it was time to teach them a lesson. He would make all of them reapply for membership and triple the joining fee. The troublemakers were all too poor to afford it.

There was a knock and Bohumir appeared in the door. "I've served the ladies some jasmine tea, sir. Can I get you or the professor anything?" There was an odd expression on Bohumir's face, Guo noticed. As if he'd come across something distasteful since the last time they spoke. Like a rat running across the kitchen floor or a cockroach clambering up the bathroom wall.

40

It felt strange to Scrimple to be in the building called Thames House. He'd never been invited here before. He'd heard the name but had not known exactly where it was located. It was an imposing old building, like so many of them in London, with a view of the river.

They were in a basement conference room that had no view but it was air-conditioned and the chairs were comfortable and there was a tray of sandwiches that had been ordered in from Pret A Manger as well as two large urns of strong tea and coffee.

"We're going to do a sort of quick debrief," Hamilton said sitting at the head of the table. "The DDG will join us soon and this is mainly for her benefit."

The others in the room were Major Rieve and Kenworthy as well as a shy bloke who'd been introduced as Dale whose job seemed to be to take minutes of the meeting on his Dell laptop.

It had been quickly established that Wendy and Lei Lei had got away shortly before the four BMW X5s from E Squadron crashed into the compound of the house. There was nothing to be done for Shady Mouse so an MI5 forensic team had been called for and they would dispose of his body according to the appropriate protocols, once they'd finished going through the house with a fine tooth comb. Scrimple and Kenworthy were both unharmed although the latter was somewhat worse for wear after his incarceration.

"Nothing that four pints of Adnams Southwold can't sort out," he'd said cheerfully.

"Are you sure you want to get back to your pub in Cambridge when Wendy is still running around on the loose?" Hamilton said.

"She'll be on a flight back to Shanghai or Beijing by now," Scrimple said grimly. "We must have blown her operation wide open whatever she was working on."

"That's the problem. We have no idea what she was working on. It was a big team. Two women, one IT guy and four heavies. It must have been something very special."

The door to the conference room opened and Sara Dodwell entered. "I may have an answer to that question," she said to Hamilton as she pulled out a chair next to Scrimple. She gave him an appraising look. Her eyes seemed to bore into him and absorb his entire essence. It was disconcerting.

"So you are Scrimple?" she said.

He nodded, feeling shy all of a sudden.

"I've heard a lot about you, over the last few years. I'm Sara Dodwell, the person who signs your pay cheque."

"Nice to meet you, ma'am," he said.

"We're all on first name terms here. May I call you Theo?"

"Nobody calls me that. It's just always been Scrimple."

The DDG nodded and turned to Kenworthy. "You're the pub landlord who used to be a Superintendent in the Hong Kong police?"

"That's right, Sara."

"Thank you both for putting up with everything that has happened to you in the last few days. Especially you, Scrimple. You didn't sign up for this. You agreed to run one of our safe houses and ended up having to defend yourself by killing those men. And you, Bob, you were dragged into this solely because of your friendship with one of our employees."

She leaned forward and waved at Dale, the amanuensis, and indicated the coffee pot. He leapt quickly to his feet to get her a cup. "Now, it goes without saying that both of you have already signed the Official Secrets Act in the past so I remind you of its contents. We can talk freely and get as much information from you as possible now but then I'd like you to go home and keep a low profile. If you prefer we can give you some protection or put you in a safe house for a few days until we have found her or know that she's out of the country and you are no longer potential targets."

The two men nodded.

Dodwell went on: "What I believe is that Wendy Shen and her Action Unit were in the UK working on an operation that involves a Chinese national who is trying to buy a lab in Porton Down. The lab specialises in anti-virals and although that all seems above board there must be something more sinister going on below the surface. I believe it has something to do with the North Korean defector you had in your safe house in St. Mary Bourne.

We had no idea how important the man is. In fact we don't even know who he really is."

"Did Wendy Shen kidnap and kill my girlfriend and the other two guys, Pacino and Tchaikovsky?" Scrimple said, with bitterness.

"Probably, but we don't know where the Korean is now. I'm waiting to get some more information from a confidential source." The DDG leant forward and touched Scrimple's arm in a gesture of empathy. "I'm so very sorry about what happened to Esmeralda."

"Thank you for saying that," he replied and there was a choking sensation at the back of his throat as the emotion welled up. He pushed it down savagely.

"You did not hear me say this, but her death will not be forgotten nor go unavenged. We will find the people responsible and make them answer for it."

Scrimple nodded solemnly.

"Now tell me everything that you know about Wendy and her team. I'd like to start with you, Bob."

Kenworthy took a sip from a glass of mineral water and ran through what had happened to him from the first time that Scrimple had called, advising him of the mess he was in. Dale typed rapidly on his laptop. Then it was Scrimple's turn. He took longer to describe his adventures starting from the moment he walked in the door of his house and found it empty.

"We should tell you," Hamilton cut in at one point, "that we are certain Winchcombe was paid off and given a passport and ticket to leave the country. That's how they knew how to get into the house, who was there and why he never answered your subsequent calls or messages.

Lesson for us to learn here is not to have only one contact person for a civilian safe house manager. We need a bit more redundancy built into the communications while still allowing for cut-outs to preserve security."

The DDG gave Hamilton a nod. "Remind me to discuss with you what to do about Winchcombe. We must find the man and bring him back to stand trial."

"I've got my guy Wesley in Cambridge working on tracing him from when he flew out of Heathrow."

"We may need some help from our friends across the river. New Zealand did you say?"

"It may just be a blind but Wesley is a bright lad and we'll see what he comes up with."

The DDG gave a grunt of agreement and instructed Scrimple to carry on with his story.

"The men you killed were enemy agents with criminal intentions so you don't need to worry about any charges being brought against you on this," the DDG advised him. "We will apply the usual pressure and the Official Secrets Act on the Hampshire and Dorset Constabularies and the files will be closed."

"No Further Action, we used to call it in the RHKP," Kenworthy interjected.

"Precisely," the DDG affirmed. "What are your plans after this?"

"I want to get back home to my pub as soon as I can," Kenworthy said. "Wendy isn't interested in me. It was always about her vendetta with Scrimple. The fellow keeps on messing up her operations. But he's always been like that. Haven't you, mate?"

"Piss off," Scrimple said but in a good-natured way. They had been friends for three decades.

"I don't have an issue with you going back to Cambridge but we'll have Major Rieve here put two men on you to watch your back in case Wendy does turn up. You don't want a repeat of what happened last year." The DDG then turned to Scrimple. "But in your case I suggest you pack your bags and go off on holiday for a few weeks. I'm told Portugal is nice at this time of the year, or Croatia or Mykonos." She tapped his arm again. "Go far away, forget about what has happened and watch your back. That would make it easier for us. Keep in touch with Gavin here on your whereabouts. We will inform you when it's safe to come back and when we've cleaned things up here."

"I might go to the Philippines. I used to be a scuba diving instructor," he said, his mind already working out what he truly wanted to do now.

"Scrimple, I hope you will come back and work for us running a safe house again. Maybe not the one in St. Mary Bourne," the DDG said. "But if you felt that wasn't right for you anymore, maybe we could find something else for you to work on."

"I think I do want to continue working for MI5." The feeling of emotion began rising up again at the back of his throat. He really needed a few vodkas and a good night's sleep. "But I could do with some time away. It's been somewhat hectic."

"You can say that again. We've valued your service on this. Be clear about that," she said and her X-ray vision ran over him once again. He could practically feel the heat boring into his bones and tissue.

"We've got you a room in the hotel up the road. Haven't we, Gavin? Let's wrap this up now." The DDG stood up and nodded at everyone to show her approval. Then she was gone.

41

As Scrimple walked into the DoubleTree Hotel lobby Jedburgh was coming out of the lifts.

"Scrimple," the Reliable Man said.

He would not have recognised Jedburgh if the man had not called out to him because he wore a designer stubble beard which was closely trimmed, slightly tinted, horn-rimmed glasses and an unruly mop of black hair that flopped over his forehead.

"What are you doing here?" Scrimple said with a gasp of surprise.

"I'm supposed to be staying in this hotel, but it's a bit of a shit-hole."

"I didn't think you were in the UK," said Scrimple. He was carrying a large shopping bag from Next because he had needed a fresh set of underwear, shirts and other things. In his other hand was his duffel bag. He missed the weight with which the assault carbines and Glocks had weighed down the bag over the last few days but Hamilton had been adamant that he couldn't keep the artillery any more. "McAlistair told me you were off in some foreign land."

"I was, until a few hours ago. Not so foreign. Just France. Working with our mutual friend Kat Pedder."

"Have you shagged her yet?" Scrimple asked and then thought it was a puerile thing to say.

Jedburgh just laughed. "Best not to shit on one's own doorstep, right?"

"Are you here because of Wendy Shen?" Scrimple asked.

"To be honest, I've no idea why I'm here. I was supposed to be in Atlanta by now, booked in for a week of cave diving in Florida. Then the big boss lady yanked my chain and here I am. On stand-by is what I've been told."

"She must want you for Wendy Shen."

"What have you been up to, Scrimple? Have you been getting yourself into scrapes again?"

"You could say that."

Kenworthy and Hamilton had opted to get the train back to Cambridge right away so Scrimple was the only one booked into the hotel and the plan was for him to get back home in the morning, pick up some things and then head off to the airport. He hadn't decided yet where he was going but a flight to Manila or Bangkok would be easy to book. Esmeralda's body was being flown back to the Philippines and the funeral would take place there. But Scrimple was nervous about attending the funeral and meeting the family because they might blame him for her death.

Seeing Jedburgh put a completely different spin on things. "Am I fucking glad to see you. How about we go somewhere for a few drinks and I can tell you what a nightmare I've been through."

They agreed to meet in half an hour because he wanted to have a shower and Jedburgh wanted to buy some bits and bobs. Before leaving Thames House, Major Rieve had suggested that two of his men stayed with Scrimple but finally it had been agreed that he was safe and anonymous in and around the hotel and only when he returned to St. Mary Bourne did he need someone to watch his back in case Wendy came after him there.

They went to a pub called The Clarence in Great Scotland Yard recommended by the Major, and had some food in the Tin Belly dining room.

"Why is it called that?" Scrimple asked the waiter.

"It's the nickname for the Blues and Royals, sir."

Scrimple nodded. "You were in the Army once, weren't you, Bill?"

"Intelligence Corps, didn't last very long. Bad fit. I did it to spite my father who wanted me to join his regiment, the Coldstream Guards."

"What did your Dad say about you joining the 'Farce' in Hong Kong?"

"He wasn't impressed. Told me there was no honour in being a policeman. 'Every man thinks meanly of himself for not having been a soldier', he used to say, to make his point."

"What did you say to that?" Scrimple emptied his glass of vodka tonic with a great sigh of relief. It was the first one and it hit the spot.

"I was a cocky lad in those days. 'A soldier's time is passed in distress and danger, or in idleness and corruption' is what I told the old man. He went red in the face and slammed the door to his study."

"Are your parents still alive?"

"No," Jedburgh said simply. "Right, tell me your story."

So Scrimple recounted his adventures again. By the end, he'd managed another three vodka tonics.

Jedburgh nodded grimly. "She's still out there. This story won't stop until she's dead."

"That's what you're here for," Scrimple remarked.

"You've been doing pretty well fighting the Yellow Menace so far without my help," Jedburgh said, giving a low laugh.

"I think I'm going to spend a few weeks in the Flips and get my head back in order."

"When was the last time you went to Angeles?"

The waiter brought them both their desserts, Bramley apple crumble with lashings of creamy custard. The pub was now completely full and there was the buzz of pleasant company all around them.

Scrimple shrugged. "Somebody's stag do, long time ago."

"Book yourself into the Pacific Breeze Hotel and let your senses cure your soul."

"What is that supposed to mean?"

"Go out and bar-fine five young ladies every night and do your bit to support the local economy." Jedburgh pointed his spoon at Scrimple. "Don't forget to take a bumper pack of Cialis with you. I think they make them in boxes of 84 now. One pill will keep your pecker up for 8 hours."

"We always used Viagra," Scrimple said and the sadness took hold of him again as he thought about his girlfriend.

At this moment a man appeared next to their table and pulled out the empty chair, plonking himself into it. He had messy grey hair, was stout as opposed to obese and wore a crooked grin and a nicely tailored pinstriped suit. He looked about their age. Scrimple was mildly alarmed until he saw Jedburgh welcome the man with a smile.

The man said, "What do you think you are doing in my local without my permission?"

"This isn't your local, Tweddle," Jedburgh said.

"It is when I'm fortifying myself for a meeting with the twats in the Department for International Trade across the road."

"Dominic, this is Scrimple."

Tweddle leant forward and shook hands. "Jedburgh and I were at school together. I'm a banker." The waiter appeared at his elbow and Tweddle said, "A Bombay Sapphire with Fever Tree, Lionel, please."

"He's a very odd type of banker. I didn't realise until we caught up once in New York in the nineties. That was a wild trip."

"It was, wasn't it?" the odd banker said.

"I nearly picked a fight with Donald Trump in Stringfellows over a lap dancer. Who would have thought then that he'd end up as President of the United States?"

"We're in for a really crazy four years," Tweddle said. "Hold on to your cowboy hats."

Scrimple stared at both of them in confusion and then drank half of his vodka tonic and waved at the waiter for another round for all of them. When in doubt about life, the universe and everything, start drinking heavily.

"Gracie," Jedburgh said enigmatically.

Tweddle raised an eyebrow in query and looked at Scrimple for guidance. He shook his head.

"The name of the lap dancer I stole off Donald Trump."

"How did you do that?"

"Official Jedburgh Secrets Act." He tapped his nose. "Have to kill you if I told you." He pushed back his chair as Lionel, the waiter delivered the next round. "I am a fair man. I don't want to embarrass the Donald. Suffice to say I used guile and subterfuge. Didn't shag her though. That wasn't allowed."

"Word on the grapevine is that Sara Dodwell has got herself a tame assassin," Tweddle changed the subject suddenly.

"That is a nasty vicious rumour," Jedburgh said. "It's fake news. Hah, I like that expression I might have to patent it before someone else starts using it."

Scrimple stared at Tweddle. "You know Sara Dodwell?"

The man nodded. "I also hear that there is a crazy Chinese operative running around the country hell-bent on destruction and filled with evil intent."

Jedburgh said to Scrimple: "Tweddle isn't a proper banker. He has some sort of a management function at MI6. They have not found him out yet as the drunken git that I know him for."

"Insulting me won't stop me from asking the tough questions," Tweddle said pointedly and put his finger into his gin and tonic to give it a good stir.

"Scrimple here killed four Chinese agents with an L119A2 assault carbine."

"I also had a Glock."

Tweddle gave a snort of triumph. "So you're the guy they're all talking about?"

"Who are?" Scrimple asked in astonishment.

"The boys and girls in my office."

"That would be the one on the other side of the river," Jedburgh said. "In the ugly building that looks as if some crazy Danish architect vomited Lego blocks."

"People know about me in MI6?"

"You are famous, after a fashion," Tweddle said. "If I didn't know that Jedburgh here is fantastically wealthy and will be picking up the tab, I'd offer to buy you a drink."

"You can take us to Boodles for a night cap," Jedburgh suggested. Tweddle laughed heartily at that. "Trust me, you're not dressed for Boodles and secondly they're all a bit stiff there. Their noses are longer than Pinocchio's and they like looking down them at anyone who isn't at least a Baronet. I'll take you to the Civil Service Club next door. They have a lovely selection of Port and are quite relaxed about their dress code."

"What is the purpose of you turning up here?" Jedburgh asked with an arched smile.

Tweddle tried to look innocent. "I'm in the intelligence business. I've come to gather a bit of product."

"Scrimple here is off to Angeles City in the Philippines to shag himself stupid. He will try not to kill any Chinese spies while he is there. As for myself I'm just stopping off in London for a few days to get a new suit made then I'm off to a new place that I've just bought."

"Where is your new place?" Tweddle asked quickly.

"That is none of anybody's business. It is high up, has wonderful views. It is remote, it is inaccessible and it was very expensive."

"Sounds like Davos," Tweddle commented.

"How else can we help you?" Jedburgh pulled his old friend's leg.

"Were you in France by any chance recently, enjoying the finer things in life?" Tweddle gave a knowing smile.

"I'd like to say 'No comment' but I'm going to go with the more traditional 'Fuck Off, mind your own business'." Jedburgh gave him a wink and put his hand in the air so that Lionel knew it was time to bring the next round.

"But it is my business. I've had an irate Frenchman busting his collar yelling down the phone at me accusing us of running an illegal operation on their turf. We're a bit miffed with your lady friend at Thames House. Five is domestic, Six is overseas. How difficult is that to understand?"

"Dominic, I've no idea what you are talking about so lay off for now. Poor old Scrimple has had a tough couple of days and we're trying to cheer him up."

Tweddle rolled his eyes in defeat. "Righty ho, I just want to say that was damned fine work and the world is a safer place for it."

"I've no idea what you are talking about but as they always say, we have to get it right every time, the enemy just has to get it right once."

42

Bohumir took a phone call as he stood in the far corner of the kitchen.

"The committee gave us the green light," Abe Berenson, his controller said.

"They did?" Bohumir walked out of the kitchen and up the stairs to a room that the staff used for coffee breaks. Nobody was there. He locked the door behind him.

"The three wise men finally listened to me and realised that this is an important one."

"But what about the British?"

"I gave them the heads up so we can beg for forgiveness, no need to ask for permission."

"Something strange happened just now," Bohumir said in a hushed voice. He held his hand over his mouth to be even more careful. "A Chinese woman turned up here saying she is Jing Jing's aunt. She's still here."

"What's strange about that?"

"I recognise the woman from our files," Bohumir said.

"These Chinese chicks all look the same. So who do you think she is?"

"Colonel Wendy Shen, she's now in charge of Department 3 at PLA Military Intelligence."

"You sure it's her?"

"As sure as I'd recognise my own mother," the Slovakian Jew said.

"So that tells us that Jing Jing is what you thought she was. She's a honey pot."

"Ah-ha."

Abe laughed at the other end of the line. "None of that matters now. You've got the green light to go ahead and terminate Guo and Professor Park."

"What about the Chinese women?"

"Leave them alone unless they get in your way."

"When do I do this?"

"Now."

"Fine, give me the clearance code."

"Wait, I've got to hit the record button. Okay. I'm giving you the clearance code: 'Habakuk, Joshua, Habakuk, Kings'. Repeat that back to me."

"I repeat. The mission is to terminate Guo and Park. Habakuk, Joshua, Habakuk, Kings."

"Don't screw it up, *Mentsh*," Abe said and the line was cut. Mossad used their own encrypted App and so the call could not have been monitored. It was still risky to make such calls because someone could overhear or there could be unknown listening devices around but the life of an undercover agent was never risk free.

Bohumir unlocked the staff room door and went up three flights of stairs to his room. It was a comfortable room, with a queen-size bed and a sofa in the corner, a television set and a built-in cupboard. It was the sort of room one found in a decent three star hotel. He was, after all, the most trusted servant in the house and had spent months working on his role. Now the play would be over.

So suddenly. Not unexpectedly but he had thought it would be a few more weeks before matters came to a head. There were three red Samsonite suitcases under his bed. One of them contained a false bottom that even an X-ray machine would not be able to detect. How they had engineered this was beyond Bohumir's knowledge, but the technical boys and girls in the Glilot head office were amongst the best in the world. Every Israeli knew that.

He snapped open the suitcase and ran his finger along the lining which identified his fingerprint. Only he could open the hiding place. A small catch appeared and he tugged on it, opening the lid to the compartment. Inside were several passports. Not one of them had his real name, but all of them showed a recent likeness of him. Sometimes he had to stop and remind himself of what his real name had once been. There were always layers, over more layers in his world. He took out the American passport and pocketed it. In case he had to move fast, it was best to have a travel document at hand.

Apart from the passports and a stack of corresponding credit cards there was a weapon. It was a polymer-framed Jericho 941 semi-automatic pistol chambered in 9 mm. A box of 50 rounds sat next to it. He loaded the magazine fully, put ten more rounds loose into his jacket pocket, just in case, and replaced the half empty box back into the secret compartment.

Five minutes later he was moving along the corridor outside Guo's study. The Jericho was tucked in the front of his waistband, hidden by the fact that his suit jacket was buttoned up.

Bohumir knocked discretely on the heavy oak door and then entered. As a butler he never waited to be told to enter. If Guo wanted privacy then the door would be locked.

"What is it?" his employer asked.

"Did Jing Jing's aunt already leave? I can clear up the tea platter."

"Yes, yes. She already left. Jing Jing is here." The girl was standing by the book shelf. Guo had many Chinese novels and she appeared to be looking for something to read. Professor Park was sitting in the chair he usually occupied and had an expression on his face that implied he was far removed from the physical world, exploring some idea which he would then rapidly type into the Samsung tablet that Guo had given him for his use.

Bohumir had not killed many men. For a member of the Kidon unit he was not considered very prolific because his speciality was long lasting, deep penetration missions. This would only be the fifth time. The first time had been the hardest - like many things in life - because you fear failure. Once you are past that initial hurdle then it becomes easier the next time you kill, because there is nothing to worry about except a clean execution.

The man from Mossad wasn't happy about the girl being in the room but he had to get on with this job now. Like a plane that is thrusting down the runway there comes a point where you can't abort, you have to push on through to completion.

He unbuttoned his jacket and grabbed the Jericho with his right hand. He brought it up and cupped his right fist in his left palm, trained the muzzle on Guo's sternum and put two bullets into the Chinese man, centre-mass. The distance was barely five metres. Not difficult for a man who had practised a lot.

Bohumir swivelled 45 degrees, trained the sights of his pistol on the North Korean and put two 9 mm rounds into his sternum. The light of life vanished quickly from the professor's eyes. By now the gun was pointing at the Chinese girl by the bookshelf. She was holding a paperback in her hand and her face betrayed shock and terror.

"Do you want to die, or not?" Bohumir asked, still using his measured butler's voice.

"What are you doing?" the girl said in outrage.

It was a strange thing to say, Bohumir thought. If she was a Chinese agent then she should have realised immediately what was happening. He had no instructions to kill her.

"Get down on the floor and put your hands behind your head. Do not move. Where is your aunt? Has she left already?"

Jing Jing began lowering herself to her knees. "She left ten minutes ago. Please don't kill me. I have nothing to do with any of this. I'm just a girl."

Bohumir grunted in acceptance although he knew she had to be more than just an innocent party. If he was right about Wendy Shen, of course. He moved smartly across the room, keeping his pistol pointed at Jing Jing who by now was lying face down on the Bokhara carpet, the one Guo had always boasted about.

"You keep still then I won't shoot you," he said to the girl as he first checked Park and then Guo to make sure they were dead. Neither of them had a pulse. Bohumir had always been good on the range and he was better in the real world. It always sharpened him up.

"You lie there for fifteen minutes, then you can get up and call for help. I am leaving now. You won't see me again. But I know who you are."

"Who is she?" the voice of Wendy Shen snapped his attention towards the door. The Chinese woman had entered the room and in her hand was also a semi-automatic pistol.

"*Do prdele*," he swore in Slovak. He should have realised that perhaps the *kurva* was still in the building.

Wendy shot first and her bullet hit him in the mouth so that his own shot went wild. Her second round took the top of his head off. Bohumir's last fleeting thought before he went to meet his maker, was that this mission was mostly successful. He'd killed Guo and Park, the world would be a safer place.

43

There had been a time in his life when Scrimple didn't get hangovers from drinking vodka. He believed the fable that because it was a pure, clean alcohol it was easier for the liver to process or some such nonsense.

But these days all alcohol gave him a raging headache in the morning. He woke up in his comfortable hotel bed wondering what he was doing here. A troop of angry Lilliputian workmen were running around his brain with hammers smashing all they could find. He staggered into the bathroom and found the painkillers. The hotel only provided three little bottles of complimentary mineral water and he'd guzzled all that already, so he drank the foul tasting tap water. They said it was safe and since he wasn't in Africa he assumed it was fine although drinking tap water at the house in St. Mary Bourne gave him the trots within an hour.

He lay on the bed and wondered if the pain in the morning was ever worth the pleasure of drinking the night before. Slowly, as he stared at the ceiling and waited for the painkillers to kick in, he tried to piece together what they had said and done.

After the Clarence they had walked up the road to the Civil Service Club where Tweddle was a member and they'd killed off a bottle of port between the three of them. Jedburgh and his old school friend had continued sparring verbally while Scrimple listened with a ruminative expression on his face, only understanding half of what they'd been talking about. Overall it had been a good evening, Scrimple concluded. He must have destroyed another large swathe of brain cells and somehow the problems of the last few days felt more removed. Everything was dull, the edges had been polished off. So by that measure it had been a cracking night out.

The phone rang on the bedside stand.

"It's about eleven thirty, sir," said Corporal Rickman, "and I was wondering if you were up yet?"

"I feel like shit but my eyes are open," Scrimple said hoarsely.

"Good night out then, was it? When would you like me to pick you up?"

"Can we do it about 1 p.m.?"

"That will be fine, sir. I'll just be around the lobby whenever you're ready."

Scrimple went back to staring at the ceiling, then eventually, when the pain had subsided, he dragged himself into the shower and then packed his duffel bag.

When they met in the lobby the first thing Rickman did was bring Scrimple up to speed on the latest dramatic developments as he'd been informed by his boss. Wendy Shen had turned up at the Chinese billionaire's house - there was some CCTV footage of her coming through the front door - and left a trail of destruction. The other servants had called the police on finding three dead bodies: Guo, the butler and the North Korean defector.

The attractive Chinese girl who'd been a guest in the house had vanished and probably been in cahoots with Wendy.

"So nobody knows where she is now?" Scrimple asked the important question.

Rickman shook his head. "They're working on it and I'll get updates as soon as they come in." He tapped his left chest pocket where he probably kept his phone.

It had been agreed that there was no need for a pool vehicle as they could take the train and pick up Scrimple's Polo from where he had left it in Andover. A taxi from an approved MI5 company was called once Scrimple had checked out and that took them to Paddington where they got First Class tickets on the train which departed at 2.44 p.m. and got them to Andover an hour and a half later.

"How long have you been in the Army then, Rickman?" Scrimple asked once they were settled. The carriage smelt of fried chicken and bleach which was an improvement on the stink of alcohol and urine that was available for the regular travellers in Standard Class.

"Since I was seventeen. Failed all my GCSEs, so it was either that or become a drug dealer around the estate." The soldier gave Scrimple a grin to show that he was only half serious but the implication was one of growing up in a tough neighbourhood.

"And before..." Scrimple searched for a suitable euphemism because there was an elderly gentleman on the other side of the aisle reading the Financial Times, "you joined the mob at Stirling Lines, which regiment were you with?"

"Royal Regiment of Fusiliers, the ones with the used tampon on their head."

Scrimple laughed at that, because he knew it was called a budgie but it did look a bit like a sanitary product. "Famous old regiment. And now you're based at the Albany Street Barracks in London?"

"That's right. We've nicked some rooms off the Artists. That's the Territorial lot. Although we get out and about a bit more. You know how it is, sir: the boss says jump and we ask how high and what's the drop zone like?"

"Rather you than me. I used to do some scuba diving. But jumping out of perfectly serviceable airplanes never made sense to me."

"You get used to it. It's the people shooting at you when you're trying to land that always makes me twitchy."

Scrimple smiled. He leant forward to make sure they weren't overheard by the elderly gentlemen. "Was Pacino a close mate of yours?"

Rickman's face tensed up slightly. "He was a crazy bastard. If he got shot that many times then he was shot trying to escape and doing his job. It's what we get paid for."

Scrimple nodded and looked out of the window. They were coming closer to Basingstoke. "I only spent a short time with him but he seemed a really solid bloke. I was looking forward to having a few beers with him while we waited for Tchaikovsky to do his interrogation. You never know if it's going to be a week or a month."

"So what's the story with you and this Chinese woman, sir?"

"Call me Scrimple for goodness' sake. I haven't been called Sir since I left the Hong Kong Police and that's a long time ago now." He then, in a lowered voice, gave Rickman a potted outline of his dealings with Wendy Shen. The soldier from E Squadron enjoyed the story.

When they arrived at Andover, they walked across town, which took them half an hour. It had been an important army base but with budget cuts over the last thirty years had fallen into disrepair and there were some rough areas. Scrimple hoped that his Polo would still be there and with all its wheels.

As they walked, Rickman scanned the road ahead and around them like a scout. Nobody paid them any attention and nobody would have realised that the lean, younger man in the black wind-cheater and running shoes with the closely cropped hair was carrying a Sig Sauer to protect the fatter, older man who carried a duffel bag slung over one shoulder.

The car was as Scrimple had left it and he was relieved. It wasn't his car. It had been leased by MI5 for him but he felt a sense of ownership and it was nice to slip into the familiar driving seat.

"So what are your plans?" Rickman asked as they left Andover and headed down the road which would bring them to St. Mary Bourne.

"I'm going to fly into Bangkok on British Airways or whatever I can book for tomorrow. Then I'll spend a few nights in Bangkok, might catch up with some friends and then I'll fly down to Phuket and go out on a liveaboard dive boat for a week or ten days. That's just chilling on a little yacht, diving three times a day."

"Be hard for Wendy to find you out on a boat."

"That's what I was thinking. Then I'll see how I feel."

"You used to live in Bangkok then?"

"For many years. I ran the office for a big trading company. It was a good life. Then they closed the office down."

"So them Thai women are supposed to be pretty wild."

"We used to call them LBFMs," Scrimple said and gave Rickman quick glance to see if he recognised the acronym. They were nearly at the safe house by now.

"What does that mean?"

"Little brown fucking machines," Scrimple explained.

"But you have to pay them?"

"You rent them for the night or an hour, you don't buy them."

"That's where I've been getting it wrong all these years," Rickman said, as he turned and stared at two men standing outside the pub. "I keep on marrying them and then they own me."

"Go down to Thailand on your next long leave or whatever you guys get," Scrimple said, activating the remote that opened the gates, "and I'll point you in the right direction."

The house was as they had left it. They had picked up some milk, bread, cheese and eggs as they passed a shop in Andover so put these into the fridge. Then Scrimple got on the internet and found a Thai Airways flight that left at lunchtime the next day and booked himself a business class seat and a return for four weeks later. After that he started sorting through some of his stuff and packed two large duffel bags. It reminded him of the year that he'd been living under a false identity and moved around a lot.

44

The DDG was in her office and she was waiting for her switchboard to set up a direct secure link with the Israeli Embassy in South Kensington. When it was finally established she got Abe Berenson on the phone: "How did we end up with such a complete clusterfuck? Can you explain that one to me?" she said tersely.

"What can I say, Sara. Sometimes things don't go as planned."

"Your guy was the butler and he was supposed to take out the Chinese guy and the Korean, correct me if I'm wrong? Whatever happened to: 'you didn't think you could get permission for that?'"

"Sara," Abe sounded shifty. "This is a recorded line so be careful what you say."

"I don't have a problem with saying what I'm saying. Why are there another three dead bodies to deal with in my jurisdiction?"

"Look, you've got to see the positive here. We got rid of the boss who was planning to go a bit crazy with what the Korean had brought to him. I'm the one who should be upset. It's one of our guys who got killed."

"The forensics people are telling us that he killed Guo and Park and then another person shot him with a 9 mm."

"Wendy Shen, the crazy Chinese Colonel who now runs Department 3."

"We know who she is," the DDG said with frost in her voice.

"So what are you doing to find her and shut this whole thing down?" Abe said at the other end of the line.

"Is that a serious question or are you trying to change the subject?"

"It's a serious question. Have you found her yet? She's with another girl, the honey pot that they planted on Guo. Jing Jing, the girl was called."

"Yes, and there is another one we know of called Lei Lei," Dodwell said.

"So, how difficult," asked Abe, "is it to track down three Chinese broads with guns?"

Dodwell said: "You are trying very hard to annoy me. We are working on this and have plenty of resources assigned."

"If you find her, why don't you let me know and I'll take care of it," Abe said quietly.

"Have you got any other Kidon units in the United Kingdom at the moment?" the DDG asked using a tone that would have made an angry headmistress proud.

There was a low groan from the end of the line. "We haven't, Sara, trust me. But if you tip me off, I could have two operatives here within a few hours."

"I will not give you the nod. Our own operatives and the police will deal with this matter and if I see any hand of yours in this I will have you thrown out of the country."

Abe was so shocked, he didn't reply for a while. "That's a terrible thing to say to me," he finally commented.

"It's a threat and you'd better take it seriously. We can recognise your handiwork anywhere and if I just so much as have a sniff of it, I will be talking to the Foreign Secretary about having you deported. And if you really piss me off I'll have you named and face checked in the media."

"You wouldn't," the Israeli spy said. Being named as an agent of a foreign power was the worst thing that could happen to a man in his position. He could never be sent to work out of any embassy again under diplomatic cover. It meant all he could do was work from a desk back at Glilot or as an Illegal. But at this point in his career being an Illegal was a huge loss of face. Returning to the head office in Tel Aviv was even worse: it was the beginning of the glide path into retirement.

"Let's be friends about this," Abe said. "All I was doing was offering help. You know. You find her, we'll clean it up. Might be a good thing. Everybody hates us Jews anyway and what are the Chinese going to do to us that they aren't doing already by financing some of our enemies."

The DDG sighed. "If you want your next posting to be Miami where the terrorists have large breasts and the Cuba Libre flows freely then do nothing that comes to my notice for the next few months. Go about your usual business. We will deal with Beryl the Yellow Peril, in our own way."

"Her name is Wendy."

"I was coining a phrase."

Abe said, "The offer is still on the table, if you need a bit of extra-judicial closure we can supply it."

The DDG said firmly, "You will not supply anything. This call is over."

She picked up her phone and her leather jacket and walked out of her office. Down a flight of stairs and along a corridor was an office that only had the letters 'ADT' on the door. The DDG pressed a buzzer because the door would always be locked since sensitive information might be on display that was nobody's business except the three people who worked in this department.

Kat opened the door herself having seen that it was her boss on the security camera.

"Where is the old bastard?" the DDG said as she walked in. There was nothing special about the office. It contained four desks, a small conference room with a projector and a white board. Kat occupied one desk and at the other desk sat a man in a wheelchair called Mike Gannion. He waved a hand languidly at Dodwell and carried on working on his computer screens. They knew each other from way back when Gannion could still walk.

"You mean Jedburgh? He went out drinking last night with his old mate Scrimple," Kat said. "Hasn't surfaced yet."

"We put him in the DoubleTree, didn't we?" the DDG said and slipped into the guest chair in front of Kat's desk. She reached back and gave Gannion a hard punch on the shoulder by way of comradely greeting.

"We did, but he told me it was a shit-hole and he moved himself to the Corinthia Hotel."

"Flash git," the DDG said irritably. "I hope he's paying for the room out of his own pocket?"

Kat nodded. "He's got a junior suite."

"That man has too much money," the DDG said.

"He claims he's spent a lifetime earning it," Kat said with the sort of expression that implied she thought it was a silly statement.

"It's close enough, a brisk fifteen-minute walk," Dodwell said. "We'll go and see him and roust him out of his bed. Where are you at with our open projects, Mike?"

The man in the wheelchair said: "We think there is another load of Semtex floating around but it's not found its way to the UK yet. I've got some data here that it may be destined for a man named Salman Ramadan. I can't identify him so far. Too common a name. But he'd be a target for Thanatos to take out."

"Where is this Salman?" Dodwell asked.

Gannion shrugged. "London maybe. There is chatter but it's just not clear enough. I'm still working it. The Americans aren't being helpful and the French have got the hump with us. Can't imagine why?"

"I may have said this before but it's worth repeating," the DDG spoke with some gravitas, "*War is so unjust and ugly that all who wage it must try to stifle the voice of conscience within themselves.*" She paused and leant backwards so she could catch Gannion's eye. "Identify the man so we can have Thanatos remove him before he gets hold of those explosives and kills a room full of innocents. Have we got a codename for him yet?"

Gannion leant forward and squinted at his screen. "Bryngwyn," he answered with a shrug.

"What is the matter with our software? Do they outsource all the coding to some company in Wales? Fine, put 'Bryngwyn' top priority. I've got a bad feeling about this one."

What the DDG was doing in this office was strictly speaking illegal. All three of them knew it, but as long as they believed in their mission and kept it a closely guarded secret, then it was a worthwhile undertaking. The DDG trusted Kat and Gannion implicitly and they trusted her. As long as none of them pulled the trigger their consciences were clear and for that tawdry work they had the burnished tool they were now calling Thanatos.

"No lunch break for you," the DDG said to Gannion. He gave a strangled laugh and pointed at the camp bed with a sleeping bag that was just visible in the conference room.

"Do you think I bother going home these days?" he said with a merry chuckle that indicated his work was all that he lived for and it gave him pleasure to be part of the greater good. He had joined GCHQ at the same time as Dodwell when they'd been youngsters together, listening in on Russian communications all day long then hanging out in the Old Restoration pub and drinking until they were thrown out. In those days they'd still enjoyed a bit of the wacky-backy and no one had a problem with that as long as you were on time with your transcripts. The eighties seemed a world far removed from the present.

"Let's go," she said to Kat and moved towards the door.

It took them twenty minutes to walk the mile to the Corinthia Hotel which was in Whitehall. The weather remained clement which was always a bonus because the month of May could be particularly rainy in London.

They called up to his room and a uniformed hotel employee helped them get into the lift because you needed a keycard to activate it. Jedburgh was up and dressed in jeans, a white T-shirt stretched tightly across his pectoral and bicep muscles and padding around barefoot on the deep, luxurious carpet.

"What is this costing you?" Dodwell asked as she sat down on the sofa.

"Does it matter?" Jedburgh replied. He looked haggard, unshaven and lacking sleep. There must have been much drink involved.

"There is a guy called Dominic Tweddle at Six who suspects that I am doing some work for you at Five," Jedburgh said as he offered them a small bottle of Perrier each and then unscrewed his own and drank from it. "Can you tell him that he's imagining things. He's seeing spooks where there are only ghosts."

"I know Tweddle," Dodwell said. "He has a good reputation. Old school."

"He's an old school friend of mine and because he's quite clever he can put two and two together and come up with six."

"I'll have a quiet word," Dodwell assured him. "You seem to have had a fun night. Have you heard the news about Wendy Shen and what happened in Belgravia?"

Jedburgh nodded. "Kat brought me up to speed earlier. Any more info? Have you got a location for them?"

"Unfortunately," the DDG said, "we've got sweet bugger all."

They discussed matters for half an hour and what else could be done on some of the open projects they had which might involve Jedburgh. Then Dodwell's phone rang and it was Hamilton.

"What have you got, Gavin? I'm here with Kat Pedder and a few other people so I will put you on speaker phone."

"My apprentice Wesley has found Winchcombe. He flew into New Zealand then flew on to Bali and he's staying in a villa he's rented on a long-term lease using a different name. He's grown a beard and seems to be rather pleased with himself."

"What makes you say that?" Kat jumped into the call.

"He's opened a bank account with 100,000 US dollars in it and bought himself a second-hand Harley."

That interested the DDG because she rode a Harley on weekends. "What model?"

"A Fat Boy, is that a good one?"

"It's what a man like Winchcombe would ride," Dodwell said with a snort.

"What do you want me to do with this information?" Hamilton asked. Dodwell glanced up at Jedburgh and he caught her eye. He shrugged, as if to say he was happy to fly out to Bali.

"Send the file over to my inbox, Gavin," she said. "We'll ask MI6 to help us on this. They can lift him and bring him back to the UK for trial."

After she'd cut the connection from Hamilton, the DDG explained: "Winchcombe is a failure of our own system. Somewhere his loyalty went awry and we didn't notice. We need to debrief him and understand what was going on in his head when he took money to sell out his own colleagues. An act that he knew might result in other people getting injured or even worse. Why would he do that?"

She turned to Jedburgh. "What you do is to protect us from the real enemy. But Winchcombe is not our enemy, he is a lost soul, so to use your abilities to deal with him would not right."

"It's all the same to me," said Jedburgh.

45

Professor Whyte received a call from Guo's lawyer, Anthony Peppard-Mills. GART's own lawyers had been whining that the draft Sales and Purchase Agreement was not to their liking and they wanted to rewrite it completely but Mrs. Block had made it clear that in her opinion that would be a terrible idea. They could not be too clever in this negotiation. It was a matter of life and death, the survival of the business. If Guo walked away - and he was a billionaire who could do as he pleased - that would be the end of GART. Nobody else was going to come riding along like a white knight with half a million pounds to cover their payroll and other expenses.

"I'm very sad to tell you," Peppard-Mills said at the other end of the phone, "but Mr. Guo met a terrible accident yesterday and has been killed. It was a traffic accident from what I have been told."

"Oh, my goodness," Whyte said. He had no idea what else to say. That was the end of the dream. The end of his wonderful venture to strike out on his own and have his own business and make a mark on his industry.

The lawyer went on: "Professor Park was also in the car, apparently, and the butler. They were both killed as well."

"That's dreadful. Where was this?" Whyte asked but his mind was in a daze and it barely mattered to him. If Guo was gone, it was all over. Mrs. Block had been adamant about that.

"A particularly dangerous stretch of the A40, I believe."

"So the deal is off then?" Whyte spoke the words that had been waiting to get out.

"Well," said the lawyer, "this is rather strange but shortly after I got news about poor Mr. Guo's death, I was contacted by a subsidiary of TEVA and they would like to make you an offer. In fact, since they knew I'd been working on the Guogene-GART merger, they wanted to offer you the exact same terms and conditions."

"The same conditions?" Whyte said, not quite sure what he was hearing.

"Correct. They are willing to honour the proposal to advance £400,000 in cash to pay salaries if you agree the text of the SPA by Friday."

"What about the amount of shares?" Whyte wanted to know.

"As I said, professor, the exact same deal, the same shareholding split, all the same clauses in the agreement. They told me they had been mulling over your research and they'd been targetting GART for some time, had just not got around to contacting you for a conversation."

"I understand," said the Professor. "So what happens next?"

The lawyer explained: "If you are amenable then I'll send over the revised version of the SPA to you and your lawyers, changing all the names and we can take it from there."

"Could we have more time to study things?" Whyte asked.

There was a sad sigh from the other end of the line. "I'm afraid not. This is the deal. It's take it or leave it. They were quite adamant that there would be no negotiations. They had another lab in their sights in Boston but once they heard how keen Mr. Guo had been to acquire GART they decided to pick up quickly on this subject. Frankly, I wouldn't," the lawyer paused to make his point as acute as possible, "look a gift horse in the mouth."

"I'll have to discuss it with the other shareholders and Mrs. Block," Whyte said stalling for time.

"You do that and call me back within an hour. Otherwise the offer is off the table."

"An hour?" the professor gasped. He stared out of his office window at his old Land Rover that now had a new tyre. Perhaps he could buy a new Jaguar XJ if the deal went through. That would cheer him up after all the stress recently. Gomeldovir had potential, it would be successful, if only someone believed in it, invested the money and if lots of people got sick with a form of coronavirus and suddenly needed anti-virals that were specifically targetted at this rare type of illness.

"The gentleman I'm dealing with," the lawyer said, "is called Mr. Cyril Dorfman. He'll come down to GART as soon as possible, if you wish to entertain their offer."

When they had concluded the phone call Professor Whyte rushed down the corridor to Mrs. Block's office. He looked through the glass into the labs and saw all his staff busy working away. All they wanted to do was develop the best drugs in the world without having to worry about who was paying their salaries and their mortgages.

He sat down in the chair opposite his Finance Director and explained to her what he'd just been told.

"Good heavens, that's extraordinary," she said, once he'd finished.

"We have an hour to make up our minds," he added.

Mrs. Block not only wore sensible shoes all the time, but overall her personality was entirely sensible. She stared hard at the man who was her boss, her fellow shareholder and also her friend.

"What do we need an hour for to make up our minds?" she challenged him.

"But… but we should negotiate. Maybe there are other companies now interested in us…"

"Lionel, if we do not take this deal, now, today, this company will be bankrupt within weeks. You know that but you've been in denial. Nobody will touch us with a barge pole. We agreed to sell to the Chinese man on those terms. TEVA is one of the most reputable pharmaceutical companies in the world and if one of their subsidiaries wants to acquire us then we must sell. It's sell or close the shop down." Mrs. Block rarely minced her words.

Professor Whyte blinked rapidly as he tried to come up with a reply. "But I haven't even met this man, Cyril Dorfman, who is he?"

"Tell the lawyers yes. Let's sign the paperwork and then we'll take the next steps." She leant back in her chair and fixed him with her firm brown eyes. "I need that £400,000 in our bank account by Friday. The offer is on the table. Take the money now."

"Very well then," Professor Whyte said. He told himself it made no real difference. They had agreed to be part of a Chinese company, now they might be part of an Israeli company. Perhaps that was after all a better thing. The more he thought about it, as he walked back to his own room, the more he decided it wasn't such a bad thing after all. If they could just get Gomeldovir to market in the next year, the world would be their oyster. He chuckled at this image. Then he thought about owning a brand new Jaguar XJ and that put a smile on his face.

46

It was about 8 p.m. by the time Scrimple had packed what he wanted to bring, and had arranged his other belongings. He'd also put all of Esmeralda's things into one of the spare rooms. He wasn't sure if the family would ask for them but the clothes and personal items would be there if anyone wanted to come and collect them.

Rickman had arrived with a small rucksack which contained his overnight stuff so most of the time he sat in the living room and kept one eye on the windows. The TV ran mutely in the corner.

"Do you think we could risk going to the pub?" Scrimple asked. "I'm starving and could really do with a pint or two."

The soldier thought about it for a few seconds weighing up any potential risk and checking this off against the orders he'd been given. Men in the Special Forces were of a different calibre to other soldiers. They had to make faster decisions on their own in the heat of battle because they often worked in teams of four or less. There was rarely an officer around who could be consulted or even blamed later if the decision turned out wrong. You had to think on your feet when the bullets were whipping up the sand around your boots.

"Pub's just across the road, innit?" Rickman asked.

"Fifty yards."

"People know you there?"

"I'm one of the regulars. It's a small village. You can't drink somewhere more than three times before everyone knows your name and your business."

Rickman gave him a nod. "What did you tell them was your business?"

"Told them I was a retired Hong Kong Policeman. If people saw our guests arrive and leave they'd think we were having friends over for the weekend."

"But now they'll have heard about the dead bodies that were found."

"I can't help that. We can just say no comment. Chances are I'll never come back and live here again so this will be my last night. MI5 will probably put the house on the market and find a new one at the other end of the country."

"You'll be running a castle in Scotland next time we meet," Rickman laughed. They decided that the risk was low to pop across the road and have a decent meal and a drink. If any of the locals wanted to talk they'd put them off. Nobody would ever hear from Scrimple again in this village after this evening.

They went out the front door and locked up carefully. Rickman studied the road and there appeared to be no threat. It was starting to get dark.

When they entered the George Inn all conversation died down. About ten men and women were in the main room. Some were not from the village so had no idea what had transpired in the last few days but the locals all looked mildly astonished to see him.

Scrimple marched directly to the bar counter. Roland the farmer was sitting on his usual stool and his eyes were as big as saucers as he realised who it was.

"What are you doing here?" he said, his pint glass paused halfway to his mouth.

Scrimple gave a low chuckle, trying to be as casual as possible. "Same as you are. We've come for a pint and a bit of company. This is my colleague, Rickman."

The soldier nodded and put his elbows on the bar, leaning back to check out all the customers. The landlord greeted them and they ordered a pint and a classic burger each.

Roland said in a low voice that was mildly tinged with awe and respect. "Did you kill those three people that were found nearby as well?" He squinted at Rickman and recognised him as one of the men who had come to his farm house after that night.

Scrimple shook his head. "No, mate. The two blokes that I killed up at your place did that. One of those dead bodies was my girlfriend, Esmeralda, but keep that to yourself. Official Secrets and all."

"Blimey, what are you doing here then?"

"To be honest, I'm just here to pack things up and will be gone tomorrow. You won't be seeing me again."

"On to another mission, eh?"

Scrimple gave him a sad smile. "Going to have a few weeks holiday and then I'll be living somewhere else." He put his hand on Roland's shoulder. "Let me say this again, thank you for putting me up that night and I'm so sorry it messed up your house."

"Is it all sorted out now?" Roland wanted to know.

"Not quite, but we got to the bottom of things and it's being sorted out by smarter people than me." He gave a deprecating laugh and, finishing his beer, placed it back on the counter top. He glanced at Rickman who was sipping his beer slowly and who shook his head.

"You go ahead, I'll just have the one," Rickman said.

Scrimple took out ten twenty pound notes from his wallet. He placed the pile in front of Frank the landlord, next to the till. "Roland here drinks on me until that money runs out."

The landlord smiled and put the cash away in the till and poured them both two more pints.

"What do people know about what happened up at your farm?" Scrimple asked Roland.

"I didn't say anything. Some people know there was a bit of a ruckus and that the police came but I didn't say anything." He leant forward and near whispered into Scrimple's ear. "They made me sign that document, you know." He gave a wink.

"The Official Secrets Act?"

"That's the one. I didn't read all the small print but they explained I should keep my mouth shut and if any journalists ever turned up just keep on saying 'No Comment' until they got bored."

"I really appreciate your help in this, once again," Scrimple said emotionally and patted Roland on the shoulder as if he were a very loyal Alsatian. Then the burgers and chips arrived and they went to sit at a table by the fireplace to eat them.

After the third pint, Scrimple decided he'd had enough. He patted his gut and thought if he did a lot of diving he might lose some weight in the next few weeks. You couldn't drink too much beer after a few deep dives because your body was full of nitrogen and you just nodded off after the second pint. Fresh air, good Thai food and hammerhead sharks. That's what he needed to put this nightmare behind him and stop feeling guilty about Esmeralda. Because he was feeling guilty. There was no denying it. He missed her and felt terrible that it had somehow all been his fault.

Although that wasn't quite true. It was Wendy's fault. Always it was that bitch's fault.

Roland had come to sit with them and they'd made innocuous conversation about the football and the usual banter about Brexit. You couldn't get away from it. "It's a bloody nightmare. I'll have to get a visa to go and stay in my villa in Spain." If Scrimple had had a pint for every time the farmer had said those words he'd be drinking free for a month as well.

Eventually Rickman had nodded at him. It was time to get back home and get a full night's sleep. Part of him was starting to look forward to getting back to Thailand. The twelve-hour flight was a shag but in business class they had flat beds and although the stewardesses always looked like someone's older unmarried sister the service was generally smooth as silk.

Scrimple shook Roland's hand and thanked him again. Told him he'd drop by and say hello when he was back and if work permitted.

They left the pub, Rickman leading. He checked the street cautiously, his hand underneath his wind-cheater where the gun was kept. There was the chirping of crickets and a Range Rover drove past them faster than the 20 mph the village signs required.

When they got back to the safe house Scrimple fiddled with the key and punched in the code on the hidden security panel. The front door opened. They'd left the lights on in the hallway. As he turned to Rickman, a shadow appeared from behind the low wall and there was a low 'phut' then another 'phut'. Rickman crumpled to the ground. Scrimple stumbled into the hallway realising what was happening, trying to get the door closed but Wendy Shen was too fast for him. She flung her body through the gap and crashed into Scrimple sending him sprawling. His head smacked hard on the flagstone floor that was only covered by a threadbare carpet.

By the time Scrimple recovered his senses, Wendy had her NP-22 pointed at his nose and two girls, Lei Lei and another one were in the house. They'd dragged Rickman's body inside and the door was already bolted.

Scrimple recognised the other girl as the one he'd seen with the fat Chinese man in the fancy London steak restaurant where he'd dined with McAlistair. What a small world, he found himself saying and then realised that he was probably concussed.

"Hello, Simple. You can't run away from me so easy," Wendy whispered into his ear and shifted the knee that was on his chest, holding him down.

47

Kat thought about it carefully for ten minutes and then decided not to. Later she thought about it again for twenty minutes and finally decided to make the call.

"What are you doing?" she asked Jedburgh when he answered. He seemed to be panting.

"I'm in the gym. I'm on my 7th set of squats. I'm super-setting with leg extensions and it hurts like being buggered by the Bishop."

Kat stifled a giggle. "Do you have plans for dinner this evening?"

"Not at the moment. I thought you'd called with a fix on Wendy."

"Nothing happening on that front," she said.

"What am I doing in London? I could be having a monster steak at the 406 on Duval and planning tomorrow's cave dive," Jedburgh said with a sigh.

"She could pop up any moment."

"That's what they always said about the fairies at the end of the garden."

"Man of little faith."

"So are you calling to check up on me or was that an invitation to dinner I missed?"

Kat said, "If you don't have any other men to go drinking with then I'm up for a bite to eat when I finish work here."

"That sounds as if I'm going to be paying."

"You are the man with the offshore bank accounts."

"My bank accounts might be legion but they are not *offshore*. I don't live in the UK so my bank accounts are onshore for me."

"Where do you pay tax as a matter of interest?" Kat asked.

"I pay tax in all the countries where I have to," he said. "This type of snide comment irritates me. I have rental income from a few properties I own in London which are rented out. So I pay tax on them in the UK. I have rental income from properties I own in Hong Kong, so I pay tax on them in Hong Kong. I have income from my investment portfolio in Singapore, I don't pay tax on that because dividend income is not taxed in Singapore. Are you insinuating that I'm some sort of slimy tax dodger?"

"You have been known to murder people for a living," Kat made her point.

"Ah, yes but tax dodging is a more heinous crime than eradicating vermin." He cleared his throat at the other end of the line. "I can't stop and chat now. I've got to finish this work-out. Come to the hotel at 7 p.m. and we'll go somewhere nice."

When she picked him up from the lobby later he was wearing an elegant dark blue suit that sat well on his broad shoulders, showed off his slim waist and his long legs. He'd trimmed his beard to the point where it was just a three-day stubble and with the horn-rimmed glasses he looked like an Italian film star from the 60s.

"That's a nice suit. Where did that come from?" Kat asked.

"Anderson & Sheppard. My mate McAlistair has an account there and I just picked it up today."

"How much did that set you back?"

"Enough to feed a small African country for a year. How about these? What do you think of them?" He stood on one foot and raised the other one briefly implying the shoes he was wearing.

"Nice, what's special about them? Not from Marks & Spencer's?"

"No, from the nice folks at John Lobb on St. James's Street." They both stared at his shoes. They were an ordinary looking pair of brown loafers.

"They're called Norwegian slippers, cobbled using my own last. No change from a £3000 note on these."

"You are a flash clothes-horse," Kat said, shaking her head in wonder.

"Quality is worth it. Lasts longer." He pointed at the door and they walked out onto the street to wait for a black cab.

"Where are you taking me?" Kat asked.

"I consulted with an old friend of mine from Hong Kong called Richard Vines. He used to be a journalist and we all drank in the same sleazy nightclub called The Cavern in those days. It was cheek to jowl every night with Hong Kong coppers, Triad gangsters, and other sorts of dodgy low life. Owned by three Brits who had made their money playing professional football." Jedburgh's eyes took on the mist of reminiscence.

"What about this Richard bloke?"

"Ah, yes. He's now the food critic for Bloomberg here in London. Has been for the last twenty years."

"I see and what did he recommend?"

"Go to Paris for dinner, is what he said," Jedburgh said and laughed to show that he was joshing. "We're going to Le Gavroche. Richard says we'll get a good feed there and he's arranged us a table."

"So we are going French again?" Kat asked.

"You said you enjoyed the food we had this week. Let's see how they do it in London."

The doorman had flagged them down a taxi which took them the two miles to Upper Brook Street. The restaurant lived up to its reputation. They sat in a cosy circular booth with plush green upholstery. They both had the eight course menu starting with *Soufflé Suissesse* and concluding with the *Eclair aux Fraises et Chocolat Blanc*. Rémi, the new head sommelier, recommended an interesting 1999 *E. Guigal La Turque* which slipped down so swiftly they had to have a second bottle.

"Would you like to hear the story of King Priam's bracelet?" Jedburgh had just said when Kat's phone began to vibrate on the table. She picked it up, frowned and said: "Yes, boss."

"Where is Thanatos?" the DDG said.

"Sitting opposite me in a restaurant where we are having dinner."

"I'm glad you are taking your job as handler so seriously," the DDG gave a chuckle at the other end of the line. "Is he drunk yet?"

"He doesn't appear to be drunk but he wouldn't be legal to drive at this stage," Kat said.

"He doesn't have to drive. He just has to shoot."

"I suspect he wouldn't shoot straight. We are on our second bottle of wine."

There was a pause at the other end of the line and then the DDG said: "Be careful you don't let his charm lull you into doing anything foolish. Remember this is a cold-blooded killer. A stone killer as the Americans like to say."

Kat tried to laugh it off. Jedburgh was pretending not to listen in to her side of the conversation. "The man is thirty years older than me, Sara."

"That's the problem. He's been practising for many years longer than you have. Don't get caught in his spider's web of mellifluous elegance," the DDG cautioned. "Remain professional and distant."

"Were you just calling to check up on us?" Kat asked, making sure that she made the words sound light-hearted.

"No, I have got a mission for him. It's not Wendy, we still haven't found her. We are on the Ganymede App, right?"

"It's on and nobody is sitting anywhere close to us."

The DDG explained: "Abe Berenson, the Israeli resident for Mossad called me earlier and confessed something he'd forgotten to mention. His guy, the butler, was the one who set up the snatching of Professor Park from the safe house for the Chinese billionaire. They hired a team of Albanian freelancers, gangsters for hire, who did the job. Abe has now come clean and given me the names and whereabouts of these Albanians."

Kat sat up and moved her coffee aside. She forced herself to concentrate and banish the wine that was in her system. "Why's Abe suddenly come up with this information? It's not like the Israelis to share anything unless they are forced to."

"I think he shat himself when I told him I'd name and face-check him if he didn't behave himself from now on. I think he's trying to curry my favour with this." The DDG gave a little grunt of satisfaction. "It's good information. I will send the details to your inbox and then first thing tomorrow morning get Thanatos to remove this loose end. They are viable targets, there are three of them and they killed Pacino, Tchaikovsky and Scrimple's girlfriend."

"We'll get onto it, Sara," Kat said firmly.

Jedburgh had taken out his phone and now that she'd finished talking he was making a call. He listened for half a minute, then shook his head.

"Thought I'd check up on Scrimple. No answer. He must be in bed by now. He always was a bit of a light-weight when it came to drinking. Probably still recovering from the night before."

"You've got some work to do tomorrow. Time to earn your crust," Kat said and leant forward to quietly explain their orders to him.

48

Rickman's body had been moved to the garage and covered with a tarpaulin. Scrimple sat in his usual armchair in the living room but his wrists were tied again with Plasticuffs. Wendy and her team were still well equipped, it seemed.

One of the girls - Jing Jing - was in the kitchen while Lei Lei sat on the arm of the sofa on which Wendy was sitting.

"My boss gave me permission to snatch you and bring you back to China," Wendy said in a conversational tone. In her lap lay the Norinco NP-22 and her legs were up on the sofa. Scrimple had to admire her calm detachment. She had more balls than a bullfighter. Nothing ever stopped her in her tracks. She kept on charging forward with whatever mission she was tasked with.

"What is the benefit of bringing me to China?" Scrimple asked. He felt much more relaxed than he should but that was on account of the beers he'd consumed. There was a sadness in his heart for the death of the young soldier. They'd been getting along well and he had been a solid, steady bloke. This woman just left a swathe of destruction wherever she went.

"You killed five of my best men, more than half my team," Wendy answered his question. "We will put you on trial for murder and being an enemy of the state. Normally we shoot spies," she gave him a cheeky wink, "but because we respect you the judge will perhaps change the sentence to life imprisonment. Forty years in prison. We have some special new camps in Xinjiang province. Do you know where that is?"

Scrimple shook his head.

"It is North West China. They are doing much work there on ideological transformation and compliance with discipline." The woman laughed and said a few words to Lei Lei that Scrimple could not understand as they were in a different dialect. "You will enjoy it very much, I am sure."

Lei Lei also laughed now and stood up to go and help Jing Jing in the kitchen.

"I just don't know why you hate me so much," Scrimple said.

"You are wrong. I don't hate you. I respect you. Much more now than when we first met in Munich. You were terrible at the sex."

"You didn't seem to complain when we did it."

Wendy considered him for a few seconds then said, "Maybe we should try sex again this evening. We have time. We cannot leave here until about five in the morning."

"Sex?" Scrimple said in astonishment.

"Every man likes sex. Don't you find me attractive any more?" Wendy gave him what could have been a pout.

"Threatening me with forty years in a Chinese prison is hardly effective foreplay. How do you expect a man to get it up when you tell him that sort of thing?" Scrimple shook his head in irritation.

"But maybe you would like to have sex with me again?" she asked and her eyes narrowed. "I will give you some of those blue pills I saw in the bedroom upstairs and you will stand up for me."

Scrimple looked away from her and shook his head gently.

"Does that mean, you do not find me sexy any more, Simple?" she demanded suddenly with more vehemence.

He sighed. "If I met you in the pub and you came on to me as you did that time in Munich, of course, I'd like to bonk your brains out."

"Bonk?"

"You know, sex."

She seemed satisfied with that. "What about Lei Lei and Jing Jing? Do you want to do bonk with them?"

Scrimple saw the trap and knew what the right answer was. "They are pretty, but they are too young. They will be boring in bed. They will just lie there and stare at the ceiling."

Wendy sat up and gave him a fierce glare. "They are both good in sex. I taught them myself. They know all the noises to make and how to make a man come in their throat."

"Really?" Scrimple said. Despite himself he felt a sudden sense of arousal at the image of the two gorgeous young Chinese girls on their knees giving a man a blow job. It was like a clip from Porn Tube.

"Guo Shu Ping was very happy with his sex with Jing Jing. She told me."

"Did you kill this Guo guy and the North Korean man?" Scrimple asked.

"No, we did not. I wanted to bring him and Professor Park back to China also with us once we knew that their work could be useful." She shook her head in annoyance at the memory. "The butler, Guo's butler, killed him. We don't understand why exactly. I had to kill him or he would have killed me also."

"I was told there was a massive bloodbath in a house in London."

Wendy shrugged.

"What was that all about?" Scrimple asked.

"It is something about a virus that can be used to kill millions of people," Wendy said tersely. "With biological weapons you also need to have cures and antidotes or your own soldiers will also die. That is what this mission was about."

"I'm still totally confused."

"Don't pretend to be so stupid," Wendy snapped at him. "I know you are not this stupid, fat man that you pretend to be all the time. You are much smarter than anyone believes."

Scrimple nodded and gave a low ironic laugh. "Yeah, right. I wish."

"The professor worked in a highly advanced lab in Pyong Yang. They have developed many interesting techniques. When he came here to England he brought all his research papers with him on a memory stick hidden in his shoe," Wendy explained. "We have all that research now, a big bag of papers that was printed out by Guo and also the memory stick. We will bring it back to China and study it."

"So the North Koreans are more advanced than what you have in China?"

"They have been specialising in weaponising zoonotic viruses for a long time. Park was a genius. I wanted to bring him back to China. We have a highly advanced lab in Wuhan that is working on this subject."

"Wuhan?" Scrimple said. He knew Hunan but was not familiar with this name.

"It is the capital of Hubei province, Central China."

Scrimple picked up on a question that had been nagging at him. "So it really wasn't you that came here and kidnapped the team while I was away and then killed them all. Including my girlfriend?"

"No, we were watching and later I sent my boys to find you at the farm. The kidnapping was arranged by Guo's butler. He hired some Albanian ex-soldiers to do it, that is what Jing Jing told me." Wendy gave Scrimple a strange sad smile. "I'm sorry that this happened. It wasn't part of our plan. We were watching Guo and waiting for Park to come to him before we decided what would happen."

Scrimple shifted his tired buttocks in the armchair. He needed to pee now. All the beer was ready to come out. "So what is going to happen now? Why do we have to wait until 5 a.m.?"

"Do you know where is Southampton?" Wendy asked.

He nodded. "Forty minutes down the road from here."

"It is the second biggest container port for shipments coming from China into your country."

Scrimple frowned because he was starting to understand.

"We will go on board a ship belonging to COSCO, the Chinese state-owned shipping line," Wendy said with a smirk. "The ship will leave from Southampton at noon today with destination Shanghai, so we must arrive just in time to board."

49

Many years earlier the Reliable Man had been tasked to kill the President of the Philippines. He'd not accepted the job because he knew the fellow and liked him despite the fact that the man was a washed up movie actor, a drunk, a philanderer and most likely corrupt on an industrial scale. But Jedburgh had met him a few times and in a manner of speaking they'd become friendly.

You don't kill your friends. Even if someone offers you a quarter of a million US dollars, which is what the fee had been. Eventually the man had been ousted and someone new had taken over who was probably also corrupt but she didn't drink or philander and was quite boring. Although her son was pretty wild and the Reliable Man came close to accepting a contract on him. That was from an irate father whose daughter the President's son had molested while they were high on *shabu* at a party in Cebu.

None of these things went through Jedburgh's mind as he prepared to kill the men who had murdered his friend Scrimple's girlfriend. It pleased him that Her Majesty's Government would - in a clever untraceable fashion - pay him £100,000 for the head of each Albanian but he would have done it for free. Because Jedburgh had always taken care of his friends and their loved ones.

The boss was called Spahiu. Another man was called Bardhi and there had been no name for the third except that he appeared to be bullet-headed which was a useful enough description. Their usual base was a house not far from Reading. They were part of a larger syndicate of Albanians that ran unlicensed hand car washes and sold drugs, mostly cocaine, on a retail basis. Spahiu had appeared in MI5's database as a man born in Tirana with military background. Not much else was known. He'd been brought in for questioning by Thames Valley Police several times but never charged with anything. The other two men were not known to the police. Albania was not part of the EU so they would not have been allowed to come into the United Kingdom without a work permit. Spahiu had one but the other two were probably illegally in the country using passports from another EU nation - Portugal was a favourite as they seemed to have lost a lorry load at some point out of an embassy's back door.

Jedburgh studied the location of the house and the surrounding area on Google Maps and another application that he favoured for reconnaissance which was not publicly available. It was five in the morning. He had woken up in his monstrously large bed in his luxuriously appointed hotel room and not been able to sleep. It would be best to get this one done quickly in case they found Wendy and he'd be called up to work on that case.

It had not been a late night. After Sara Dodwell called, the mellow mood of the evening was spoilt. There was a whiff of death in the air and so they had finished their coffees and gone their separate ways. He'd kissed Kat chastely on the cheek as he always did and been in bed by midnight.

The men lived in a village called Shinfield which was located just south of the M4 motorway. As Jedburgh studied the aerial pictures a smile crept across his lips. The detached house was part of a small middle-class estate and had a large garden that bordered on a forest and farmland. The garden was surrounded by a six foot high wooden fence. At the back of the house was a patio. This felt like a job that could be done with a sniper rifle. He hadn't been that keen on ringing the door bell and trying to take out three men with a hand-gun - although the element of surprise and a decent suppressor would have probably made it workable.

Being a man who planned ahead, Jedburgh had already arranged for some appropriate weaponry to be at hand for the moment when they located Wendy and her team. Downstairs in the hotel store room, embedded in what appeared to be a carrying case for a musical instrument was the new Israeli sniper rifle, the IWI DAN 338. He'd taken delivery of the rifle a few months ago - the SAS had started using it recently so a few spare ones had found their way to other units - and spent many happy hours getting used to the trigger pull, the optical sights and its odd-looking razor-back futuristic design.

It was a bolt action rifle that fired the powerful Lapua Magnum cartridge, weighed about 8 kg, had a folding stock and an effective range of 1200 metres. Today his range would be around 400 metres, he estimated. The scope he had fitted on the weapon was a Vortex Optics Viper which was a bit fiddly but he had got used to it.

In preparation for a quick deployment he'd also rented a car which was in an underground garage in Shepherd's Bush. By 9 a.m. he was turning off the M4 and heading into Shinfield. It took him another half an hour to find a suitable place to park in the woods. He was dressed as a rambler, had a rucksack over his shoulder and wore practical water-proof hiking boots.

By 10 a.m. he'd found a perfect location, built a small hide underneath a tree, far from the beaten track along which he'd come, and with a clear line of sight of the back of the Albanians' house. He unfolded the DAN 338, arranged the tripod, fixed the Vortex sights and tightened the screws and had a quick peak at his target.

It was a warm day again and the patio doors were open. Inside the living room he could see one man matching the photo he had of Spahiu sitting by the dining table talking on the phone. Several other phones lay on the table in front of the man. Most of them were cheap throwaways. The type of phone that defined any gangster or drug dealer in the age of the smart phone.

The optics were so good that it felt as if Jedburgh could reach out and pick up any one of the phones himself. He could even make out the words 'Alcatel' on one of them.

He was prepared to lie and wait all day, all night and the next day. That was the lot of any sniper in the world. He had two water bottles, one filled with water, one with Lucozade - that sticky, old-fashioned English energy drink. He had three Mars Bars and three Cliff bars. There was no need to eat anything else. He'd had a fine meal the night before. That could last a few days. To keep from getting bored he had one ear piece plugged into his left ear and listened to a play list that he'd put together on Spotify. It was mostly 70s rock and 80s pop and reminded him of younger, simpler days.

He lay and watched, listened and thought about his life. Two years ago he'd gone deer stalking in Moidart on the West Coast of Scotland. They had walked for three days. They had got soaked to the skin, the rain vicious, finding all the weaknesses in his Barbour and the other gear that was supposed to be waterproof. They had lain up for 8 hours until the great deer had presented itself and Jedburgh had taken one shot. The guide had given him a probing look and said in his Highland brogue: "You've not just hunted deer, have you, sir?"

The hours went by and Jedburgh saw Bardhi and the bullet-headed man appear. But they were never all three in the same room together and that was what he was waiting for.

A woman arrived and began serving a late lunch. She seemed young but her face was harassed and she didn't speak much to the men. Finally all three men were at the same table. The bullet-headed man was talking, explaining, expostulating, while the boss, Spahiu, stared at him, unimpressed by what was being said. Bardhi leant forward and put a hand on Spahiu's arm, then joined in the conversation. The woman appeared and cleared the plates away.

In Jedburgh's ear the band Journey was singing *Don't Stop Believin'*. He hit the pause button. It was nearly time. The forest noises became louder.

The sniper checked the wind, did the calculation in his head, made the adjustment on the scope. The rounds were so powerful they would not notice any glass they had to penetrate first before they reached flesh and bone. But the angle was good and the patio doors were open wide enough for a clean shot.

He adjusted his eye on the scope; he took the slow deep breaths; he watched the men as they sat close to each other at the dining table.

Then he fired the first round. Spahiu's head exploded. The second round: Bardhi's head exploded. The third round found its mark.

He watched for a minute or two. There was no movement from the fallen bodies. The woman came in from the kitchen and stared in horror. She would have heard the bodies fall and perhaps the strange sound that a bullet makes when it disintegrates tissue, but nothing else.

50

Major Tom Rieve believed that in battle a sixth sense was not a figment of a soldier's imagination. It was what made a good soldier a great one. Sometimes you just ducked for no reason and then realised that if you had not ducked an enemy round would have taken your ear off. Listening to your instincts was not something foolish. It was part of the kit that you were issued with.

What his instinct was telling him this morning was that there was something not right about Corporal Rickman missing his evening check-in call. There should have been a brief message at midnight saying, 'all in order'. There had not been. He'd made a conscious decision not to be paranoid and give Rickman the benefit of doubt but when there was no message at 6 a.m. Major Rieve called Rickman at a minute later and only got his voicemail.

He left a short, terse message to call back within ten minutes with an excellent explanation for missing his check in call. But the Major knew that Rickman was a dependable soldier. You didn't pass selection for the SAS by being even ten seconds late for any task. You didn't survive ten years in the Regiment by being sloppy about standard operating procedures.

There was something badly wrong in St. Mary Bourne. Rieve called Scrimple's new mobile and the house number but got no reply. By 0630 hours he was pulling himself into one of the BMW X5s with two of his men and he'd left a message for the DDG and Kat Pedder telling them he had a bad feeling about Scrimple and Rickman and was already on the way to Hampshire.

The phone did not ring. He tried Rickman's and the other numbers again a few more times. On a scale of 1 - 10 this was a 9, a high degree of certainty that the situation was FUBAR, as a Texan Captain of his acquaintance always said.

The soldier nicknamed Grandarse - because he was the slimmest, leanest man in the Squadron - was driving. Rieve instructed him to put the blue light and the siren on and to step on it. The German SUV flew down the right lane of the M3 without any effort. Its 3-litre diesel engine was designed to cruise calmly along the Autobahn at 140 mph and Grandarse was not even doing 120 mph. But for the UK that was as fast as the road surface allowed. The other man in the back was nicknamed Viscount - on account of his posh public school accent; he'd been thrown out of Wellington at the age of 16 and signed up for the Parachute Regiment as a private. All three of them were grim-faced. They had already lost Pacino and it felt as if they might have lost Rickman.

Unless, perhaps, it was a false alarm or they could get down there fast enough to stop whatever had happened from getting worse.

When they were near Basingstoke, the Major called Hamilton.

"Are you still on this case with Scrimple, Gav?" he asked.

"Yes, all hands still on deck trying to track down what's left of that Chinese Action Unit," Hamilton said cautiously.

"I've left a message for the DDG and Kat. We are on our way down to St. Mary Bourne. We've lost contact with our guy who was watching Scrimple's back. Nobody is answering their phones."

"Oh, shit," Hamilton said. "I can try and get into the CCTV cameras around there but there was very little coverage if you remember. Wesley, come here!" he yelled at someone who must have been in the office with him. "All right, Tom. What else can we do?"

"Just wait until we get there. We're not far away. I hope it's a false alarm but if it is then Rickman will be looking for a new career if he just overslept and forgot to send his routine signal."

"Is he that sort of bloke?" Hamilton asked.

"Of course not," Rieve said tersely, and then cut the connection.

When the X5 reached the safe house, Viscount jumped out the back and found the coded panel that opened the gates. The SUV shot in and they had their hands on their assault carbines in case there was anyone hostile waiting for them.

But there was nothing except silence. They ducked down behind the car's engine block, did a quick visual recce and then advanced on the back door. It wasn't locked. They found the house empty. But there were signs of recent occupation and Grandarse swore the place smelt of women and a hint of perfume.

After they'd cleared all the rooms they checked the other buildings and found Rickman's corpse hidden under a tarpaulin which had been used to cover over a pile of logs for the fire.

"Fucking bollocks," Viscount said and shook his head. "Boss, you better come here."

The Major stared at the body of his soldier. His lips pursed in fury. He squatted down and examined the wounds. There were two neat entry points in centre mass. Good shooting. Someone must have surprised Rickman and he'd had no chance. The Major nodded to himself.

"Get on the phone, Grandarse. We need Rickman taken care of." He stood up and walked back out to where the BMW was parked. He leant his elbows on the bonnet and dropped his chin on his chest. "We should have known that she would be coming after Scrimple. It's him she's obsessed with."

"What's that, boss?" Viscount said. He was standing with his assault carbine in both hands waiting for further instructions.

"Talking to myself," Rieve said. "Let's have another look at the house and see if we can pick up anything useful. Wendy Shen and her team must have turned up here last night, jumped them, taken out Rickman, he's been dead for hours, and then left with Scrimple."

They walked back into the house and walked through all the rooms more carefully hoping to find some useful evidence. It was in Scrimple's upstairs bathroom that

Rieve found something on the mirror above the washbasin.

It was written in lipstick, probably Scrimple's girlfriend's, a dark, almost brown colour. In messy capital letters the man had written: "Being brought to Southampton docks. Boarding COSCO ship leaving at noon for Shanghai, China. S."

Rieve took a photo of the mirror and the writing first, then called everyone, one by one.

Hamilton and his colleagues were already at work on finding out what ships were leaving Southampton for China that day by the time the DDG called back.

"Good work, Tom. We need to stop that ship from sailing," Dodwell said. "There's more going on here than just the kidnapping of Scrimple. She is not just exfiltrating. Her mission is done or she wouldn't be leaving yet."

"How many ships would that shipping line have in Southampton?" Rieve wondered out aloud. "Probably not so many?"

"You'll find there will be a lot more than you can imagine. People have no idea of the amount of ships that ply between Asia and Europe just to bring us all that crap we buy in our supermarkets," the DDG said. "Hamilton will get back with some answers on that one. If we can identify several most likely targets we'll stop them all from leaving until we've searched them. You need to mobilise your entire available manpower to assist on that. Got it?"

"Yes, ma'am."

"I'm not your mum. I'm just the woman who will be blamed if this goes horribly wrong."

Rieve gave an ironic chuckle at that, received further instructions from her and then hung up to make some more calls.

Hamilton rang back ten minutes later and said: "We've got a list of 16 ships that are leaving for China today. Eight of them are owned by the COSCO line, China Ocean Shipping Company with its head office in Beijing. They only own 1,114 ships," he added with a little dry laugh, "so having only ten in Southampton today is a good result."

"That many?" Rieve said, surprised. "Can we stop them all from shipping?"

"We'll give it a damn good try. I'm going to get on the phone to the Harbour Master."

"Do you have the authority to do this?" the Major asked sceptically.

"I suspect the DDG is already on the phone to the Home Secretary as we speak. She isn't known to sit around on her hands waiting for others to do their job."

"We'll set off for Southampton now. It's about half an hour from here if we put our foot down. Mostly motorway."

"There's one ship leaving at noon. That should be our first priority target. It's a vessel called COSCO Superbia. She's a big lady," Hamilton read from his screen. "366 metres long and she can carry 13,000 containers."

"It will take us weeks to search that," Rieve said, feeling suddenly depressed. It was starting to sound a bit more complicated than just setting up a road block and searching some lorries. He got off the phone and turned to his men.

"What's the score?" Viscount asked.

"Fucked Up Beyond All Recognition," the Major said, shaking his head. "Let's hit the road."

51

The container terminal of the Port of Southampton was located on the west side of the complex. It was a vast messy, confusing conglomeration about ten miles inland. Scrimple had heard someone say in the pub once that it was situated at the confluence of the rivers Test and Itchen, both famous for excellent trout fishing, a subject of great passion to some men in St. Mary Bourne.

Wendy had driven while Scrimple was wedged in between Lei Lei and Jing Jing. It was a disconcerting journey because although he was terrified of what the future held for him, he could not avoid being conscious of how attractive both of the girls were whose shoulders and knees touched his constantly during the journey.

The traffic had been smooth since they'd left shortly after 5 a.m. and within an hour they had pulled up near the huge monstrosity that was the ship named COSCO Superbia. Containers were stacked eight storeys high along the entire length of the hull. The conning tower poked out from amongst the forest of metal boxes in the middle and towards the back of the superstructure what appeared to be an enormous rectangular-shaped beige and blue funnel rose up from the hidden deck. At the back of the ship its name was prominently displayed on top of the smaller name of its port of registration: 'Hong Kong'. For a moment Scrimple's heart trembled with a tiny sense of optimism. If they called at Hong Kong before Shanghai, might there be a chance of escape? He looked at the grim faces of his three female captors and doubted there would be any chance.

It was already dawn by the time they had been ushered up along a gang plank into the bowels of the ship by a Chinese crewman wearing an orange hi-vis buoyancy jacket and a light blue uniform. The man hadn't smiled or batted an eyelid at Scrimple's hands being cuffed in front of him and Lei Lei prodding him to keep him moving with something hard that was hidden underneath the jacket she held in her hand. They had ascended fourteen flights of an internal staircase - Scrimple panting and his legs screaming with pain towards the end - until they had been shown into what seemed a small canteen. There were four tables bolted to the floor, a kitchenette along the far end of the room and a large fridge containing cans and bottles of non-alcoholic beverages. Wendy helped herself to a can of Fanta and put a bottle of Harrogate Spring water in front of Scrimple. He nodded his thanks.

Ten minutes later the Captain appeared. He was a stern-faced Chinese man in his early sixties wearing a similar light blue uniform.

It was clear that Wendy had rank over him. He spoke respectfully to her in a dialect that made no sense to Scrimple. It wasn't Cantonese, nor was it Mandarin or Shanghainese which he could recognise without being able to understand. The Captain seemed to be welcoming his guests, probably asking them to stay in the galley until the ship had left harbour and also entirely ignoring the fact that Scrimple was obviously a prisoner. Was abducting foreigners something they did on a regular basis besides delivering containers of toys, clothes and electronics to the markets of Europe?

"You want food?" Wendy asked and waved towards the countertop at the end of the room. "Captain say we can have noodles and sandwich. Later they will cook lunch for all the crew and show us our rooms."

The Captain practically bowed himself out of the galley and Lei Lei went to put the kettle on and make them some pot noodles. She brought Scrimple some cheese and ham sandwiches wrapped in clingfilm which didn't appear appetising but he had nothing else to do and felt a bit hungry. Lei Lei cut off his Plasticuffs so he could eat.

"How long is the journey?" Scrimple asked between mouthfuls.

"Maybe fifty days," Wendy said and gave him an odd look.

"That's quite a cruise," Scrimple said.

Wendy laughed. "You are stupid. We will get off at Algeciras, which is the next port of call. Then we fly from Spain directly to China. Do you think we want to waste fifty days to get home?"

"I guess not," he said. Perhaps if they had to get through an airport there might be a chance for escape?

Wendy seemed to guess his thoughts. "We will have a private plane from Seville." She laughed at the expression on his face. "Do you know what is Netjets?"

He shook his head.

"It is something big companies or rich people use to travel more conveniently. You can rent hours on a plane. Our Department has a Netjets account. It was my idea a long time ago." It seemed she wanted him to be impressed.

"Sounds like a clever idea," he said.

"We will fly in comfortable way," Wendy said. "On a plane called a Bombardier. We can fly directly to China. No stop anywhere."

They sat there for several hours. Jing Jing and Lei Lei chatted in low voices with each other. It felt as if Jing Jing was gossiping, because every once in a while Lei Lei would burst out in a peel of laughter. Wendy sat in a chair by the door and stared at her phone, reading messages, then typing replies. Hardly any noise penetrated to the galley but occasionally it felt as if something large and heavy bumped into the ship. Scrimple assumed they were still loading containers. Were the containers full or empty? If they delivered all the products from factories in China what did they send back to Asia from the Europe? Surely the containers were empty? But that would not make sense. You can't just ship empty containers. It would be like flying a plane empty. What were they sending from the UK to China? There was no manufacturing in the UK any more. Not anything of note or value that the Chinese would want to buy.

"What are they loading onto the ship here?" Scrimple asked Wendy. She glanced up irritably at him.

She thought about it for a while then said: "Captain told me they are shipping Land Rover, Jaguar and Mini cars to

China. Nearly all containers full. British cars very cheap now because of the Brexit matters."

Scrimple nodded. "That makes sense. I didn't think they would be shipping Melton Mowbray pork pies or cheddar cheese."

"Why do you care?" Wendy snapped at him.

"No reason. I was just wondering."

The Captain appeared at the door and there was a worried expression on his face. He spoke rapidly to Wendy and she shot words back at him. Scrimple sat up with interest. Something wasn't quite right and that made him feel excited. The conversation went on for a while. Lei Lei and Jing Jing had stopped and were listening intently to what their boss was saying. The older man explained something at length and seemed to give them some alternatives. He obviously wasn't happy. The presence of Wendy and the rest of them was now suddenly an irritation. Wendy kept on interrogating him and they seemed to be discussing alternatives. Finally they reached a conclusion or some form of agreement.

"What's happening?" Scrimple asked.

"Shut up," Wendy shouted at him. She turned to the two girls and gave them rapid instructions. They nodded, jumped up and began grabbing their bags. The Captain had disappeared from the door and the earlier sailor was there who stared blankly at them. When the girls were ready he led them off leaving Wendy and Scrimple.

"The Harbour Master has refused permission for any ship owned by COSCO to leave here without being first searched," Wendy finally explained. She glared at him.

Scrimple worked really hard to suppress his smile. It was as if an entire football team of little men were running around in his chest celebrating winning the World Cup. Was this as a result of his final, hurried message on the bathroom mirror or just somehow a happy coincidence?

"You and me will go off the ship and hide away somewhere else. The girls will stay here. It is a big ship but if they are found they can pretend to be part of the crew." She pulled the semi-automatic from her holster at her back and pointed the muzzle knowingly at Scrimple. "You will come to China with me. I will find another route out of the country. The Captain says there are a lot of COSCO ships so it will take time for the police to search them but ours will be the first one." Her eyes narrowed and she stared at Scrimple. "How did they know about COSCO?"

He shrugged and tried to look innocent.

"I am happy to shoot you, Simple," the Chinese woman said. "But that will be too easy for you. You walk ahead of me. We will go off the ship the way we came on, go back to the car and then drive away. There is still time, the Captain says."

She shucked a rucksack on her shoulder and waved at the door, indicating that she wanted Scrimple to start walking. He did as he was instructed. They began walking down the same fourteen flights of stairs, this time it was easier, especially as Scrimple felt a glimmer of hope. Now there was only Wendy and him, the odds had been evened out and he had one tiny ace up his sleeve. Once they'd arrived at the bottom of the stairs, Wendy had draped her jacket over the NP-22 and given Scrimple an angry nod to remind him that the gun was not going to waver from the small of his back.

They walked back across the gangplank. A Chinese sailor waved them along, giving them a mildly curious glance. Otherwise everything else was as normal. Containers were being loaded by giant cranes. Cars and lorries were going about their business. The SUV was still where they had left it, in a small car park outside one of the office buildings that seemed to be occupied by several freight forwarding companies. Scrimple was walking a few paces ahead of Wendy. There was no sign of any customs inspectors or police. The lights on the SUV blinked as Wendy hit the remote to pop open the door locks.

Scrimple paused and turned to look at her. Their eyes met and she scowled, waving at him to continue walking with the hand that held the gun but was still shrouded by her jacket.

He didn't move. Instead he flicked the catch on his belt buckle and felt the handle of the push dagger come loose into the palm of his hand.

"Move," Wendy barked at him, her eyes flashing with irritation. This was not going according to her plan and as always she'd be blaming Scrimple.

He didn't move. The gun was less than a metre from his belly. He did as Major Rieve had told him. Every feeling of fury that was contained in his body was channeled into his next action.

Scrimple swatted Wendy's right arm aside with his left hand and with his right fist - the short triangular blade protruding between index and middle finger - he punched into the centre of her throat. An angry, vicious bellow that every Berserker Viking would have recognised came from his mouth, came from the depth of his gut, and the dagger penetrated deep into the Chinese woman's cartilage.

He sat on her arm until she dropped the gun. He picked it up and turned it on her as he sat on her diaphragm, pushed the barrel into her mouth, ready to fire. But the blood was gushing from her throat and he could see that life was fading fast from her. There was no need to shoot her. The blade was deep inside her gullet and only the handle was visible.

Scrimple watched as she died. Her eyes flickered with shock, then fear, then - as she understood what he had done to her - there was anger, and then came the end: the moment when the eyes glaze over. The moment when that immortal part of oneself slips away from the body, and what remains is bestial.

Scrimple looked up and saw a small crowd of men and women in hi-vis jackets standing around in a rough semi-circle, horror written on all of their faces at what they had just witnessed.

Then there was the screeching of tyres and a black BMW X5 pulled up. The doors were flung open and Major Rieve jumped out accompanied by two other hard-faced men, and Scrimple thought, perhaps, this business was finally over now.

52

"The wench is dead," Jedburgh said holding up his pint glass in a toast.

"Thou hast committed fornication," Hamilton added with an erudite smile, holding up his glass of beer. "But that was in another country."

"The wench is dead," Scrimple and Kenworthy repeated and they all drank deeply from their glasses. They were sitting at the corner table next to the bar counter in the George pub in Girton. Drinks were on the landlord. It was a celebration.

Things had been hushed up very fast. So fast that no news outlet except the Sun had managed to get hold of the story of the vicious stabbing that had taken place at the Southampton dockyard. MI5 assumed that some of the witnesses had called The Sun newspaper's hotline hoping for reward money for a good, juicy story. But The Sun's excitement had been very short-lived when they were instantly slapped with a Defence and Security Media Advisory Notice which was still an effective mechanism that controlled publication of any news that might be detrimental to the security of the realm.

"So what happened to the two little tarts?" Kenworthy wanted to know.

"They were never found," Scrimple said, staring into the bottom of his empty beer glass. "They searched the COSCO Superbia as best they could but they reckon the girls slipped off in the confusion and found a different way of leaving the country."

"I've got to say this," Kenworthy commented, pointing at the young fellow who was working behind the bar this evening to get more beers lined up, "if you've got to be kidnapped and tortured it could be worse than by a six foot super-model babe from Shanghai like that Lei Lei."

"She didn't torture you," Scrimple pointed out.

"What the fuck do you think this is then, tosser?" Kenworthy said pointing at the bandage on his face where he'd been cut.

"That wasn't Lei Lei, it was the other two bastards."

"I was still tortured," Kenworthy insisted.

"Yes, you were tortured. And I'm really sorry about that."

Jedburgh, sitting tucked into the corner, with his back against the wall, said: "Give credit where credit is due. Scrimple sorted those two bastards out for you, Bob. They're done and dusted. Dancing around in *Diyu* by now."

"What, pray, is *Diyu*?" asked Hamilton.

"That's chog hell," Jedburgh explained. "You're probably not allowed to use the expression chog any more are you? Not politically correct. You'll have to sign some form and refer yourself to an internal investigation."

Hamilton gave a dry laugh. "You're not entirely wrong. But what we say in the pub stays in the pub."

"Will you be applying to the Chinese government for a refund on your plane ticket for missing your flight to Bangkok?" Hamilton asked Scrimple with a smirk.

"I fucking well should, shouldn't I?" Scrimple sat up and bristled.

"They might not see it that way. They've spent millions on training Wendy Shen and that entire Action Unit and all they've got left now is two cute little ladies who can work as honey traps," Hamilton said. "You'd better be careful, they might come after you and get you in a threesome and frot you to death."

Scrimple thought about that for a while. "Be one of the better ways to die," he decided. "I'm off to Thailand tomorrow and I'm going to go into hiding on a boat in the middle of nowhere on the Andaman Sea. I'll stick to local lasses. Only LBFMs for me from now on. If they're tall and pale skinned, I'll give them a wide berth."

"What are you going to do then, Jedburgh?" Kenworthy asked. They all had fresh pints in front of them. After a few more drinks they'd move into the other part of the pub and have a Thai meal. But Scrimple was already looking forward to Thai food in Thailand. He wanted to forget about all recent events. He wanted to forget about the pain that came when he thought about Esmeralda. He just wanted to get back to his ordinary boring life. After a few weeks in Thailand, he had decided, he might go and visit his son in New York. He was still in two minds about whether he really wanted to continue to work for MI5. For now he'd leave that decision hanging.

Earlier, when they'd been on their way to the pub Jedburgh had pulled Scrimple aside and told him that he'd cleaned up a loose end: the men who had killed Esmeralda. He hadn't provided any further details. He just confirmed that it had been sorted.

Jedburgh frowned. "I had a cave diving trip booked which I might still be able to do now. Then I'm going to do a bit of furniture shopping for a new house I've bought."

"Where's that then?" Scrimple asked.

Jedburgh shrugged. "I'll invite you sometime, once it's all decorated."

"Oh, it's like that is it?" Scrimple said, pretending to take offence.

"Yes, it's like that." He laughed to show he didn't mean any offence. "I'll give you a number to call in case you want to keep in touch. Or in case Wendy's two little nymphettes turn up."

"They won't," Scrimple said with more conviction than he felt.

Hamilton's phone that was lying on the table next to his beer glass began to vibrate. He stared at it and recognised the number. He excused himself and stood up to walk out and take the call. Two minutes later he came back in. His face was pale. Scrimple didn't think he was a man who was easily shocked but he seemed upset.

"I've got to go, gentlemen. A bomb has just exploded during a pop concert in Manchester. Some teenage pop star called Ariadne or something. Twenty-two people dead so far, most of them teenage kids and two hundred wounded. It's a fucking bloodbath. It's all hands on deck. Gotta get back to the office. We should have seen this one coming."

If you enjoyed reading this book then look out for the next instalment in the series, coming later in the year:

BURN CONTROL

Printed in Great Britain
by Amazon